PROLOGUE

As is predictable every year, when snow blankets the northeast in frigid weather conditions, South Florida's climate remains balmy. In the winter of 2008, the area's customary blue skies and temperatures in the low eighties bathed tourists and snowbirds alike in their speedos and panama hats while morning mimosas did their best to melt the problems of the world away.

However, just as the warm weather drew thousands of vacationers who wanted nothing more than a fun and relaxing time, the area's year-round residents still had to go about their everyday routines.

In a modest home in a middle-class neighborhood, Darren Handel, the newly appointed prosecutor for the District Attorney's office in Fort Lauderdale, is starting his day with a morning shower while the rest of his family eats their breakfast in the downstairs kitchen. Knowing that he still has thirty minutes before he has to drive his ten-year-old daughter, Denise to school, Darren remains in the shower, enjoying the relaxing feeling of the hot water cascading over his body.

Unfortunately, Darren's Zen moment is interrupted by the obnoxious sound of his cell phone buzzing on the bathroom countertop. With a sigh, he shuts off the water and steps out of the shower to grab his Android. Clicking on the call, he hears the voice of his new boss, District Attorney Benjamin Stack.

"Darren, I need you to go Executive Airport right away. Jane Lewis, our state AG, is arriving from Tallahassee in twenty minutes. I need you to pick her up and bring her to our office for an emergency meeting about the container of dead Asian girls that was found yesterday at Port Everglades. The shit has hit the fan, Darren. The governor wants all it taken care of ASAP."

Unable to conceal his exasperation with the early morning order, Darren's tone of voice reveals his irritation. "Mr. Stack, I don't know if I can go to the airport now. I have to drive my daughter to school, and I can't..."

Ben Stack is not a man who tolerates dissension. He cuts Darren's protest off before his new subordinate can say another word. "Look, Darren, you weren't my first choice for the open prosecutor position. If your father wasn't a judge with so much influence in this town, you'd still be a public defender. You now have eighteen minutes left," he warns. "Get your ass to the airport." After that, the line goes dead.

With some effort, Darren holds back his urge to throw his phone onto the tile floor. Forgoing his usual routine, he hastily climbs into a new business suit.

Downstairs, ten-year-old Denise is calmly eating her waffles while her four-year-old sister, Abby tosses

STUCK IN TRAFFICK
The Novel

by
FRANK A. RUFFOLO

Based on the Screenplay, *Stuck in Traffick*
by
Rose Warner, Frank A. Ruffolo, Rico Cameron, Zane Pappas

milk-soaked Cheerios onto the floor.

When Darren rushes into the kitchen, the first thing he sees is his wife, Gabriella on her knees, cleaning up the mess. Although he is still-agitated, the D.A. stoops to kiss Denise on the forehead while he grabs a piece of cold wheat toast from a plate. "Gabby," he says to his wife's back, "my boss just called. I have to leave right now pick up Attorney General Lewis at Fort Lauderdale Executive Airport. Her plane arrives in less than ten minutes."

Gabriella shakes her head with annoyance and then looks up at her husband. "We're in Coral Springs, Darren!" she says. "There's no way you'll be there in ten minutes! Does your boss think you can fly?"

"Yeah, I know," Darren replies while moving a stray hair from his wife's eyes. After planting a kiss on her cheek, he adds, "But I have to go. Denise will have to walk to school today. It's only a couple of blocks."

"She's only ten!" protests Gabriella.

"It's okay, Mom," says Denise quickly, trying to try to head off a fight. "Daddy needs to go to work early, so I'll walk with Tammy from next door."

Gabriella looks at her daughter thoughtfully; taking her time considers her options. "All right," she says finally, "but just this once."

While mother and daughter were negotiating, Darren was already out of the door. He couldn't wait for Gabby to make up her mind, so he left the solution to her. Now in his car, he cringes at the condition of the old Toyota and prays that it will start right away. "I hope the AG won't notice the cracked windshield," he mutters as he passes Denise, who is now knocking on Tammy's front door.

Up in her bedroom, Tammy's mother rolls off her new boyfriend for the second time that morning when she hears the knocks at her front door. "Tammy, get the door!" she yells downstairs as she grabs her robe from the floor. But her boyfriend isn't ready to let her go yet. Reaching for her arm, he pulls her back and mounts her like a racehorse.

Downstairs, Tammy bounds to the door at her mother's request. When she opens it, she squeals with delight at the sight of her next-door neighbor on her doorstep. "Wow!" she exclaims happily. "You're really going to walk with me today?"

"Yeah!" smiles Denise. "My father had to leave for work early, so I finally convinced my mother to let me go with you!"

"Oh, that's great! Um, my mother isn't down yet. She's sleeping in," says Tammy. "She, ah, doesn't feel well. Wait for me get my books. Then, we can go."

While Denise lingers on the doorstep, a white Ford Econovan with missing plates cruises slowly down the street.

The two young girls begin their walk a few minutes later, laughing and giggling at some secret, girlish gossip. Just before they reach their elementary school, an Econovan stops alongside them at the curb. Still talking earnestly to each other, they don't see the two large men who have slid open the back door until they grab them and cup their mouths closed.

Happy with their newest acquisitions, the van

speeds away like a thief in the night, and the girls' muffled screams are heard by no one.

CHAPTER ONE

The 2017 calendar says it's winter, but in Broward County, Florida you'd never know it. The weather outside is warm, and the beaches are crowded.

Darren Handel, now a Fort Lauderdale District Attorney, is sitting in his well-appointed fifth-floor office near the county's jail and courthouse. The office overlooking the New River is a far cry from the bachelor apartment Darren has occupied since his daughter, Denise, disappeared nine years ago.

When the frantic search for Denise slowed without any clues about her whereabouts, an unrelenting heartache took up residence in both of her parent's hearts, and they grew apart. Not long after that, their marriage ended. To this day, neither Gabriella nor Darren has recovered from that tragic event.

According to the terms of the divorce settlement, Gabriella was granted sole custody of Abby, their younger daughter, and several years after Denise disappeared, the young girl began to suffer heart problems. Now, Abby's heart is so weak that the thirteen-year-old's doctors have told her parents that she will need a heart transplant one day. Gabriella has been dealing with Abby's declining health along with her new husband, with only occasional help from Darren.

On his own for many years now, Darren often feels overwhelmed by his lonely life. As a divorced man without custody of his remaining child, he retreats to his office when he feels particularly abandoned. Oddly, his workplace has become a sort of sanctuary for him. Long hours of hard work have helped him keep his mind off his personal troubles.

Today, Darren is staring out of his office window at the river below while one of the area's touristy cruise ships passes by, filled with happy-go-lucky snowbirds.

As he watches the tourists waving at people on-shore, Darren's mind wanders to thoughts of his older daughter. For too many times to count, he has hoped that she's still alive, and he tries for the nth time to imagine what she may look like. After all these years, Darren still harbors much anger and regret for his actions that fateful morning, and his thoughts are dark. Absorbed by his feelings, he doesn't hear the soft knocks on his office door.

Sally Griffin, a middle-aged black woman, cracks the door open and peers inside. "Mr. Handel, are you all right?" his secretary asks sheepishly. "Bob Knox is here. You know; that reporter from the Broward Times. His appointment was for two o'clock, and he's been waiting for almost an hour."

Hastily called back to reality, Darren turns away from the window. "Oh, sorry, Sally. I was thinking about Denise. Ah, send him in. And get us some water, will you? Thanks."

Bob Knox, a fire hydrant of a man with a shaved head and a thin mustache, has come to Darren's office to interview him for an article he's writing about the D.A.'s commitment to eradicating human trafficking from the city and the county. During the interview, Knox also wants to address persistent rumors that Darren is about to run for higher office.

Sweating profusely, the reporter greats Darren with a quavering handshake, and gratefully accepts a bottle of cold water from Ms. Griffin.

While Darren waits for Knox to take a seat in one of the tufted leather chairs in front of his desk, he looks more closely at the man and can't help but notice his flushed appearance. "Mr. Knox, you look out of breath. Are you feeling well?" he asks.

"Yes," answers Bob, a little more composed after drinking half the water in his bottle. "I forgot to take my meds today; I have some heart issues. My cardiologist put me on a strict diet, but I'll be okay." He takes another long drink of water before declaring, "Now that's enough about me. Let's talk about you."

Bob Knox is all business. He smiles profusely while he takes out a recorder and asks his first question. "Mr. Handel, you have made the elimination of human trafficking for sex and organ harvesting your main objective as district attorney. Is this a reaction to the death of your daughter, Denise?"

Disturbed by the reporter's brashness, an unwelcome explosion of anger wells up inside Darren. "Mr. Knox!" he seethes indignantly, "How dare you assume that my daughter is dead!"

Delighted by Darren's response, Bob Knox withdraws his smile. Satisfied that he pushed the right button with his initial question, he adopts an innocent tone. "Mr. Handel, haven't you been informed?" he asks. "Your ex-wife, Gabriella Hoffman, has petitioned the court to have your daughter declared dead. She's been missing for nine years now. Don't you two talk to each other?"

"Oh, not again," moans Darren, cupping his head in his hands. "That woman is going to drive me crazy! She's been trying to have our daughter declared dead for years now. She wants the money from a trust fund that was set up for Denise. Look, Bob, I want to end the human trafficking of young children for sex and organ harvesting; it's a stain on society. That's what I wanted to talk about today. But now, I'm going to have to postpone this interview to contact my attorney." Standing, he grabs Bob's elbow and leads him firmly to the door. "Make another appointment with Ms. Griffin on your way out," he adds as pleasantly as he can.

Bob nods his head to indicate his agreement, but he insists on having the last word before the door closes on him. "Mr. Handel," he says quickly, "there's a rumor going around that you're interested in running for governor. Is that the real reason you're pioneering this cause?"

Darren frowns but doesn't respond to the reporter's second jab. Instead, he stares daggers at Knox and shuts the door not so gently on the man's smirking grin.

Alone again, Darren scurries over to his desk to dial his secretary. "That fat bastard wants to schedule another appointment," he spits into the phone. "Not on my watch! Do your thing and dismiss him. Then, get

Dan Nichols on the phone. I need to talk to him right away."

Darren sits down at his desk and turns his head rapidly to try to relieve the tension in his neck. It's a quirk he developed to calm himself down. When his intercom beeps, he hears, "Mr. Handel, Mr. Nichols is on Line Two." Grabbing the phone receiver, he shouts, "Dan! My fucking wife is at it again, still trying to get Denise's money! Handle it! Make her stop!"

Message delivered, Darren slams the receiver down with a satisfying thump. "Ha," he mutters quietly. "Slamming down a desk phone is so much more satisfying than clicking a cell phone."

In contrast to the balmy weather in sunny South Florida, winter has definitely arrived in the northern Chinese city of Chifeng. In a bamboo and mud brick hut on one of the many rural farms scattered across the countryside like a patterned quilt, farmer Li Tang and his wife, Tam Su, huddle together in their kitchen trying to stay warm. Dressed in a mixture of new world and old world clothing, the couple moves as close as they can to their small earthen stove, the only heat in the home. Li Tang wears a conical straw tag hat on his head with a red polo shirt, old jeans, and homemade sandals cut from truck tires. Tam Su is more traditional in a long Hanfu dress. Both of them are shivering.

Sleeping nearby are the couple's two children—a son, Jin Tang, eight months old, and a daughter, Lu Tang, who just turned nineteen. Although Tam Su and Li Tang are only in their forties, their hard lives and weather-worn appearances make them look fifteen years older than their years.

While the children sleep, the couple talks at a wooden table, one of the few pieces of furniture in their earthen-floored home. Speaking in hushed tones, they are discussing a familiar problem—their inability to keep food on the table, and clothes on their children's backs.

With tears and deep sighs, the father finally agrees to the unreasonable and unthinkable thing that he knows he must do to save his family and his farm. Turning to his wife, he says, "We can no longer feed both children, so we must send Lu to the United States. I know of men who will take her there. They say wealthy Americans need house workers, and they will pay us well. Lu must leave this farm to make a better life for herself. I will bring her into Chifeng in the morning."

Rising from the table, Li adds more wood to the stove. Then, he holds Tam Su tight as husband and wife retire to their bamboo mats, each of them crying as silently as possible so they won't wake their children.

CHAPTER TWO

As Darren sips his morning cup of *kopi luwak* coffee, an extravagant, $100-per-cup brew popularly known as civet-poop, he looks out over downtown Fort Lauderdale from his high-rise apartment across the river from Las Olas Boulevard. The coffee, made from beans that were previously digested by an Indonesian civet, is one of the few luxuries he permits himself.

Disappointed by the clouds that are blocking his normally spectacular view, Darren turns away from the window and recalls that he heard about an early season cold front that would bring rain ahead of some frigid-by-South Florida temperatures of fifty-eight degrees by the following day. Swallowing his last drop of coffee, he glances at his Rolex and is surprised by the time. "Dammit!" he exclaims. "That meeting with Detective Ballard is in ten minutes!"

Quickly unplugging his five-hundred-dollar coffee maker, he grabs the keys to his Audi and tucks a folder into his leather briefcase. On the way down to the building's covered garage, he hopes for light traffic during his commute to the Fort Lauderdale police station.

Detective William Ballard, a black man in his thirties, is in charge of Fort Lauderdale's Vice Unit. As he pours himself a cup of coffee from the eighteen-dollar coffee maker in the unit's squad room, his superior taps him on the shoulder.

"Don't you have a nine o'clock with the D.A.?" asks Lieutenant Jeffers.

"Yeah, well, you know how that goes, Boss," replies Will with a roll of his eyes.

Late for his first appointment of the day, Darren hastily wends his way toward Ballard's desk through a sea of humanity in the vice unit squad room. Typical of every day, the unit is abuzz with uniformed and plainclothes officers interviewing suspects and perpetrators. As Darren walks on, he notes with some distaste that many of the persons being questioned—male as well as female—are dressed in the unofficial street uniform of the shortest skirts and highest heels imaginable.

When Detective Ballard catches sight of the D.A., he greets him with a curt, "Let's use Lieutenant Jeffers' office. I want him to be in on the meeting so I won't have to repeat our conversation." Ballard had hoped for an apology from Darren for his tardiness but when the D.A. doesn't offer one, he mutters, *"Typical,"* under his breath as he leads the way to the meeting.

When they arrive at Jeffers' glass-walled office, the men arrange themselves around a small conference table, and Darren wastes no time in getting down to business. Opening his case file, he displays a single photograph to the two law enforcement officers. "His name is Eral Rosenbaum. He owns a condo in downtown Fort Lauderdale and a financial services company called Solstice Investments on Las Olas Boulevard." The photograph is of an older, balding man. "A hooker who turned state's witness last week in a murder case gave us his name. She said he supplies young women for discreet services for special clientele, but we can't find any criminal record on him. The only things we know are that he's a member of Temple Beth El, which happens to be within walking distance of my apartment, and that he considers himself to be a pillar of the community. Detective Ballard, I need your department to thoroughly investigate Rosenbaum. As you know, I've made it my duty to wipe out sex trafficking while I'm in office, so if this guy is dirty, I want his ass in a sling. Any questions?"

Ballard takes a close look at Eral's photo and then glances quickly through the file. "You're right, this guy looks clean. How do you know that witness of yours wasn't lying?" he asks. "Maybe a john pissed her off."

Darren cricks his neck before responding. "Eral finances a shelter for the homeless. My sources on the street tell me that some of the vagrants who've used his facility have ended up missing. It may be that they left town, or it could mean something else, I just don't know what. I happen to think the guy is dirty, and it's your job to prove me right. This meeting is now over. Good day, gentlemen. Happy hunting."

Grabbing the case file out of Will's hands, Darren

makes an abrupt exit, leaving Ballard and Jeffers baffled by his brusque behavior.

"All that guy wants is a fast track to the governor's mansion in Tallahassee," gripes Will, irked by Darren's insistence that Rosenbaum is guilty without having any evidence to back up his assertion. Will glances at his boss to see if he'll make one of his usual quips about people in high places, but when Jeffers says nothing, he waves his hand and sighs. "Okay. Looks like I'll have to head down to Solstice to visit this Rosenbaum dude. I need to get a financial advisor, anyway."

Surprised by that last comment, Jeffers raises his brows at Will. "You have a chunk of money stashed away somewhere, Ballard?" he asks sarcastically. "You need a large wad of dough if you want to hire a financial advisor, you know."

"So give me a raise," retorts Will with a sly grin. "Look, I'm gonna have one of the undercover guys pose as a homeless person. He can check into the shelter to scope it out. Meanwhile, why don't you work on my raise?"

"Yeah, I'll get right on that," replies Jeffers with a smirk.

Even after a one-hour bus ride down National Road 111 to Chifeng, Lu Tang and her father still have an almost forty-minute walk to their destination—a warehouse located in an alley behind several of the town's older buildings.

The father and daughter do not speak as they walk. They concentrate instead on bobbing and weaving through the city's crushing traffic—mopeds, cars, bicycles, and pedestrians are everywhere. The walk is a somber and sorrowful one for each of them. The pair trudges on like condemned prisoners heading toward the gallows.

When the pair finally enters the warehouse, the first things they notice are the absence of light, and the unmistakable squeals of rats. When their eyes adjust to the darkness, they are horrified to see hundreds of rodents scurrying around to protest the intrusion of their space. Although Lu and her father are used to having rats around, seeing so many of them in one place is unnerving.

The old building is also cold and dank, and the farmer and his daughter are shivering in their thin clothing. Lu is wearing a tattered overcoat over a soiled Hanfu dress and worn sneakers, but none of that is keeping out the cold. Her young breasts are pointing the way under the threadbare fabric of her modest clothing.

Li, dressed in a tattered coat of his own, is doing what he can to stay warm. He has pulled the collar of his coat tightly around his neck in a feeble attempt to retain what little warmth his polo shirt and jeans are providing him. With a small bundle of Lu's clothes wedged under one arm, he has gripped his daughter's hand tightly and pulled her close.

Soon, a man approaches them through the darkness. "Is this your daughter?" the man asks Li gruffly.

Before responding, Li inhales deeply and exhales slowly. He knows that he must now do what every fiber of his being is telling him not to do. "Yes," Li replies slowly. "This is Lu Tang. She is nineteen. She is a good worker."

The sleazy little man smiles and touches Lu's face. Then, he runs his hand down her side and stares at her chest. Reaching out, he unbuttons her coat to get a better look. "Yes," he says approvingly. "She looks strong. She will do just fine. She will work out well."

Reaching into a back pocket, the man removes an envelope and hands it to Lu's father. "Here," he says. "Go back to your farm and take that bundle with you. We will supply suitable clothing and everything else that is necessary. Now say goodbye, and leave us."

Knowing that this is the moment he has been dreading, Li Tang's face contorts into an expression of extreme pain. He gasps at the thought of leaving his only daughter to an unknown fate, but he feels that he has no other choice.

Li holds his daughter close, and they both cry hot tears. "This is your chance to get away from all this, my little flower. Leave China and go to America. Be happy," the father whispers through tears streaming down his face.

The pair clings to each other tightly, but Li knows that this embrace must end. He looks into Lu's eyes for a long moment and then pushes his daughter away and runs out of the warehouse.

When the father is out of sight, the man grins at Lu and takes her by the arm. "Come," he says. "We will clean you up and get you ready with new clothes. Yes, you will make a beautiful worker. Come with me now."

At many times of the day, parking on Las Olas Boulevard is local nightmare, and in late afternoon, it's almost impossible. The short street features high-end boutiques and trendy bars and restaurants, but there aren't enough places for customers' vehicles.

Luckily, Vice Detective William Ballard has found an empty spot in a municipal parking lot behind a long building of pricey storefronts. Faced with putting money in the parking meter or using his law enforcement privilege, he decides to take the easy way out. Reaching into the car, he leaves the blue lights flashing in the grill of his sedan so he won't get a ticket.

The evening is warm, almost seventy-five degrees, but a cool breeze is announcing the impending cold front. Tonight, Detective Ballard will visit Eral Rosenbaum as William Ballard, private citizen.

After a backward glance at his car, he exits the parking lot and merges with throngs of tourists and locals who are scurrying around on the street's narrow sidewalks.

Recalling the directions he looked up beforehand, Will easily locates the office of Solstice Investments in a tastefully decorated courtyard between two brick buildings.

Opening the door, Will steps into a tiny reception area. There are no chairs, just a fake plant, a small sliding glass window, and a door with no knob or handle. Looking around, Will contrasts his surroundings with the type of business the company professes to be. It's not a very impressive entrance for a company that professes to make people wealthy. Nevertheless, he approaches the window and signs in at the ledger, entering the time he arrived and the name of the person he is scheduled to see.

A few minutes later, a young, well-dressed Asian receptionist slides the window open and crosses his name off the ledger. Then, she places an interoffice call.

When the call ends, the girl says, "Ah, Mr. Ballard, you come in now," as a loud buzz sounds and the knobless door swings open.

As Will passes through the doorway, he feels as if he is entering another dimension. All of his senses go on overload as he takes in marble and hardwood floors, rich oriental rugs, and exquisitely decorated ornaments of brass and gold—a far cry from the starkness of the waiting area he just left.

The person who greets Will grabs his attention right away. She is an older girl, or perhaps a young woman, and she is dressed very provocatively in a tight leather miniskirt, an equally tight blouse that is unbuttoned just enough to make it interesting, and chic six-inch heels. Her dark hair is expertly styled, and her makeup is flawless.

The girl beckons Will forward and he follows her, speculating on the way that the D.A. may be right about the guy he's about to meet. This girl and the other one look too young and too alluring. Something is not right. When the girl stops at an office doorway, she bids Will to enter, and then sashays away.

Inside the office, Eral Rosenbaum, the firm's owner, is proudly seated behind a large teak desk with a finely wrought coffee table and two upholstered chairs in front of it. As Will's sharp eyes rove around the large room, he immediately notices what seem to be original Picassos and Dalis on the walls, along with other expensive items.

"Mr. Ballard, please have a seat," declares the financial advisor. "I'm Eral; we spoke on the phone. How may I service your needs?"

CHAPTER THREE

Lu Tang is now in the back of an old box truck with five other teenagers, all of whom are dressed in the latest western fashions. Lu and the four girls and one boy were sold as household servants to wealthy persons in the United States. That is what they all think, however.

As Lu sways along with the truck's movements, her mind wanders from her father's farm to the riches she believes await her in America. She occasionally glances at the others in the truck, wondering what their circumstances are.

After being in the truck for a while, Lu begins to notice that four of the other youths seem to have formed a bond with each other. She realizes that they have been sitting together and talking together in whispers for a while, but that they are actively shunning the fifth youngster, a young albino male. Lu thinks that the genetically-challenged youth knows that he is not welcome.

In Chinese society, Albinism is believed to be bad luck, but on the black market, the condition is considered to be a rare jewel. The children's slaver knows that in America, many cults and Satanic worshippers believe albino blood is a treasure worthy of sacrifice, so the profiteer counts himself lucky to have caught this particular young man in his net.

The three-hour ride to the youngsters' destination is a rough one at best. The old truck travels from unpaved roads to paved roads and back again on its way to Jinzhou, China's northernmost seaport, one of the largest Chinese cities on the Yellow Sea. Located north of the Korean Peninsula, the city proudly possesses two railway stations and a large airport which serve a wide range of government-controlled industries.

When the children arrive in Jinzhou, the slaver has arranged for them to be taken directly to the next mode of transportation on their journey to America—a small, rusting cargo ship hidden in a secluded cove in Jinzhou Bay.

Late in the afternoon, the box truck stops in front of a dilapidated building near an inlet, and the children are ordered to enter the structure. Inside, the youngsters join a group of youths who are already there. Obediently, the youths are standing inside a cavernous room where the only illumination comes from the waning sunlight that is streaming through the room's glassless windows like a strange laser show.

All of the children, including the ones already there, are frightened, so all thirty of them huddle together, even the outcast. Shivering with fear, Lu Tang and the others try their best to block out the unnerving sounds of hundreds of squealing and scurrying rats all around them. Too afraid to speak, the only noises the children make come from the occasional coughs and sneezes they can't contain as the stench of mold and dirty water assaults them.

"Mr. Rosenbaum, you came to me highly recommended," says Will. "I'm a single parent with a young daughter, and I've invested well. I want to take advantage of your expertise in preparing for my future expenses—my daughter's education and my early retirement." Will pauses for effect and sighs. "But before we continue, I need to tell you something. My wife has been gone for over five years now, and the absence of companionship has made me notice the bevy of beautiful young women working here. I haven't dated much, so my interest is piqued, so to speak. How do you get any work done with all of those distractions?"

Eral smiles and sits back in his chair. "Mr. Ballard, please call me Eral. If we're going to work together, we'll need to be on a first name basis. As for the beautiful women you see here, I have made it my mission to help newly-arrived immigrants adapt to our country by offering them employment so they can hone their talents and become solid citizens. Now, I reviewed the biographical information and financial details you emailed me, and I must say that I'm impressed. You have amassed some very decent reserves, considering your career as a postal worker."

Will chuckles and continues the charade. "The bulk of my money is from an inheritance. My late uncle invested in some major companies, and I was his favorite, well, his only living relative, so he bequeathed all of his stocks to me. My job has nothing to do with my portfolio."

Will's explanation is interrupted when the young girl in the tight leather miniskirt who brought him to the office enters the room with a silver tray filled with bottled waters and sodas. Stopping near Will, she bends over seductively and deposits her tray onto a small cocktail table at Will's right. Then, she smiles at him alluringly and hands him a cold bottle of Perrier.

Fascinated by the young girl, Will's eyes automatically wander to where every man's eyes wander, and Eral notices. So does the girl. Before she leaves the room, she winks beguilingly at Will.

To get Will's attention back to the business at hand, Eral clears his throat loudly, but Will's is focused on the young girl's backside.

"Will," says Eral, "it will take me a couple of days to come up with a suitable strategy for you and your daughter. Is there anything else you would like from me at this time?"

Reluctantly, Will turns his head away from the girl. "Yes," he says thickly while he adjusts himself in his chair. "Her name and phone number."

Prominent Fort Lauderdale rabbi Herbert Katzoff is a portly man in his early sixties. Today, he is in his office with Doctor Ethan Waterford, a fit and trim, square-jawed specimen of a man who looks as if he stepped off the cover of GQ magazine. The doctor recently gave up his lucrative practice to become CEO of UNOS, LLC, a non-profit corporation.

Rabbi Katzoff's office is downtown, inside a small building next to Temple Beth-El, his congregation's place of worship. This meeting is Doctor Waterford's first with the rabbi, and he is all smiles. "As you know," he says haughtily, "UNOS is compiling a database of worldwide organ donors. With your keen interest in organ donation and your many contacts in Fort Lauderdale, I fully expect that our new South Florida office will become our most fruitful. Our company has recently begun to include all of our donors' DNA information in our database, something I know that you've already been doing. We know that information will help us to provide the perfect matches for our donated organs."

Rabbi Katzoff nods his head. "Yes, it has worked quite well for us. Doctor, I'm planning to hold a party with some very influential people. I would like to promote UNOS and announce our new business agreement, and I insist that you attend. We can raise a sizeable amount of money together and boost interest in your company at the same time. In addition, I can guarantee that you will gather more organ donor names for your international database at the gathering. I'll have my secretary forward you the details when they're finalized."

"That's wonderful," agrees Doctor Waterford. "I will definitely attend. Most of our organs are provided at no cost to the recipients, but as you know, there is a significant expense involved in delivering organs on time and in the best condition. We also incur extra fees when we have to expedite the delivery of organs that are needed on a rush basis, so all fundraising efforts are greatly appreciated."

The men continue to discuss their mutual business interests for the next quarter hour. Then, Katzoff stands to end the meeting. "You know that South Florida is eager to help in any way we can," he says. "Together, we can supplement your database and help your cause. I have many friends in high places; many friends who are financially secure and eager to help. If the Almighty is willing, we will be successful, Doctor Waterford, very successful."

The rabbi shows Doctor Waterford out and then makes two quick phone calls.

"Nick? It's Herb. Meet me at the Cheesecake restaurant on Las Olas at eight tonight." When he ends that call, he makes another. "Rocco, come to my office today at four thirty sharp. Don't be late. I have an important task for you."

With an inward confidence that contrasts with his outward appearance, a disheveled man in his late thirties walks into Rosenbaum House, Shelter for the Homeless. Dressed in ragged and soiled clothing, the man is unshaven, and it appears that he has not bathed in several days.

The scruffy-looking man is Sergeant Fred Staten, who has been sent to the shelter by FLPD to pose as a homeless veteran. His orders are to investigate any possible connections Eral Rosenbaum may have to the area's missing persons.

Sergeant Staten is unopposed as he passes through the reception area but when he appears in a section beyond the lobby, he is intercepted by a young woman.

"Oh, you, poor man," says the woman soothingly. "Come on in. Let's get you to a shower, and I'll find you some clean clothes. After you're cleaned up, someone will assign you to a bed. Oh, and I'll bet you're hungry! Dinner isn't until five, but I think I can rustle you up a sandwich and some water from the kitchen. Come on now; what's your name?" asks the woman as she takes Fred by the arm.

"I'm Fred," says Staten, "and I really need to pee!"

In his younger days, Rocco Despirito, a dark and hairy Sicilian, was a soldier for the Genovese family in Brooklyn and an inmate in New York's prison system. After his release, he moved to Florida and continued his criminal activities on his own.

As he strolls across the campus of Temple Beth-El smoking a long De Nobili cigar, Rocco appears to be a fish out of water, but this stocky, former mobster definitely knows where he's going. He stops in front of the building next to the temple and takes one last puff of his De Nobili, then puts the cigar out on the sole of his Italian leather shoes and places the stub into the pocket of his silk suit jacket. After that, he enters the building and proceeds confidently past the receptionist to Rabbi Katzoff's office.

Knocking twice, he enters the office unannounced and surprises the rabbi, who is having his pipes cleaned by a blonde teenager.

Rabbi Katzoff is not pleased by the intrusion. Frowning at Rocco, he pushes the girl's head away and orders gruffly, "Go away and come back in fifteen minutes."

With a hearty laugh at his poor timing, Rocco seats himself in a comfortable chair in front of the rabbi's desk and ogles the young thing as she walks past. "Herb," he says with a grin, "how's it hangin'?"

Katzoff scowls and adjusts his pants. "Fuck you," he says to Rocco. Then, he reaches over his desk with a file for Rocco. "I got a job for you. Her name is Brooke Schoenfeld. She's one of our organ donors, a perfect match for a liver. Make it happen, and quick. We need that liver within twenty-four hours. Capeesh?"

"Twenty-four hours?" smiles Rocco. "That don't give me a whole 'lotta time. I'm gonna need an incentive for this one."

Herb knew this was coming, so he tries to negotiate a reasonable price. "Hey, we have overhead here," he protests. "What do you need to get this job done?"

"I'll make it easy on ya," says Rocco, leaning back in his chair. "Get that young blonde back in here and have her do me. After I'm done with her, she can finish you. CAPEESH?"

The Irish Pub facing the New River is one of Darren Handel's favorite watering holes. Located across the river from his high-rise condo, he goes there often to enjoy a cold Guinness.

This afternoon, Darren is relaxing at one of the establishment's outdoor tables, watching a wide-ranging size and style of boats sail by on the river. As is his custom, he closes his eyes and tries to imagine what his long-lost daughter may look like now—assuming that she's still alive. Suddenly, his reverie is interrupted by a shrill voice.

A woman, dressed to look fifteen years younger than her years, approaches Darren's table with an outstretched finger pointed at his head. "How dare you stop me from getting that money!" she screams. "Remember Abby, your other daughter? She's getting worse! I need that money for her medical bills!"

Instantly, the crowded pub's patrons turn their gazes away from the view and toward the show before them. When the customers realize that their popular district attorney is the object of the woman's scorn, many of them whip out their smartphones to capture the moment.

Darren knows that he's on display. With considerable effort, he attempts to hold back his temper, which is boiling within him like a volcano waiting to explode. "Good afternoon, Gabriella," he declares as matter-of-factly as possible. "I'm fine, how are you? I'm curious—how did you know I was here?" Changing his mind about that, he says more quietly, "Oh, never mind. You know very well that most of that money came from my family and that it belongs to Denise. It was part of the settlement we agreed on after you decided to end our marriage and marry your hairstylist."

"I still have bills to pay, you bastard!" seethes Gabriella.

"It's obvious that you haven't changed your spending habits at all, my dear ex-wife. I just gave you ten grand. What did you spend it on, Botox?"

"You really are a bastard, you know that?" snarls Gabriella.

"Listen to me carefully," seethes Darren in a low voice. "You are not getting Denise's money. At any rate, Abby is on my insurance plan. You don't have any medical bills other than your Botox and his Viagra."

Fortunately, just as Gabriella gears up to respond to Darren's insult, Detective Will Ballard appears out of nowhere and steps between the D.A. and his ex-wife. Flashing his badge, Will asks, "Is there a problem here?"

Staring daggers at Darren over Detective Ballard's shoulder, Gabriella snarls at him through gritted teeth. "You will hear from my lawyer, you bastard." Then, she pushes Ballard out of the way and storms down the brick path along the river while cell phone cameras flash across the walkway.

Will locks eyes with Darren and shakes his head. "I can arrest her for assaulting an officer, you know."

"Yeah, but that would make her even more ornery," sighs Darren with a hand on Will's shoulder. "You gotta admit, though, she sure has a tight ass. Sit down. Let me buy you a beer."

The two men enjoy each other's company while they guzzle beers and exchange pleasantries. As their conversation continues, dusk becomes darkness, and their discussion turns to comments on the numerous couples walking past them in the evening air and the endless parade of expensive boats and yachts passing by on the river.

Sometime later, Will brings up business matters. "Mr. Handel, I sent Sergeant Staten to Rosenbaum House earlier today. He's posing there as a homeless person, so I hope we can learn something about Rosenbaum's operation. I also paid a visit to Rosenbaum myself and pretended to be a potential client. My gut tells me that you may be right—the guy seems dirty. He has a slew of beautiful Oriental girls working in his office, and damn, the way those girls dress and act, it's hard to tell how old they are. He may be pimping them out, so I showed interest in one of them and got her name and phone number. I'll call her to see where it leads."

Darren listens attentively to the detective's report while he finishes his fourth beer. "Good," he says, swaying slightly in his seat, "we need to get that fucker off the streets. Maybe he can get me some info on Denise. Want a refill?"

Will shakes his head and wonders whether Darren is too drunk to go home alone. "No," he answers, "I gotta leave and call that girl. Look, you okay to drive? Need a ride home?"

Darren shakes his head and calls the waiter over. As Will watches warily, the young district attorney places a late night order for an Irish whiskey and a plate of bangers and mash.

When the waiter leaves, Darren says, "I walked here from my condo. You think I'll get a WUI on my way home?"

"No," says Will, rising from his chair, "but you could get mugged. I'll call a uniformed unit to stick around. You can use them to get home later if you want. Talk to you tomorrow."

"Yeah, talk to you tomorrow," responds Darren with a pronounced slur to his words. "Can't wait to see the social media reaction to Gabriella's stunt. Should be pretty interesting!"

Rabbi Herbert Katzoff is also enjoying a few drinks tonight. The rabbi's drink of choice this evening is Chardonnay, and he is sipping it at a local bar. When he spots Judge Nicholas Handel across the room, he waves the judge over and orders his friend a drink.

Judge Handel, Darren Handel's father, is in his late sixties. The elder Handel is tall, fit, and trim with salt and pepper hair that is cut in a flattering style. The judge presides over one of the county's juvenile courts and works closely with Child Protective Services.

Rabbi Katzoff hands the judge a glass of single barrel bourbon, neat and slides off his bar stool.

"Thanks, Herb," says Nicholas. "Why did you call me here tonight? Anything I should be concerned about?"

Rabbi Katzoff sips his wine and smiles. "They're holding our table," he says. "Come on; we'll talk where it's more private."

Drinks in hand, the gentlemen walk to the reservation desk and then follow a young hostess to a booth in a back corner. The location is perfect; the din of voices and clanking dishes is sure to mask their conversation.

When their waiter leaves the table, Judge Handel gulps down his bourbon in preparation for the fresh one that will be coming soon. "Herb," he comments with a sideways glance at the rabbi, "you look like the cat that ate the canary. What's going on?"

"You've heard of UNOS, haven't you?"

"Yeah, that's the multinational outfit that's trying to legitimize, for lack of a better word, worldwide organ donations. Where are you going with this?"

Herb snickers. "Well, I met with Doctor Waterford today, the new owner and CEO of that business. He's opening a regional office here in South Florida, and we're going to help him with organ donors and fundraising."

Judge Handel is still laughing when the waiter brings the drinks they ordered.

"Give us a few minutes to order our meals," says Herb, also laughing. The waiter nods and leaves the table.

When they are alone, Herb raises his wine glass in a toast. "It looks like the foxes are in charge of the henhouse!" he chuckles happily.

Nick raises his glass of bourbon in solidarity. "Henhouse, whorehouse...it's all just semantics, right?"

Darren Handel is feeling no pain. Several of the restaurant's patrons snap photos of him as he pays his tab. Knowing that he is always on camera, Darren rises from his table and steps unsteadily off the restaurant's terrace. Then, he turns back toward the outdoor area and takes a low bow.

With the patrons' laughter in his ears, Darren staggers down Fort Lauderdale's Riverwalk toward the Andrews Avenue Bridge, the boundary between the old and new sections of Riverwalk.

At the railroad crossing, a young police officer approaches out of the darkness. "District Attorney Handel, do you need a lift, sir? Are you okay?" he asks.

Darren smiles and gives the young officer a firm handshake. "I'm fine, son," he slurs. "The night air will do me good. I've walked this way many times before. Go catch the bad guys, okay?"

The young officer nods and disappears back into the night.

Minutes later, Darren is walking erratically through Old Riverwalk, a quiet area that has become known as a favorite hangout for certain ladies who earn money the only way they know how. This stretch of the New River is undergoing renovation, but empty storefronts and walls covered by graffiti can still be found near the few bars and restaurants that have remained in business.

Darren is well known around this area of the

city. Ever since his divorce, he has spent more time than he should at Old Riverwalk.

As the drunken D.A. continues his unsteady progress toward Andrews Avenue, three women of various ages and races circle him like a pack of wolves. Darren looks at each of them and puts his arm around the youngest of the three. "Hi Crystal," he says drunkenly, "haven't seen you in a while."

Although Crystal has just turned sixteen, she has made herself up to look twenty years older. Tonight, an exceedingly short skirt barely covers her rear end and black fishnet stockings mask her extensive leg tattoos. She rubs against Darren's chest, making sure her newly-enhanced breasts peek out from her blouse.

With a look of appreciation at the girl's offerings, Darren reaches out and grabs one of her nipples. "Is it still twenty-five bucks, Crystal, or have you increased your price to pay for your new tits?"

"Normally, it's fifty just for me," Crystal coos into Darren's ear," but for old friends, a fifty tonight will get you a BOGO."

With a knowing grin, Darren grips Crystal's arm and sidles up to an older Asian woman—"older," meaning in her early twenties. Taking advantage of Crystal's two-for-one special, Darren heads for the Andrews Avenue bridge with a girl on each arm.

After Will left Darren at the restaurant, he returned to his apartment in Pompano Beach—a small, two bedroom unit decorated in early IKEA.

The first thing Will always does when he comes home late at night is check on his daughter, Calista. This evening, when Will poked his head into Calista's room and saw that she was safely fast asleep, he tiptoed up to the bed and kissed her forehead, an action that always ends in him brushing away a few stray tears. Calista is the only family Will has and she looks so much like his late wife that it sometimes takes his breath away.

Calista has never said anything to Will about these late night paternal visits, so he prefers to believe that she doesn't know that he's still checking up on her.

After leaving Calista's room, Will glances at his Timex in the dim light of the hallway outside her bedroom door. The time is one fifteen a.m., still early enough to make his call.

Fishing through his wallet, Will removes the business card he received from Eral Rosenbaum and walks into the living room to dial the number on the card. Mei Lan Zhao, the twenty-something Chinese immigrant with legs that won't quit, answers on the first ring.

"Hello, Mei Lan," says Will softly, not wanting to wake Calista. "This is Will Ballard. We locked eyes this afternoon in Mr. Rosenbaum's office, and I asked him for your number. You're very attractive. Can we meet for dinner?"

Will listens for a moment and then responds, "Great. I'm looking forward to it."

Unbeknownst by her family, Denise Handel is not dead. She is very much alive and living in a large house nestled high in the Rocky Mountains.

This evening, Denise is sauntering down a marble staircase, gently caressing the brass banister as she goes. She has perfected her long, slow steps in seven-inch heels over a long enough period of time to know that her silk robe is parting just enough to show tantalizing portions of her flimsy navy blue teddy at the most opportune moments. Along with developing a provocative gait, Denise has learned how to apply generous amounts of makeup to hide the dark circles that linger under her sunken eyes. At nineteen years old, Denise has become an old pro in this mansion's harem.

Halfway down the staircase, Denise stops to survey the large room at the bottom of the stairs, currently filled with political figures and international dignitaries. For a brief instant, an image of her father, Darren Handel, flashes across Denise's mind, but that image is fading more and more every day. As she looks over the people in the room, part of Denise wants to scream and run far from this house, but that part is also fading. The women of this harem are prisoners, held under lock and key and made passive, dependent, and submissive by daily distributions of Vicodin.

While Denise enjoys her daydream, an older man in an Armani tuxedo spots her on the stairs and bounds up the steps, two at a time. Grabbing her arm, he snarls, "What are you waiting for? Senator McMaster is anxious to meet you, so untie your robe, smile, and get to work!”

CHAPTER FOUR

The thirty children have been waiting for hours in the stillness of the dark and cold building in Jinzhou. They are scared and their hushed words, spoken in their native Mandarin, are disturbing the pigeons that have taken shelter in the old warehouse. The birds' cooing and flapping wings periodically send the children's eyes upward.

Suddenly, footsteps in the distance grow louder, and the rats become silent.

Xian Li Sun, a modern-day pirate and human trafficker, emerges from the gloom flanked by two muscular and well-armed guards. The look on Xian Li's face makes it plain to the children that this man is the leader and that he is not one to be trifled with.

Xian Li takes his time studying the group in front of him. With dark and menacing eyes, he looks silently over each child until he spots the albino boy. Poking the guard to his left, he orders, "Take the freak outside; he's worth thousands. We have special plans for that one." Then, he addresses the other youths. "For the rest of you, the voyage to your new lives begins now. I am the captain of the ship that will take you to America. You will do as I say, or you will never get off the ship. It will take more than one month to reach the United States, and you are expected to learn English during the trip." He barks another command to one of the guards. "Take them to the ship and show them where they will stay." Pointing to Lu Tang, he says, "I will take care of that one."

Xian Li walks over to Lu Tang, who is wearing a black hoodie over skinny jeans and pink sneakers. Xian lifts the hoodie off Lu's head and discovers to his delight that she is older than the children he usually sees on these missions. Older, and more beautiful. "Well," he says appreciatively, "you are an exceptionally fine looking young lady. You will do very well in the United States, and if you behave and do as you are told on the ship, you will have a very comfortable ocean voyage. Come with me."

Xian Li puts his arm around Lu Tang and nudges her toward the waiting ship, but she freezes in her tracks and stares at Xian Li in wide-eyed fear.

Xian Li is not happy. He grabs Lu's arm and holds it tightly, causing Lu to grimace in pain. "Maybe you did not hear me," he snarls. "Behave, and you will see America. Defy me, and you will die. Do as I want, and your trip will be most rewarding."

At five a.m. the next morning, a knee jammed into Darren's nose jolts him awake. Startled, he tries to focus his bloodshot, hangover eyes on the culprit and struggles to understand what he is looking at. A pale white inner thigh sporting a tattoo of a hand with one finger pointing toward the owner's crotch is dangerously close to Darren's nose. For a short time, Darren is surprised by the sight, but then he remembers.

Looking around at the sea of humanity surrounding him, Darren sees arms, legs, and breasts, but can't figure out which belongs to whom. Darren's tongue is asleep, his teeth itch, and his stomach is queasy. He hopes that his current condition is only the result of a hangover and not the early symptoms of something he contracted from his frequent romps in the sack.

Pulling himself free from the tangle of flesh in his bed, Darren heads unsteadily into the bathroom. When it burns as he pees, he sighs and whispers, "Oh, fuck," and then makes a mental note to have that checked, again.

Ambling back into his bedroom, he pulls on his underwear and shakes his "guests" awake. "Let's go, girls," he orders. "Rise and shine. You need to leave now, before the rest of the building wakes up." Moans of protest fill the room, but the two pros are experts at pulling themselves together quickly.

Crystal locates her clothing on the floor and dresses while her partner from the previous evening hits the bathroom. "That was fun, Darren; we should do this more often," Crystal says with a crooked grin. "Two more times, and it's on me." Reaching out, she grabs Darren's crotch and squeezes it.

The Asian beauty is already dressed when she walks out of the bathroom, so both girls waste no time in heading for the door. "See you soon, Stud," calls Crystal over her shoulder.

Panicked by the girls' quickness, Darren dashes for the door and reaches it before Crystal does. Opening it quietly, he stares down the hall and is relieved to see that the way is clear. Ushering the girls out, he closes the door firmly behind them and inhales a deep and cleansing breath on his way to the shower.

That same morning, Darren's ex-wife is making oatmeal in the large kitchen of the house she shares with their daughter, Abby, and her new husband, Ted Hoffman.

Upstairs, Abby has just stepped out of the shower. Although she's not yet twelve, she sometimes acts as if she's going on twenty-four and can't wait for her body to catch up. Looking herself over in the mirror, she smiles with satisfaction at her pubescent breasts, which are coming in nicely.

Abby's smile is short-lived, however. A flash of pain across her chest prompts her to hold her breath tightly until the pain eases. Abby is concerned, as these flashes of pain are becoming more frequent, and seem to be lasting longer.

When the pain finally eases, the pre-teen splashes cold water on her face and closes her eyes to steady herself. While she waits for her breathing to stabilize, a familiar voice drifts up from the kitchen.

"Abby? Hope you're ready!" calls her mother. "It's getting late, and you haven't eaten breakfast yet!"

Abby opens her eyes. "Okay, Mom," she calls out

weakly. "Be right down." Toweling off, she mumbles, "Hope Daddy can find me a new heart soon, like he promised he would."

Tied to a secluded pier in mainland China, a small tramp steamer has finished loading its cargo of woven silk and other fine fabrics, as well as human trade. Registered in Shanghai, the Essex is a 10,000-pound vessel that will traverse the Pacific Ocean toward the Panama Canal and then sail on to the Bahamas. In the Bahamas, the legal and illegal cargo will be off-loaded, and the captain will receive his payment.

Immediately after everyone boards the ship, Lu Tang is assigned to a private room next to the captain's quarters. At this point, she doesn't know why she has been singled out from others. Not yet, anyway.

All too soon, Lu will understand why she has been chosen, and she will know what she will be required to do on this voyage—whether she wants to or not.

Across the globe, Mandy Goldman, a fifteen-year-old blonde troublemaker with more beauty than brains, is sitting in the breakfast nook of a five-million-dollar house on a wide canal in Coral Ridge, Florida. Pounding her fists on an expensive teak table, she screams across the kitchen, "How long does it take to make fucking Eggs Benedict?!"

"Be patient," responds her Filipino cook softly, trying to soothe the savage beast in his employer's family. "I need to make it right, so you won't throw it at the wall again."

Mandy glares at the nanny through blank eyes. "Don't tell me what to do!" she screams back. "You're the hired help! I tell *you* what to do. Now, where the fuck is my breakfast?!"

Aaron Goldman, the wealthy philanthropist and international financier who owns this house, enters the kitchen just in time to overhear this latest tirade. "Now, Mandy," he sighs, "we've talked about how you should treat the staff. I can't keep hiring new people, you know."

When the nanny delivers the eggs to Mandy, he waits near the table with his eyes closed, fully expecting an outburst from the young girl.

Mandy pokes the egg, sniffs it, and then reluctantly tastes her breakfast. "Well," she comments dryly, "you finally did *something* right."

Unable and unwilling to control his daughter, Aaron only shakes his head at her bad behavior, reluctant to discipline her any further. "You need to hurry," he says. "The driver is waiting to take you to school."

"But, Daddy," pouts Mandy, listlessly pushing the eggs around on her plate, "I *hate* that charter school! The students there are so mean. Why can't I go back to the Academy?"

"It's your own fault," clucks Aaron's new wife, joining the family in the kitchen. "You were expelled from the Academy, remember? And if you don't shape up, the charter school will end up kicking you out as well. If that happens, you'll have no choice but to go to the public high school."

Mrs. Lisa Goldman is dressed to kill, as usual. Closer in age to Mandy than to her husband, she twirls around to give her audience a good view of her five-hundred-dollar hairdo and her newest designer outfit. Then, she leans over and kisses Aaron on the cheek. "Honey, I'm leaving now to meet Vivian for breakfast at the club. After that, her driver is taking us up to Palm Beach for some shopping on Rodeo Drive. Ta-ta!"

Mandy stares at her stepmother with evil on her mind, but when her father turns to her, she quickly adopts a childishly pleading look. "Daddy," she whines, "can't you just give the Academy some money so they'll let me back in? I *really* hate this charter school!"

Sighing again, Aaron kisses his daughter on the forehead. "I have to go to a meeting. I'll call them later."

Mandy shares a pouty face with her dad, but as soon as he and his wife are out of the house, all hell breaks loose. The spoiled child picks up her eggs and flings them, bone china and all, past the cook's head. The harsh sound of fine china crashing against granite and stainless steel reverberates jarringly throughout the luxuriously decorated home, but Mandy ignores it all. Scraping her chair against the floor, she rises petulantly from the table with her street-hooker uniform of fishnet stockings, tattered denim miniskirt, dyed halter top, and heavy makeup on full display.

"I can't eat this *shit!*" she snaps. "I'll tell Jose to stop at McDonald's on the way to school!"

Mandy's current school, a state-of-the-art charter school, is inexplicably located only a few miles away from a sprawling complex of pale yellow buildings and broken-down cars—one of Fort Lauderdale's Section 8 Housing districts.

Living in a one-bedroom apartment in one of the subsidized units is Tara Smith, one of Mandy's schoolmates.

Tara lives with her mother, Jenny Smith, a middle-aged bleached blonde who is working three jobs while attempting to get her GED. Recently divorced from Tara's father, Jenny is currently on probation for soliciting in order to make ends meet. Although Jenny is struggling financially, she intends to do everything she can to keep custody of her daughter.

Tara and her mother are very close. When the fifteen-year-old is not attending classes at the nearby charter school, she is looking for ways to make her mother's life as easy as possible. This morning, she is making breakfast.

"Hurry up, Mom!" Tara shouts. "You gotta take me to the bus and get to work on time! Oh, and don't forget, you have to go to that guardianship class the judge told you to attend!"

Jenny rushes into the kitchen wearing the uniform of the fast-food restaurant that is her morning job. "I'll try to go to the class, Honey, but I don't know if I can. I'll get fired if I take any more time off." When she sees that Tara is cooking breakfast, Jenny feels miserable but knows that she must decline. "Oh, that looks so good," she says plaintively, "but I'm not hungry right now. Put it into the fridge. I'll grab something at work later, and you can have that for dinner."

Tara doesn't believe that her mother isn't hungry. She knows that she is trying to conserve their food, but Tara doesn't let on that she sees through her mother's protests. Instead, she finishes cooking the scrambled eggs, places them between two pieces of toast, and wraps the sandwich in plastic wrap. "Here, Mom," Tara says obstinately, "you can take it with you."

After placing the frying pan in the sink, Tara grabs her backpack. "Let's hurry," she says. "I don't want to have to listen to Mr. Levy complaining that I'm late again. He's such a nerd!"

Randal Levy, the student counselor at Mandy's school, is standing in the schoolyard, oblivious to his surroundings while he texts on his cell phone. Today, he is wearing a corduroy sports jacket with a yellow shirt, an out-of-fashion tie, and ill-fitting jeans. A model of the latest fashion trends, he is not.

Although Randal is one of the school's morning monitors, he is thoroughly ignoring the confusion that is the daily morning routine at the school. Unobserved by the monitor, a long line of private vehicles is snaking its way to the drop-off area while a row of yellow buses, fresh from picking students up, are parked nearby.

Calista Ballard, Detective William Ballard's thirteen-year-old daughter, is already inside the building, reading an announcement on the school's bulletin board. Her friend, Abby Handel, soon joins her at the board, and the two girls enjoy some gossip.

Spotting the girls from the other end of the hallway, Mandy Goldman approaches, eager to make her presence known. "There she is!" she shouts. "Dead girl walking! Hey, Abby! Why don't we have a good, heart-to-heart talk? Oops, we can't, can we? Ha, ha, ha!"

Although the entire school knows about Abby's heart problems, kids being kids, they find Mandy's taunts funny and laugh along with her.

Abby winces at the harsh words and tries to concentrate on her mother telling her to be strong, but Mandy's comments hurt.

Unfortunately for Mandy, her jibes have been heard by Randal Levy, who has just entered the building. He is dismayed by the exchange, and by the other students' reaction to it. Shoving his ever-present phone into his pocket, he walks up to Abby and smiles compassionately at her. Then, he turns his attention to Mandy. "Ms. Goldman," he says stiffly. "Into my office. Now, please."

With a roll of her eyes, Mandy flashes Abby a one-fingered salute and heads toward the familiar office. As she passes Levy, she declares with a sneer, "I have free speech, ya know!"

Still at the bulletin board, Abby dismisses Mandy's vulgar display and turns to Calista, who is reading a lengthy notice. "Abby!" proclaims Calista enthusiastically. "Let's enter this talent contest! Whaddya say?"

Denise hasn't slept all night. It's now five a.m., and she has been preparing for hours. Knowing that no one should be awake at this early hour, aside from a lone security guard monitoring the surveillance equipment, she quietly opens the window of her small bedroom.

The cold mountain air rushing into the room makes Denise gasp, but she ignores the chill and drops the bedsheets and pillowcases she painstakingly tied together outside of the window.

Dressed only in jeans and a sweatshirt, Denise ties one end of her improvised rope to her bedpost, dons a black hoodie, and grabs the backpack she secretly filled with essential items.

With a long look at the bottle of Vicodin tablets sitting in its customary place on the bedside table, she sighs and leaves it behind as she climbs out of the window.

Slowly, slowly, Denise makes her way down the linen ladder from her second-floor bedroom. The materials she tied together don't quite reach the ground, so she drops the last two feet onto the snow, startling a family of raccoons scavenging by the light of the moon. The animals' squeaks and shrieks break the quiet of the estate's grounds, making Denise even more nervous than she already is.

Inhaling deeply, Denise wills herself to calm down. With no time to spare, she goes on with her plan, creeping around to the front of the mansion, making sure to avoid the security cameras mounted high on the brick façade. Denise studied the cameras' bright LED floodlights from her window every night for months while she plotted her escape.

Unfortunately for Denise, she doesn't know that there are more cameras hidden among the tall Aspen trees surrounding the compound.

With her feet making scrunching noises in the snow, Denise slips quickly across the lawn and through the bushes that hug the stone walls around the perimeter. When she reaches the wall, she hunkers down between the bushes and the wall. She plans to wait there, near the main gate, until the early morning delivery of new supplies or new sex slaves.

She knows that trucks arrive every other morning at five fifteen a.m. sharp. There are no guards outside of the property at the moment, so Denise hopes that she can make a dash for freedom using one of the trucks for cover before the security guard inside can react.

Regrettably, the night guard has already noticed Denise creeping toward the front of the mansion. Keeping his eye on one of six monitors, he activates his shoulder microphone to issue an order. "Hey, Joey, Denise is at it again. She's in the bushes at the right of the gate. Yeah, I know. Sure don't want to be her right now."

Cowering in the dark, Denise hears a sound that chills her to the bone more than the cold air and the raccoons ever could. It is the sound of three German Shepherds bounding toward her, howling like the dreaded hound of the Baskervilles.

Curling up into a ball to protect her face and legs, she waits, fearing the moment they find their target.

Fortunately, or perhaps unfortunately for the hapless girl, just as the dogs converge upon her, the two guards running behind them whistle for them to stop their attack. The larger of the men reaches down and yanks Denise off the ground. "Let's go, ya little bitch!" he bellows. "It's time for another attitude adjustment!"

"Rabbi," calls Herb Katzoff's secretary when he returns from a bar mitzvah class. "Judge Handel is waiting in your office."

Surprised, the rabbi looks down at his watch. "Really? He's an hour early. Oh, well, bring us some coffee, will you please, Mrs. Gerber?"

In a former closet that the school insists is an office, Randal Levy sits quietly behind a metal desk that has seen better days. He's playing a waiting game, hoping that Mandy will be the one to start the conversation about why she's there. That is not going to happen, however. Mandy isn't at all concerned about being in trouble with Randal Levy. She is calmly staring down at her cell phone, completely ignoring the school counselor.

As the minutes tick by, the sound of Mandy's tapping fingers is the only noise in the room.

When it doesn't look like Mandy will come around, Randal leans over the desk and grabs the phone out of the girl's hands.

"Hey!" yells Mandy. "That's a new iPhone! It cost my dad a bundle, and I need it back!"

Without a word, Randal places the phone in a drawer and slams it shut. "You'll get it back when you start talking," he announces. "Now I'll ask you again. What is going on between you and Abby Handel?"

With a frown, Mandy leans back in her chair and crosses her legs—a favorite motion that she knows will hike her miniskirt up her thighs. She steals a glance at Randal to see if he's looking at her legs but is disappointed when she finds that he is not. "Abby's a little bitch," she pouts. "She's milking her condition for sympathy. I hate her guts."

Randal stares sadly at the troubled young girl in front of him. "I think you meant to say that she's drawing attention away from you. Mandy, I'm giving you one week of detention. Be in my office at two p.m. every day this week. We'll discuss your behavior at that time. Now go to class."

Mandy uncrosses her legs in a very un-ladylike way, which lets Randal know that she has gone commando. Standing, she puts a smirk on her face and stretches out her hand. "My phone?" Randal shakes his head. "You'll get it back after today's detention, if I think you deserve it. Have a nice day, Ms. Goldman."

Furious, Mandy's face turns beet red and her temper lets loose at full volume. "You just wait till my daddy hears about this!" she screams at the top of her lungs. "You're going to lose your job for this! He'll make sure of it!"

Storming out of the office, Mandy slams the door behind her and seethes with rage as she makes her way to her first class of the day.

Seated behind his desk, Randal grins as he takes out his cell phone and opens his messaging app.

Sergeant Fred Staten has woken up on the cot he was assigned to after dinner the previous evening. He is grateful for the new underwear, the faded blue jeans, and the old Florida Marlins T-shirt that some shelter volunteers gave him last night.

Turning his head on the pillow, he spots his old clothes on the bottom shelf of a small table near his cot. It looks like they've been washed and folded.

In this ward of Rosenbaum House, Shelter for the Homeless, Fred's bed is one of twenty-four cots arranged into two rows of twelve. With communal bathrooms and showers at one end of the room, the ward reminds Fred of his Marines basic training barracks.

Fred's bed is the last one in his row, which gives him a good view of the entire room. Sitting up, he notices that two of the beds that were occupied the night before are now empty.

An older man with long, greying hair and a scruffy beard is lying on the cot next to him. With a stretch and a yawn, the man turns over and swings his legs onto the floor. "Breakfast is great," he declares.

"It'll be served in half an hour."

Fred nods. "Where are the guys who were in those empty beds?" he asks.

"Don't ask, won't tell," states the older man. "Happens all the time. Some just leave; it's a fucking shame. Look, I gotta pee. Word to the wise—keep your mouth shut. If you don't, you may disappear too." The old man farts, scratches himself lazily, and heads for the bathroom.

Remaining in the bed, Fred stares pensively at the empty cots while the other men in the room slowly awaken to the new day.

CHAPTER FIVE

Judge Handel is relaxing in a tufted leather chair in Rabbi Katzoff's office with his legs splayed apart in the all-too-typical position commonly known as man-spreading. As Handel absentmindedly scratches himself, Katzoff moves behind his desk and takes a seat.

Herb intends to ask his friend why he arrived so early for their meeting, but the judge speaks before he can ask his question. "I hear you have another large shipment of Oriental works of art coming in soon," says Handel. "When can I sample the merchandise?"

Katzoff smirks at the judge's question; he knows what his friend means. "Yeah, that's the problem," he frowns. "You're always sampling the merchandise. Why don't you have Rosenbaum fix you up?"

Judge Handel stands to adjust himself. "I need the fresh stuff," he asserts. "Rosenbaum's whores are rode hard and put away wet."

The rabbi chuckles at the foul expression, then suggests an alternative. "Do a hand laundry for a while, Nick. The new merchandise won't be here for a month. Listen, I'm going to host a party for UNOS; they'll be here in time for that. But give Eral a call anyway. A few newbies came in recently from San Diego."

"Fuck him," grates the judge. "How about that

cute blonde you got? You know, the one who can suck honey through a straw?"

"You're too much," needles Herb. "All right, I'll go get her, but remember—I'm first."

Denise tries to raise her head and look around, but the harsh artificial light and the repugnant images that keep fading in and out of her drug-filled mind prevent her from focusing clearly. She's shivering in this cold room and feeling nauseated. The overwhelming odors of body fluids and disinfectants are making her feel sick.

Knowing that she is naked, Denise tries to sit up again to locate her clothes but her hands and feet are handcuffed to the four corners of the dirty bed. When she lies back down, she hears laughter coming from somewhere outside of the room and a moment later, the man who ordered her to work at the party walks in.

"You are a pimple on the face of progress!" snarls the man, dressed elegantly in a custom-made Armani suit. "If you weren't so popular with our clients, I'd take your kidneys and leave your body for the coyotes! You gonna behave now? Or should I send the men back in?"

Denise raises her head high enough to spit in the man's face. "Fuck you!" she screams. "And the horse you rode in on!"

"Well, well, well," laughs the man as he wipes his face with a starched handkerchief. "I guess that horse is gonna be you, then."

Fred Staten estimates that he is one of about fifty homeless men, women, and children at the morning's communal breakfast.

The meal is being served in a large room filled with worn metal tables and scratched benches. At the far end of the room, Fred sees a stainless-steel food service area staffed by cooks and others. He doesn't know if they are volunteers or paid employees.

Fred watches as more food is set out for the shelter's occupants in the large and nearly silent room. The place is full, but no one is talking. The only sounds Fred hears are slurping and chewing noises coming from hungry people who don't have time to chat. He watches with interest as helpers bring individual meals of oatmeal, toast, sausage, and juice to each seated person.

Surprisingly, the woman he met the day before sits down at Fred's table. As covertly as possible, he studies the woman whose nametag says "Lorinda" and wonders if she's involved in any illicit activity. Curious about this morning's missing men, he decides to strike up a conversation. "Lorinda?" he asks. "I don't know if you remember, but we talked yesterday. How long have you been volunteering here?"

The woman tilts her head and smiles. "I've been here about a year now, ever since I graduated from college. But I'm not a volunteer; I'm employed by the shelter. I have a degree in psychology. How long have you been in Fort Lauderdale?"

Fred looks up at nothing, pretending to think.

"I recently returned from Afghanistan," he responds sadly. "My wife took everything and split, so now I'm here. Hey, tell me something. There were a couple of young Hispanic men in my ward last night, but this morning, they're gone. Are they okay?"

"Oh, I don't know anything about that," says Lorinda. "All I heard was that ICE came in early this morning with a warrant. You done with breakfast now, or are you still hungry? I'll be happy to get you more food, but if you're finished, there's an orientation briefing I need to hold with you in my office. We need to do that before I can start the process of getting you back on your feet and out of here."

Inwardly, Fred wonders, *Does "out of here" mean vertically or horizontally?* But outwardly, he smiles and asks, "More orange juice, please?"

"Sure thing," replies Lorinda as she flags down a volunteer to put the order in for Fred.

While Fred waits for his juice, the shelter's psychologist finishes her oatmeal. Looking around the room, Fred wonders how many of the people who come here end up missing.

Darren's first stop of the day is his urologist's office. He has dutifully peed in a cup and is now awaiting the results. While he passes the time, his mind fills with images from a recent, particularly active night, and his blood rushes to where it must go. It stings.

Minutes later, Doctor Richard Lackerman walks

into the examination room and busies himself at a computer terminal. "Well, Darren," he says, turning around to address his patient, "you lucked out this time. No STDs. However, you do have a urinary tract infection. I'll prescribe an antibiotic and you need to drink lots of liquids, especially cranberry juice and water. Lighten up on the alcohol, and watch where and with whom you come into contact—understand? The infection should clear up in a week or so. Remember to take all of the medication, even after the pain subsides. I'll see you back here in ten days. Make an appointment at the front. And Darren, if you don't slow down, or at least use a condom… Well, you know what's out there."

Lackerman walks away from his patient, thinking, *Like father, like son.*

At school, Tara slams her locker shut and slumps down onto the tile floor. She is crying and doesn't care who sees her.

"What's wrong, girlfriend? Boy troubles?" asks Mandy Goldman, appearing out of the blue. Mandy should be at detention with Mr. Levy, but Tara's predicament looks interesting.

"No, it's my mom," says Tara, wiping her eyes with the back of her hand. "They want to take her away and put me in foster care. The judge told her to do something that she can't do because if she does, she'll lose her job! Oh, I don't want to lose my mom!"

Tut-tutting sympathetically, Mandy plops down and places her arm around Tara's shoulders. "You know I got your back, girl; my father has money, remember?" Brightening at a sudden thought, Mandy gushes, "Hey, I know what you need—a new outfit! Let's meet up this weekend, and I'll treat you!"

Tara begins to express her appreciation, but Mandy cuts her off. "Uh-oh!" she exclaims. "You better move your ass, or you'll miss the bus!"

"Oh, no!" says Tara, gathering her books in a hurry. "But don't you also have a ride waiting?"

"Naw," smirks Mandy with a roll of her eyes "I gotta sit with Levy for a while. I got detention."

"Oh, Mandy, you gotta stop picking on Abby," admonishes Tara. "Her dad is the D.A.!"

"Yeah, I know," Mandy grins over her shoulder on her way to Levy's office, "and he ain't bad looking, either."

A few paces away, Mandy thinks of something else and walks back to Tara. "Look," she whispers, "I'm having a little fun with Abby. If you want to be in my posse, you need to screw with that little freak, too. Or better yet, screw with her dad. I know I would. Ha, ha! I'll call you Saturday, and we'll hit the mall together!"

Bewildered by Mandy's brazenness, Tara stares at her schoolmate's back as she struts down the now-empty hallway. Then she shrugs and rushes to catch her bus.

Fred waits quietly while Lorinda fumbles through a stack of papers on the desk in her cluttered office. The psychologist employed by Rosenbaum's homeless shelter is a brunette in her mid-twenties, but with her long hair gathered into a tight bun and a below-the-knee A-line skirt and frilly blouse buttoned up to her neck, she dresses as if she's thirty years older.

Fred is usually a patient man, but he has been watching the psychologist fuss with her desk for long enough. "The nameplate on your desk says "Miss Vitale," he blurts out in an attempt to get her attention. "So that means you're not married, right? What do you do for fun, besides hanging out here, of course?"

Lorinda's face blushes a deep shade of pink. She likes Fred. He doesn't look like the riff-raff she usually sees at the homeless shelter.

"Let's talk about you, first, shall we?" says Lorinda, looking at Fred with hazel eyes. "You'll only be allowed to stay here for two weeks, so we need work as quickly as possible to get you on a path to success. We have job placement programs that you can sign up for, and we work with several rental properties to find you decent housing."

Fred nods but doesn't reply.

"Okay," resumes Lorinda. "The first thing you need to do is fill out this questionnaire. It shouldn't take long, and I'll leave you alone to complete it. I'll be back in fifteen minutes."

Lorinda hands the form and a pen to Fred. Then she stands, straightens her skirt, and walks toward the office door. As she passes Fred's chair, he openly ogles her backside and makes sure that the young psychologist notices what he's looking at. When Lorinda doesn't say anything about his brazen stare, he drops his eyes down to the form and works hard to suppress a smile. *She's my way into this shit,* he thinks happily.

When Fred can no longer see Lorinda, he jumps up and checks the hallway. Finding it empty, he closes the door softly and scrambles over to Lorinda's desk. Opening several drawers, he rifles through the contents, looking for information about the shelter's operations.

Finding nothing incriminating, Fred sighs and places a call to Detective Ballard on the desk phone. Making the conversation as short as possible, he fills Will in on what has transpired so far and then rushes back to his seat to complete the questionnaire.

When Lorinda returns, she sits down at her desk and reaches out for the form, but Fred doesn't hand it over right away. He is momentarily stunned to see that Lorinda's blouse is no longer buttoned all the way up to her throat.

"I'd like you to attend a class this morning," states Lorinda nonchalantly, not meeting Fred's eyes. "It will help you to integrate into the community, and it will give me time to review your qualifications. I want to see if I can set you up with a job as soon as possible."

"That's great," says Fred. "I'll be able to earn some money so I can take you out to dinner."

Surprised and pleased by Fred's interest in her, a flush of pink creeps up Lorinda's neck and colors her cheeks.

Once again, Darren finds himself in Lieutenant Jeffers' office with Detective Ballard. "Sergeant Staten is in the shelter," confirms Will, updating both men on the status of the investigation into Eral Rosenbaum. "He said two men were missing when he woke up this morning, and someone who works there told him that ICE agents picked them up early today. I called ICE, but they said they haven't been at the shelter in a while. Fred is befriending a shelter employee to see if he can get more info, and he wants to meet me this afternoon at the parking garage near the performing arts center. The shelter is less than two blocks from there."

"Okay," nods the lieutenant. "Anything else?"

"Yeah. I posed as a client and met Rosenbaum. It didn't take long for him to hook me up with a young Asian girl. I called her, and we have a date for dinner." Will looks at Darren. "I think you're right, Mr. Handel. Rosenbaum is probably dirty. Now, we just have to prove it."

The staring match picks up where it left off, and Randal is patient for a while. He waits to see if Mandy will break the stalemate, but when she doesn't, he grabs his phone and starts to text.

Mandy sits sullenly across from him, watching Randal engaged with his phone. When minutes morph into almost an hour, she can't take it anymore. She breaks the silence, letting Randal know that he has won round two. "Hey," she complains, "you said you were going to give me back my phone."

Randal replies without looking up from his phone. "I said I would give it back when you decided to talk. So talk."

"I have nothing to say to you."

Randal places his cell on the desk and looks hard at the young girl in front of him. "Then I get to keep your phone until you do talk to me. You have ten more minutes of today's detention. Why do you bully Abby Handel and everyone else in this school, except Tara Smith?"

In defiance, Mandy stares at the floor and then at the ceiling. Finally, she gives up and looks at Levy. "I hate this school, and I don't want to be here!" she declares haughtily. "None of my friends are here! Abby is an easy target, and Tara is worse off than me! Satisfied? Now, give me my phone!"

"Well, that's a start," comments Randal calmly. "But you'll have to keep coming to detention until you show some remorse." Reaching into a drawer, he retrieves Mandy's phone and tosses it to her. "Go home now. We'll do this again tomorrow, but you'll have to leave me your phone in the morning."

Finally freed, Mandy jumps up from her seat, tosses her head with a sneer at the counselor, and storms out of the office.

Mandy's recurrent theatrics do not impress Randal. With a sad shake of his head, he looks down at his phone and starts texting again.

CHAPTER SIX

Bob Knox, the Broward Times reporter, is once again breathing heavily and sweating profusely. It's odd because he's not doing any physical activity; he's just sitting at his desk in an air-conditioned building, finalizing his opinion piece on Darren Handel.

Bob wipes his brow and stands to try to catch his breath but when he attempts to walk away from his desk he feels lightheaded, and the floor rushes up to meet his face. For a brief moment, he hears the muffled voices and screams of his coworkers, but everything rapidly fades into a thunderous silence.

Rocco is in Eral's office, reviewing profiles of the latest group of homeless people sheltered at Rosenbaum's facility. One in particular catches his eye and he looks through it more closely. This one is a veteran, a Special Forces soldier, with no family or next of kin.

"Found a new donor?" asks Eral when he notices Rocco's raised eyebrows.

"Fuck no; this one's too good," responds Rocco. "Take a look for yourself. Then contact Lorinda for me, will ya?" Rocco hands the folder to Eral. "I've seen enough for today. Gotta go. I'm gonna get that liver for ya now."

Fred has been at the shelter for several days now and wants to see if he can get more information from Lorinda. He stops at her office for a chat but when the psychologist doesn't notice him standing at her door, he takes advantage of the moment. Looking her over, he discovers that she's still dressing modestly and wonders why she's trying to hide her age.

Sensing someone's presence, Lorinda looks up from her laptop. "Oh, hello, Fred," she says. "Do you need something from me?"

"No, no. I was just wondering... It's such a nice day that I thought I'd take a walk along the river. Do you feel like taking a break? There's a little area near the Performing Arts Center that I like to visit. I go there sometimes to watch the yachts go by."

"Sounds lovely," smiles Lorinda. "I'd like to join you, but I can't today. Maybe we can do it tomorrow. Enjoy yourself, but be back by five for dinner."

"Okay," waves Fred. "Tomorrow will be great."

Fred is disappointed. He was hoping to ask Lorinda some questions and thought she might be more agreeable to answering them if she was away from the shelter. He has a meeting with Detective Ballard in a couple of hours and wanted to see if he could talk to her before then.

When it's time for his meeting with Ballard, Fred

is surprised by the slightly cooler weather outside the shelter—the humidity is low and the temperature feels like it's in the high 70's—a typical winter day in Fort Lauderdale.

Fred walks toward the Performing Arts Center garage as cars and buses whizz by. Inside the garage, he takes the elevator to the top floor.

The outdoor parking area at the top is uncharacteristically empty today. There is only one car in sight, an unmarked "piece of shit" police sedan with Will Ballard leaning against its front fender.

"I like your fashion statement," clucks Will as Fred approaches. "You never looked so good."

"Yeah, this shirt's definitely too big for me," Fred affirms, looking down at his faded T-shirt, "but there aren't many choices at the shelter. Listen, I tried to get the skinny on the men who disappeared but whenever I bring the subject up, everyone except one guy clams up and changes the subject. This guy is a shelter regular, an old Vietnam Veteran. I'm going to try to talk to him tonight."

"Okay, good," says Will. "Just don't blow your cover."

"I won't. I also noticed that there seem to be a lot of goons around that place. They act like they're security, but there's way too many of them for a homeless shelter. Doesn't seem right. Oh, and everyone has to give a DNA sample when they sign up. They say it's for medical reasons, but..."

Detective Ballard shakes his head. "Be careful, Fred. You don't want to become one of the 'chosen' ones, ya know?" When Fred nods in reply, Will says, "You know, I also have some interesting news. I had a meeting with Eral Rosenbaum, and it looks like he may be pimping out young girls. I arranged a date with one of them to see if I can get her to turn him in. Let's meet again in forty-eight hours so we can compare notes."

The two officers nod and shake hands. Then Fred walks back to the elevator while Detective Ballard waits a few minutes in the parking lot before leaving in his police-issued, POS "piece of shit" sedan.

At the end of each day, Rabbi Herbert Katzoff looks over his calendar for the next day's appointments. That is what he's doing when his secretary, Mrs. Gerber, rushes into his office.

"Oh, Rabbi, I'm so glad you're still here!" announces Mrs. Gerber excitedly. "Mrs. Knox is in the waiting room, and she's very upset about her son!"

"It must be about his heart," states Katzoff, sitting back down in his chair. "Send her in."

As Mrs. Gerber turns to leave, a sobbing Barbara Knox hurries past her into the office. Herb recognizes Mrs. Knox as a portly woman in her late sixties, with a full head of gray hair and no chin.

Feigning compassion for his congregant, Rabbi Katzoff walks around his desk and guides the distraught woman to a chair.

While the woman blows her nose with a tissue from a box that Katzoff offers, the rabbi comfortably perches himself on the edge of his desk. "Now take a deep breath and tell me what's going on," he urges. "Remember, the Almighty will console you in your time of need."

Barbara Knox takes a deep breath and looks at the rabbi through bloodshot eyes. "It's my son, Bob," she winces. "He had a massive heart attack today and is in critical condition. The doctors stabilized him, but it's his heart, Rabbi. It's failing! The doctors have been trying for a long time to get him to lose weight, and he did lose fifteen pounds, but... Oh, I need your help! They say he needs a transplant!"

Hiding a smile, Katzoff slides off the desk and walks back to his chair. After composing himself, he turns to Barbara with a serious expression. "Don't worry, Mrs. Knox, I'll start the process immediately. The transplant bank has probably put your son on a waiting list while they search for the proper match, but their methods could take some time. In the meantime, I'll check our own resources. I don't think we'll have a problem finding your son a donor heart. Mrs. Knox, you have been a loyal member of our temple for many years, but I need you to know that this course of action will come with a price. Let me find your son a heart. We'll talk about the fee later."

Fred is on his way to the meeting he arranged with the homeless Vietnam Veteran from the shelter. He's a bit uneasy since the Vet demanded that they meet secretly, so he's taking his time, making sure that he's surveying his surroundings as he goes. He's a little early when he arrives at Esplanade Park, so he takes a seat on one of the steps that slope down to the edge of the New River to admire the large yachts as they glide past. The scene is alluring, and Fred easily gets lost in it.

"Hey, we need to talk," says a gruff voice behind him.

Turning toward the sound, Fred sees the old veteran standing behind him dressed in clothes similar to his. The man's face bears signs of the hard times he endured. He has deep scars and haunted eyes; it seems as though he's still staring down the Mekong Delta.

Without another word, the man sits next to Fred and stares at the water. Fred wants to let the man lead the conversation, so he waits for him to speak first.

"Young men disappear without warning," the gruff voice says. "Shit is getting real in there. Lucky my body's a bit ragged; they don't bother me much. Watch your six, my friend. Don't take any medications they try to give you. I thought I should warn you."

"Have you told anyone else about this, or reported it to the police?"

"Everyone thinks I'm a crazy old man; no one believes a fucking word I say," he replies with a laugh. Then he stands up and cracks his neck. "Watch your ass, friend, and get out of there as fast as you can." With a wink, he adds, "Lorinda has the hots for you, you know." Laughing again, he pumps his fist and turns in the direction of the shelter.

Fred remains at the water's edge, thinking about what he has learned so far. When the sun begins to set, he makes his way back to the homeless shelter.

"I'm glad I found you!" declares Lorinda when she spots Fred. "I have some good news for you! You already have a job and an apartment!"

"Wow, isn't that a little quick..." questions Fred until Lorinda cuts him off.

"I'll tell you all about it in the morning," Lorinda says, waving off his hesitation. "Be in my office at eight."

Fred is surprised to see that Lorinda is dressing a little more daringly today. She is still wearing a high-necked blouse but she has unfastened the two top buttons. Fred makes no secret of staring at her as she walks away.

Later that evening, Eral Rosenbaum is impatiently waiting in Rabbi Katzoff's office for a meeting the rabbi unexpectedly called earlier that afternoon. He's been there for over twenty minutes now, and he's not happy. It's late, and he can't stop fidgeting in his chair.

Staring at his Rolex for the tenth time, he mumbles a not-so-silent, "Fuck it," and decides to leave. However, just as he moves toward the door, the rabbi breezes in.

"Sorry I'm late," apologizes Herb as he slips past Eral. "I was hoping that I could have a quiet evening tonight, but a couple of interesting things happened this afternoon. I just left one of my synagogue members; her husband died suddenly. I went to her house to comfort her, but she wouldn't let me leave. She tried to seduce me, and if I didn't need to see you, I would have gotten laid. Sit down," he orders, pointing to a chair. "I have an emergency."

Eral returns to his seat as Herb pulls out the chair behind his desk and sits down.

"I need a heart, ASAP," Herb declares. "I don't have a match in my database right now, so I need you to do a bio check at your shelter." He grabs a manila folder off his desk and hands it to Eral. "These are the bio-markers. Do your magic within forty-eight hours, and you'll get a nice bonus."

Eral smiles and opens the folder.

The tramp steamer Essex is on course for Panama. Built in the '60s, the ship is an older one, but it serves its purpose. When the vessel reaches Panama, it will wait in line to enter the Panama Canal at the Miraflores Locks near Panama City, and then head for the Bahamas.

Lu Tang is in Xian Li's cabin, as she has been every day since the ship got underway. The captain has always found a reason for the girl to be in his room. Today, Lu is sitting on the floor between the captain's bunk and his built-in desk, busily polishing his shoes. She is not wearing much as she goes about her work—only a push-up bra and lace panties, the captain's preferred outfit. Lu does her best to shine her captor's footwear while the old steamer's engines rumble and the ocean air swirls around the room.

Xian Li's cabin is small, but it is twice the size of the cabin that Lu was assigned for the duration of this voyage. Because it is the captain's quarters, it contains a private bathroom and shower, one of the only luxuries on the ship.

Xian Li is currently on the bridge, and Lu hopes against hope that he will remain there until she is finished. Not long after the ship sailed away from the Chinese coast, the captain showed Lu over and over again what she was expected to do in order to survive her journey.

While Lu works at her task, she reflects on her family and her previous life and cries. Deep in her soul, she hates Xian Li for what he is doing to her, and she often fantasizes about how she would like to murder him for what he has already done, and for what she knows he will continue to do. Then again, she knows that she could never hurt anyone, so she dismisses those thoughts and wipes away her tears, concentrating instead on the promise of the United States, where she has been assured that everything will be better.

Too soon, the door to the cabin opens, and Lu rises to acknowledge her tormentor. Without a word, Xian Li orders her into his bunk.

And just like that, Lu Tang's abuse continues.

CHAPTER SEVEN

Denise Handel's punishment for her latest escape attempt has finally ended, and she has been allowed to return to her room at the mountain mansion. She is not alone in the room, however. Gloria Ashton, a retired nurse practitioner and ex-Las Vegas call girl, is examining her thoroughly.

Gloria is in her early sixties but still shows signs of her younger beauty—a plus in her favor, and one of the reasons why she was hired at the brothel. The primary reason for her employment is that she has no family obligations so she can be on call 24/7 to take care of the ladies housed there.

"Well, Miss D," Gloria says dispassionately, "you have gonorrhea again. I'll give you a shot of Ceftriaxone and take you off duty. You'll be on your back again in a couple of days. Enjoy your time off."

While Gloria prepares a hypodermic needle, Denise's overlord enters the room. Impeccably dressed in one of his many designer suits, Guido Testoni leers suggestively at the nurse and inspects her from top to bottom. "My dear Gloria, you're looking fine, as usual. If you were only a little younger..."

Gloria is proud that she is still attractive, but she has no time for Guido and his smarmy behavior. She pays no attention to him and continues to prepare Denise's injection. When Guido realizes that he's getting no reaction, he shrugs his shoulders and turns to the matter at hand. "What's going on with her?" he asks, pointing a manicured finger at Denise. Still ignoring the man, Gloria orders Denise to lower her Daisy Duke shorts so she can inject the girl's left buttock.

After the shot is administered, Gloria takes her time discarding the used hypodermic needle. Then, she states flatly, "Mr. Testoni, Denise has gonorrhea again. I'm taking her offline for a few days. She should be good to go next week."

"Well, that's convenient," responds Guido, his calm demeanor surprising both Denise and the nurse. "We were planning to transfer her out of here, anyway."

Startled, Denise struggles to hide her joy at hearing that she will be leaving the brothel. Her fledgling happiness is dashed by Guido's next comments, however.

"You've become too much trouble here, bitch, so we're sending you to our property in Florida. That will be your last chance. If you give them any problems at all down there, you'll be dealt with even more severely than here. Capeesh? Now pack up your shit. You leave in twenty-four hours."

Without a backward glance at Denise, Guido turns toward Gloria and leads her out of the room. In the hallway, he pushes her against the wall and whispers in her ear. "You're still hot, Gloria. I'd do you right now, but you better check my men, too. They had an 'attitude adjustment' party with Denise."

Left alone in her room for the first time in a couple of weeks, Denise sits cross-legged on her bed and giggles, not believing her luck. Thinking about her father in Florida, she vows softly, "I'm going to see you again, Daddy, even if it's the last thing I ever do!"

At eight a.m. the next morning, Fred sits in Lorinda's office, alone. He has been anticipating this meeting, and Lorinda is late. All night long, he couldn't help but wonder what arrangements she had made for him so quickly. To pass the time, he thinks back to when he woke up that morning. None of the other men were missing, but he is still undecided about whether that is a good thing or a bad thing.

Hearing a noise, Fred looks up to see Lorinda entering her office in a hurry. Today, she is wearing jeans and a polo shirt, and the way she applied her makeup makes her look younger and more glorious. However, looking at Lorinda in a new outfit reminds Fred that he is still wearing the same jeans and T-shirt that he received when he arrived.

"Sorry I'm late," Lorinda huffs, a little out of breath. "The Andrews Avenue Bridge was up, and traffic was a mess."

After putting her purse down, Lorinda walks over to a file cabinet behind her desk and removes Fred's folder. Fooling with the drawer to try to get it to close properly, she eventually gives up and slams it shut instead. "Sorry about that," she declares. "I need a new file cabinet, but money is tight around here."

Sitting down, Lorinda opens the folder and skims the front page. "Fred, I have good news. Your military background has piqued the interest of our founder, Eral Rosenbaum. He's offering you a position as a security officer on his staff. He has also arranged a small apartment for you off Andrews Avenue. You have an appointment to meet with him at his office at ten this morning. One of our drivers will take you there and wait. After the meeting, he'll bring you to your apartment. I'm so happy for you, Fred! I hope this gets you back on your feet. Mr. Rosenbaum only chooses the best. Perhaps, after you get settled, we can celebrate your lucky break."

"Wow," gushes Fred smiling widely in simulated gratitude, "this is fantastic! Thank you so much! Security is right up my alley. And I'd love to celebrate with you! I was hoping we could get together sometime soon."

Lorinda grabs an envelope out of her center desk drawer. "I knew you'd be happy. Let's have breakfast in the dining hall before you go to your meeting." Standing, she hands Fred the envelope. "Here. Mr. Rosenbaum knows that you'll need some money to set up your apartment and get food and clothing. He's calling this a signing bonus."

Fred rises from his seat to accept a rather thick envelope. When he glimpses what's inside, his eyes go wide at the sight of a stack of freshly printed one-hundred-dollar bills. "Good Lord!" he exclaims. "There must be thousands of dollars in here!"

Fred knows that he's being bought, but he's not sure if Lorinda is in on the deal or not. To keep the young psychologist in the dark about his suspicions about the homeless shelter, Fred continues to act as if he's thrilled and completely surprised about this stroke of good luck. Reaching for Lorinda, he gives her a long hug, a hug that Lorinda does not want to end.

"I'll meet you in the dining hall in a minute," says Fred. "I just have to make a quick trip to the restroom."

Fred needs to update Will Ballard with the information he just received, so he detours to the men's room to place a furtive call. Happy that the room is empty, he ducks into an empty stall and powers up his phone, hoping that the battery will last long enough for his conversation. He's had to keep the phone out of sight all this time, so it hasn't been charged for a while.

"Will, I'm in," Fred says softly when the detective answers. "Eral offered me a job on his security team. He also got me an apartment and gave me a boatload of cash. I'll call you tonight with the details."

"Hot dog!" he hears through the phone. "I'll let the D.A. know. But call me after midnight, okay, buddy? I have that date with one of Rosenbaum's honeys."

"Yeah, well, don't do anything I wouldn't do," responds Fred as the low battery warning sounds on his phone. "Shit, I gotta go."

Thirty-something marketing guru Brooke Schoenfeld is in a hurry. Her morning workout ran longer than usual, so she fears she'll be late for work. Because she needs to go home first to shower and change, she is texting furiously to try to cover her ass for being late for her daily meeting. She is not paying much attention to the road, so she doesn't see the white Ford Econovan that has been following closely behind her Lexus since she left the gym.

When she turns off Federal Highway, she accidentally jumps the curb and crashes into an empty bus bench and a shopping center retaining wall. Thankfully, her car's airbags do their thing, but Brooke is temporarily stunned.

In the shopping center, several bystanders have seen the crash. Jumping into action, they swarm Brooke's vehicle to offer their assistance.

In the Econovan behind Brooke, Rocco Despirito has also seen the crash. Thinking quickly, he pulls his vehicle behind Brooke's car to block it from the street and directs his men to grab their target. Rushing toward the damaged Lexus, two men pull Brooke out of the car and take her to the van. Brooke is in a daze, so she doesn't understand that she's being dragged out of her vehicle.

"Hey!" shouts one of the witnesses. "What the hell are you doing?" he asks. But the thugs ignore the busybody and shove Brooke inside the van.

Rocco knows that he's going to have to do something about the upset shopper. "Hey," he shouts out of the car's window. "There's no problem; she's our boss's daughter! Thank God we were following her to the job site! We're gonna take her to the hospital now. We'll be back later to deal with the car." Waving to the confused bystanders, Rocco drives the van away while the thugs sedate their captive.

"Did you see that?" exclaims an older woman. "Are they really going to take her to the hospital?"

"That's what they said," says the male shopper as he dials 911, "but there were no plates on that van."

One block away from the crash site, Rocco pulls out his cell phone. "Target acquired," he announces. "We'll arrive in five minutes. She made it easy for us. Let Katzoff know that we have his liver, and get the team ready for extraction."

CHAPTER EIGHT

The following day, Randal is back in the schoolyard, texting as usual while the students file in for class.

In the middle of the crowd, Mandy has paired up with her friend, Tara, but she is not content. She is searching the throng for Abby, and Abby's pal, Calista. When she spots them a short distance away, she grins wickedly and forms her hand into a gun-like position and points it at them.

Assuming that no one else saw the gesture, Mandy puts her head together with Tara's and shares a private laugh.

The incident wasn't as stealthy as Mandy thought, however. Randal saw it all. Threading his way through the crowd of students, Randal catches up to Mandy and Tara before they enter the building.

"Morning, ladies," voices Randal sternly, holding out his hand in front of him. "I saw everything. Hand over your cell phones. And both of you need to see me at the end of the day."

"Mr. Levy, I can't," protests Tara. "If I miss the bus, I'll have no way of getting home! My Mom works three jobs, so she can't come and pick me up. She'll get fired if she does!"

"Cool it, Tara, he don't give a shit," snaps Mandy. "I'll have my driver bring you home."

Resigned to having detention yet again, the girls grudgingly hand their phones over to Randal. Then, they giggle and slither off to their first classes, both of them sashaying down the hallway as if they were strutting down a fashion catwalk.

Randal shakes his head at the girls' lack of remorse and turns to head to his office, but he bumps into the school's vice principal instead. The VP, who was standing behind him the entire time he was reprimanding the girls, looks serious.

"Randal, you need to let up on Mandy," orders Mr. Sullivan. "Her father practically paid for this place. He won't like this at all."

Randal glances down at several new text messages on his phone and shrugs. "Obviously, you've mistaken me for someone who cares what that man thinks," mutters Randal, low enough for only the vice principal to hear.

A makeshift operating room has suddenly sprung to life in a wing of the large house owned by Rabbi Katzoff. While the two thugs from the van drag Brooke Schoenfeld into the room, unlicensed medical personnel finish prepping a table to receive her. The surgery team is definitely out of place in this neighborhood of expensive homes situated on a wide section of Fort Lauderdale's iconic Intracoastal Waterway.

Brooke is still semi-conscious from the concussion she received during the crash, so she puts up no struggle as the men strap their victim to the table and cut off her clothes.

"This is for a liver, people!" instructs the surgeon to his assembled team. "If we do it fast, we won't need to keep her alive while we take it out!" To the thugs, he says, "I have a splitting headache. Ice the body down and shoot her in the head. I don't want to hear the screams. Tell Katzoff that the liver will be en route to Jackson Memorial in thirty minutes."

Suddenly, Brooke regains consciousness. She blinks at the bright, overhead light and tries to speak, but she becomes confused and feels very cold. Shivering, she opens her mouth again, but no sounds emerge. Brooke Schoenfeld feels very, very cold for several minutes, until everything goes black.

Will Ballard has just hung up with Fred Staten when he hears Lieutenant Jeffers shouting for him to come into his office. "Shut the door," Jeffers states. "I just got off the phone with Handel."

"What's goin' on?"

Jeffers takes in a deep breath and lets it out in a sigh. "We got another missing person. A woman named Brooke Schoenfeld had a car accident on Federal Highway. Witnesses say she was abducted from her car by three men in a white van."

"Don't tell me. No plates, right?"

"You got it. Tracking a white van with no plates is like finding a needle in a stack of needles. Handel wants Rosenbaum picked up, STAT."

"Will rises from his chair and paces his boss' office, deep in thought. "Fred just got a job offer from Rosenbaum, and this evening, I have a date with one of the girls in Rosenbaum's harem. Fred and I are going to talk later tonight, after my date."

"All right," replies the lieutenant. "We've been told to wrap this investigation up fast, but the both of you need to do good police work first, understand? We need hard evidence that can't be tainted or overturned by a slick lawyer."

The dining area of the dilapidated steamer Essex is sad, gray-walled room. With a sour smell of ocean air, fish heads and rice, it seems more like a bad dream than a place to eat. At mealtime, it's hard to hear anything over the din of Mandarin Chinese spoken by the ship's rowdy crew members.

Lu always eats alone during the nightly mess. Although the crew and the other captive children openly avoid her, all of them talk about her and the captain. The crew just likes to gossip, but the children shun her because of the special treatment she is receiving on this voyage. None of them knows what Lu has been forced to do to receive her privileges, however.

While the Essex is pulled through the Panama Canal like a dog on a leash, Lu Tang sits at her lonely table and closes her eyes. She often retreats into dreams of her family and the promised "streets of gold" in America. Lost this way in pleasant thoughts, she cringes when one of the ship's officers whispers in her ear.

"The captain wants to see you in his cabin."

At those dreaded words, Lu lowers her head in submission. Rising from her table, she leaves her food uneaten and follows the man, all the while trying to ignore the taunts of the other children as they laugh and throw food at her.

It is time for Fred's meeting with his new sponsor, Eral Rosenbaum. The homeless shelter's driver couldn't provide him with any information on Rosenbaum, so he doesn't know what to expect from the man.

When Fred enters the stark reception room of the address Lorinda gave him for Solstice Investments, he instantly notices that there doesn't seem to be an exit into the rest of the building, except through a door on the far wall that has no visible handle. Will Ballard told him about this room, but he is surprised, nonetheless.

Walking up to the small glass window, he taps lightly on it, and it instantly slides back to reveal a young and lovely Oriental girl. "Excuse me," says Fred pleasantly, "I have an appointment with Mr. Rosenbaum."

"Ah, yes, you are Mr. Staten," responds the girl

with a smile that Mona Lisa would admire. "Mr. Rosenbaum will see you soon."

Noting the girl's youth and beauty, Fred grins slyly, knowing that he must be on the right path.

With no chairs in the room, Fred leans against a wall to wait for his summons, but Eral Rosenbaum doesn't delay. He opens the knob-less door and beckons to his newest employee.

"Please come in, Fred. It's so nice to meet you. Lorinda speaks very highly of you."

Following Eral, Will arrives in an office filled with marble figurines and priceless works of art, just as Will described. Standing before Eral's desk, he adopts a sheepish grin and waits in silence for what he fully expects will happen next.

"Sit, sit," urges Eral. "Welcome to my staff."

Fred tries to get a read on Eral, but the man's blank stare reveals nothing. "Mr. Rosenbaum," says Fred in his most agreeable voice, "I want to thank you for offering me this opportunity. I also want to thank you for the cash. I fully intend to pay it back." Inwardly, Fred thinks, *Yeah, you just wait for that payback.*

Eral gives a good impression of a Cheshire cat as he rests his chin on steepled fingers. "I need a man of your experience to work at my shelter," he says quietly. "We get a lot of, shall I say, 'undesirables' there, and they need to be weeded out from the others."

Fred's bullshit meter is on high alert as his thoughts travel back to the men who were missing from his ward; however, he continues to exhibit a grateful demeanor. "Yes, sir. I will do my best to make you proud."

"Good," nods Rosenbaum with a smile that doesn't reach his eyes. "Rocco Despirito, my security chief, will take you to your apartment and get you settled in. I'll let the shelter driver know that he is no longer needed here. We'll take care of you from now on. Please follow me. Lillian in our HR department has some papers for you to fill out. You'll meet with Rocco after that, and he'll explain what he expects you to do for us."

Later that day, Will clears the dinner table after an early meal with Calista.

"Are you ready yet?" Will shouts after he shuts the dishwasher. "We need to leave soon! You don't want to keep Abby waiting, do you?"

A muffled voice returns to him from the bathroom. "Just doing my hair, Dad! I'll be right out!"

As Will places their leftover pizza in the refrigerator, Calista joins her father in the kitchen dressed in her favorite jeans and sweatshirt, with an overly large and fully stuffed backpack slung over one shoulder.

"Girl, you're only sleeping over there for one night," remarks Will. "What the heck you got in there?"

Calista places her hands on her hips and rolls her eyes. "Are we going now, or not?"

With a shake of his head, Will grabs his keys and gives his daughter a playful, but firm kick in the butt.

Laughing together, the pair exits their apartment and climbs into Will's car for the ten-minute ride to Abby's house.

Will walks Calista up to the door of the well-maintained Hoffman home. The entrance to the house is impressive. Large double doors made of high-quality wood contain frosted-glass side panels and a brass, lion-head knocker.

Responding to the doorbell, Gabriella Hoffman swings the door open and greets Will coolly. "Detective Ballard. Abby is looking forward to having Calista sleep over tonight." Sensing some tension in the air, Will is relieved when he hears a high-pitched voice behind Gabby. "Calista!" the voice says. "Come on up to my room!"

Recognizing her friend, Calista's face lights up, and she rushes into the home without saying goodbye to her father. Will notices, and frowns. "Our little girls are growing up," he observes. "Thanks for agreeing to have Calista stay here tonight. I don't go out often."

"Well, they're such good friends, it will be good for them," responds Gabriella. "And I'll get them both to school in the morning. Um, Will, I think I should apologize for the other night."

Momentarily puzzled, Will remembers the scene at the bar. "Oh, no need," he replies with a wave of his hand. "I know you two are having a rough time. I was just trying to cool things down."

Flushed with embarrassment, Gabriella offers another weak apology. "Well, we're a hit on social media, that's for sure." Then, she changes the subject.

"I know Abby is looking forward to performing with Calista in the talent show."

"Talent show?" asks Will. "Calista didn't mention anything about that. Teenagers! Well, goodnight, Gabriella. I'll call you in the morning. Thanks again."

"Enjoy your date, Will."

Will grimaces as he turns away from the door. *Yeah, some date.*

Judge Nicholas Handel's last hearing of the day is the Jennifer Smith custody case. Hilda Tarsey from Child Protective Services has joined him in his chambers.

Hilda has been with Child Services for many years and is well known by court personnel as being very protective of her young clients.

"Your Honor," expounds Hilda, "Jennifer Smith has not gone to the parenting classes you ordered her to attend. She is in direct violation of your order."

The judge looks up from the Smith file to consider what Hilda has said along with everything he has read. "Put Tara in foster care," he says. "Tell Mrs. Smith that I'll give her ten more days. If she doesn't comply with the court within that time, she will lose permanent custody of her daughter."

Judge Handel hands the file back to Tarsey, who nods and leaves his chambers. When he is alone, he reaches for his cell phone. "Herb," he says quietly, "I got a new young pussy I'll probably be sending your way soon. Her name is Tara Smith."

Will is relieved that Calista will be at her friend's house for the night. He doesn't know how long the date will last, or how it will go.

When he arrives downtown, he parks his car behind a hotel on Las Olas Boulevard and walks over to the central pay station. When he's on duty, he doesn't usually have to pay for parking, however tonight, he needs to maintain the ruse of being a private citizen out on the town for the evening.

Will strolls toward Rosenbaum's office, using the time to mull over the questions he wants to ask his date. He hopes to persuade the girl to give him as much information as possible about Rosenbaum's operation.

The short Las Olas strip is crowded tonight with locals and tourists. Many are window shopping at the trendy stores while others are eating and drinking at the area's many restaurants and bars.

Will has arranged to pick up his date, Mei Lan Zhao, in front of Eral Rosenbaum's office. Although he knows that he only arranged the date because of the case he's on, he's still a man, and he is eagerly anticipating seeing the pretty young thing again.

Walking with purposeful strides, Will enters the cobblestone alcove that leads to Eral's office, but he stops dead in his tracks when he beholds the young girl waiting for him. Mouth agape, Fred stares at Mei Lan and momentarily forgets that he's on duty. The girl's name means beautiful orchid and is indicative of her delicate features. The Asian beauty is tall and lean, with twin, store-bought assets that could make a blind man see. Tonight, she is wearing a tight skirt slit halfway up her thigh paired with a silk blouse that is unbuttoned just enough. Her face is framed by shiny, pitch-black hair flowing delicately off her head and caressing her shoulders. Her long legs, which end god knows where, are accented by six-inch heels that cause her hips to sway side-to-side in a magical dance.

The beautiful young woman smiles demurely at Fred's reaction. With her eyes locked on Will's, she walks up to him and places a slender arm around his shoulder. Leaning over, she whispers, "My, my, if you do not close your mouth, something can fly in."

Will works hard to extricate himself from his imagination. "Mei Lan," he says hoarsely, "you ah, look incredible. You're no match for this old man."

"Oh, do not condemn yourself," Mei Lan smiles. "You are quite handsome."

Will knows that the beauty has been generous in her description of his physical attributes, but he accepts her compliment and takes her arm. Proud as a peacock, he escorts his date out of the alcove and onto the Boulevard.

"I thought we'd go to the bar at the Riverside Hotel for some cocktails and then try that new French Bistro across the street for dinner," explains Will.

"What my man want is fine for me," coos Mei Lan. "I very much like French food."

When the couple enters the hotel, they stroll toward the bar through a crowd that parts to let them pass. Men and women alike gawk at Mei Lan.

After receiving their drinks, Will guides Mei Lan to a loveseat near a gas fireplace. The detective wants to sit somewhere that will afford them some privacy from the rest of the people in the bar who are trying to hook up for the night.

When she settles into her seat, Mei Lan sips her wine and stares calmly into the fire. Between sips, she licks her lips seductively.

Will watches his date with a knowing grin. "Mei Lan," he says, "tell me about yourself. Where are you from? How long have you been in Fort Lauderdale?"

The beauty looks at Will but doesn't respond right away. She resolves to reveal only the most basic information, nothing more. "What can I say?" she finally answers. "I am from small village near Beijing. My family saved money to send me to U.S. to go to school. I do not like cold, so I come to Florida. Mr. Rosenbaum give me job when I arrive."

Will stares into Mei Lan's eyes and detects the lie. "So Mr. Rosenbaum hired you and all of those other Asian women who work for him? I guess a lot of Chinese parents want their children to come to America for their education. What a coincidence that you were able to get a job at the same place where so many other young and attractive Chinese women work. It's so fortunate that you met Mr. Rosenbaum," he adds sarcastically.

Mei Lan fidgets uncomfortably as she listens to

Will. There is something in his tone; she suspects that he is not buying her story. "Yes, it is a happy thing," she claims. "You do not believe that my family want to help me get good education?"

"Oh, of course I do. It's like all those other Asian children we find dead or dying in shipping containers at the port," says Will. "Those parents, like yours, wanted a good life for their children and they accepted a lot of money in return for sending them away from home. They trusted the people who paid them, as I'm sure yours did. But I think what really happened is that you were sold into a modern-day slave trade and brought here to work off the money your family received." Watching Mei Lan's expression pale, he adds, "You're not really here to go to college, are you? You're working off your family's debt at Eral's business. Isn't that right?"

Surprised, Mei Lan covers her mouth with her hand, prompting Will to reach into his pocket for his badge. Showing it to Mei Lan, he says, "I'm a Fort Lauderdale Police Detective, and I'm investigating Eral Rosenbaum. I would like you to come to my office so we can talk about Mr. Rosenbaum and his company."

"Police?" Mei Lan protests. "You send me to jail? I have done nothing!"

"No, no, you are not going to jail," declares Will firmly. "We have testimonies from other women who have told us about Mr. Rosenbaum, so you are not alone. Talk to us and we will help you and protect you from him."

With unseeing eyes, Mei Lan stares into the fire

and blinks through tears that are now streaming down her face. Knowing that her mascara is probably leaving behind a trail of woe, she whispers, "I look terrible now. I must fix my face. Then, I will go with you. Mr. Rosenbaum is not a good man."

Will nods and walks Mei Lan to the ladies' room. When she goes inside, he leans against the wall to wait for her.

Inside the restroom, Mei Lan splashes water on her face and tries to fix her makeup while fresh tears fall. As she dabs at her eyes, a middle-aged woman exits a stall and stands next to her at the sink. "Whoever that man is, he's not worth it," she advises. "You need to dump his ass."

Mei Lan smiles wanly at the woman and pretends to fix her hair while she waits for her to leave. When the door closes, Mei Lan scans the bathroom to make sure it's empty and then pulls a nail file out of her purse. Staring at her wrist, she knows it's going to hurt, but she still jabs the file deep into the skin on her left arm. Grimacing in pain, she gasps at the blood that begins to stream down her arm and hand. The sight of so much blood makes her faint, and she crumbles to the floor.

Outside of the ladies' room, Will continues to wait for Mei Lan. He doesn't pay much attention when a woman walks past him to enter the bathroom, but when she lets out a blood-curdling scream and runs out, Ballard runs in.

The sight of Mei Lan on the floor with all that blood causes Will to go into action. With one hand, he grabs as many paper towels as he can and applies pressure to the open wound. With the other hand, he dials 911 and provides his police code to the dispatcher to summon an emergency response team.

Will holds Mei Lan tightly and tries to comfort her as she drifts in and out of consciousness. "Nice try," he says quietly, "but you missed your artery. You're probably gonna be okay."

"Help me," moans Mei Lan.

Minutes later, the hotel lobby swarms with EMT and police personnel. When two EMTs arrive, Will stands aside to let them do their work.

"She's a lucky one, Detective," says one of the EMTs. "You want to come with us to the hospital?"

Will shakes his head. "I'll assign a uniformed officer to guard her there. She's a material witness in a criminal investigation, so the D.A. will want to keep her safe."

As the emergency technicians wheel Mei Lan out of the bathroom, Will gives a nearby cop his new guard duty assignment and then calls the D.A. "Mr. Handel? Sorry to bother you at this late hour."

"No problem, Detective, I just got home. It's been a long day. What do you need?"

"My date with one of Rosenbaum's honeys proved fruitful and she may be willing to help. However, the stress may have gotten to her. She tried to commit suicide, but luckily, she failed. She's on her way to Broward General now. I sent a uniformed officer with her."

Darren responds, but his tone is anything but jubilant. "Got the son of a bitch?" he declares blandly. "I'll send one of my investigators to the hospital in the morning. If all goes well, I may be able to convene a grand jury soon."

"I won't go!" cries Tara, hugging her mother in the living room of their small apartment. "I want to stay with you!"

"I'll get you back, honey. I'll go to those classes, I promise," weeps Jennifer as she holds her daughter tightly.

Standing nearby, Hilda Tarsey clears her throat and clicks her pen impatiently. "Well, you haven't attended any of them yet," she grouses. "You have less than two weeks to accomplish the task Judge Handel gave you. If you don't do it by then, you'll more than likely lose custody of your daughter." Turning to Tara, she declares, "We need to go now. Get your suitcase."

Tara glares at Ms. Tarsey through bloodshot eyes. "Fuck you!" she yells at the woman. "Fuck the judge! And fuck Child Services!"

Calista and Abby are enjoying their time together. Sitting on the floor of Abby's bedroom, they painted each other's nails and changed into their pajamas to talk while they comb each other's hair.

"Calista," pleads Abby, "are you ever going to tell me about that guy?"

"There's nothing to tell," replies Calista, blushing. "We met in a chat room. He sounds real nice and wants to be friends."

"Yeah? What else?"

"He goes to the Heritage School. He's seventeen and has his own car." After a slight pause, Calista adds, "He wants to meet me."

Abby raises her brows in surprise. "Calista, you don't know him. You need to be careful, especially if your dad finds out and goes all Five-O on you."

With a laugh at Abby's comment, Calista says, "Yeah, well, I don't know if I want to meet him right now, anyway. Maybe later; who knows? Hey, let's think about what we're going to do for that talent show."

"Okay. Hmm... how about a dance routine?" says Abby, rising off the floor a little too quickly, which makes her dizzy. Feeling like she might faint, she collapses onto her bed.

"Hey! Are you okay?" asks Calista. "Should I call your mom?"

Abby shakes her head. "I'm fine. This feeling comes and goes; I just need to hydrate. It goes with the territory, I guess. I'll take a drink of water, and then we can work out a routine."

That night, when Will finally makes it home to

his empty apartment, he stares longingly at a photo of his late wife and sighs. Then, his phone rings.

"Ballard," he answers.

"Hey, it's Fred. They set me up in my new apartment and also gave me a car. Rosenbaum wants me for some security work at his homeless shelter. I'll find out more in the morning. How'd your date go?"

Will sighs again. "She tried to kill herself after I told her that I knew what was going on. Luckily, she didn't do a good job of it. She's at Broward General now and will probably testify against Rosenbaum. Looks like we may have got him. The D.A.'s office is sending one of their investigators in the morning. I'm going to be there when he talks to her. If he likes what he hears, they'll convene a grand jury and get that prick off the streets. Whatever you can find out on your end will be great. Let's talk again tomorrow night."

CHAPTER NINE

The next day's early morning darkness provides too much cover for the wicked. The Essex has docked in the Bahamas, and Lu and the rest of the children have been ordered off the ship. The crew is now waiting for their legal cargo to be offloaded.

Sitting in the back of a truck that had been waiting for them, the children are once again in the dark, wondering what will come next. Out of necessity, most of them have sought comfort with each other, but Lu is sitting off to the side, alone. The children still want nothing to do with her.

After a while, the truck drives away from the dock and disappears into the gloom. It's on its way to a small cove where a go-fast boat will take the youths to a private beach on Florida's east coast.

At the Hoffman house, Abby and Calista are eating their breakfast of waffles with butter and molasses while Gabriella tidies up the kitchen. "Finish up, girls," Gabby orders, "it's almost time to leave."

Unexpectedly, Calista's ever-present cell phone rings and after a quick glance at the screen, she answers it in a flash. "Morning, Daddy! How was your date?"

Will grimaces at the thought that his encounter the previous evening was a normal date. "It was fine," he lies. "Did you have a good time with Abby?"

"Yeah, but Abby's mom is gonna drive us to school now, so I can't talk. I'll take the bus home, as usual. You're gonna have to fill me in on all the details of your date, you know! See ya later!"

Calista ends the call abruptly, leaving Will staring at his Android. "Guess I gotta make up some details," he mumbles.

Will glances at the clock in the kitchen and realizes that if he doesn't leave now, he's going to be late for the D.A. investigator's interview with Mei Lan. As he rushes out of the kitchen, he forgets to turn off his coffee maker.

At the same time Will is driving toward Broward General Hospital, a Learjet is landing further north, at West Palm Beach Airport. The private plane taxis to a hanger in a remote area of the airport and stops. With its engines still whining, three people exit the plane—two large men, and a young girl.

Although each of the men is much larger and stronger than the girl, both of them take firm hold of the girl's arms. They know all about Denise Handel's reputation for trying to escape, and they don't want to take any chances of losing her. They guide her firmly toward a waiting limousine, and while one of them opens the rear door, the other one shoves her inside and slams the door closed. The larger of the two walks around to the driver's side and taps on the window, giving the driver the thumbs up sign.

As the car speeds off, the two men turn back toward the jet. On the way, the smaller one remarks, "For all the trouble that one's caused, she should be dead by now. She must be a great lay!"

Will Ballard is not in a good mood. Although he rushed through the terrible morning traffic to make it to Broward General Hospital on time, the D.A. investigator is not there. While downing his second cup of vended coffee, he paces the lobby impatiently and watches each person who enters. Suddenly, he stops and mouths, *Oh, fuck!* Will just remembered that he left his coffee maker on, and that irritates him even more. Keeping a watchful eye on the steady stream of people coming through the hospital's doors, he goes on high alert when an obese man in a tight suit walks toward him.

"You must be Detective Ballard," says the man, stretching out his hand. "I'm Kevin Ingram, Associate D.A."

This guy looks a little too green, thinks Will unhappily. *Could he really be with the D.A.'s office?* "You must be new in town. I haven't met you before."

"Yeah, I, ah... This is my first case. Shall we go? I don't want to keep Ms. Zhao waiting."

Will mouths another, *Oh, fuck,* as he follows the newly-minted attorney to the elevators.

Fred is back at the homeless shelter, having driven there from his new apartment in the green '72 Dodge Dart he got from Rosenbaum. Although the car has 300,000 miles on it, its slant six purrs like a kitten, and he didn't see much rust when he did a quick walk around.

Psychologist Lorinda Vitale was just getting out of her car when Fred drove in. With a smile and a wave, she walks over to his car. "Glad you're on board," she says happily. "I'm going to enjoy working with you. Hey, I like your car! It's an oldie, but a goodie!"

"Yeah, Mr. Rosenbaum gave it to me. I have no idea where he found it. She runs damn good for a car that's over forty years old. And it even has AC!"

Lorinda grabs Fred's arm on the way to the employee entrance. "Mr. Despirito's office is behind the kitchen; you can't miss it. It's the only door at the end of the hallway on the left. Good luck today!"

With another smile and wave, Lorinda turns toward her office, leaving Fred looking down the hallway. When he sees the door she mentioned, he cricks his neck, exhales, and walks toward it.

As the sun continues to ascend in the morning sky, its golden rays shine brightly over a grand, 30,000-square-foot mansion in the coastal city of Boynton Beach. Bathed in the sun's light, the stately mansion surveys the ever-changing expanse of the Atlantic Ocean like an English castle overlooking the moors in Northern England.

Well beyond the breaking waves, a forty-three-foot Midnight Express powerboat is sweeping down the coastline from somewhere north of the city. When it comes within sight of the Boynton Beach house, it cuts through the breakers and idles at the mansion's dock.

Aboard the boat, the Chinese captain grabs a suppressed Glock and points it at each of his passengers. Raising his voice to be heard over the motor, he shouts in his native Mandarin. "Time to tread water or die! That house on the shore is your destination! Every one of you—get the hell off my boat!"

Although the young passengers are frightened, they are eager to get back on land. Taking the lead, Lu dives headfirst into the surf, and the others follow. Everyone, that is, save one. A terrified little girl remains huddled in the bow, and she is refusing to move.

The scar-faced captain is furious. He cares nothing for the children he pilots to this house on a regular basis. All he wants to do is be on his way so he can collect his payment. With his Glock pointed at the youngster's head, he repeats his command. "Leave now, or die here! It's your choice!"

The other youths are swimming toward the beach, so they don't know that one of their number has not left the boat. When they reach the shore, they are met by several of the mansion's servants, who offer them towels and speak to them in their native tongue.

Although the youths are wet, the servants order them up to the house.

At the top of a set of stairs that leads to a pathway over the dunes, Lu turns to take a last look at the powerboat and is surprised when she sees a flash of light in the bow. Still looking at the vessel, her surprise turns to horror when a body falls overboard and the powerboat speeds back out to sea. Lu has no chance to react to what she just saw, as someone pushes her forward at that moment and she is compelled to continue to walk up to the house. Lu and the rest of the children are eventually led into the servant's quarters where they are made to wait again, with no explanation.

While the newly-arrived youths survey their surroundings and dry themselves off inside the house, outside the house, a white limousine is gliding through the gate. The limo slithers up the home's brick-paved drive lined with Italian cypress trees and comes to a stop in an elegantly designed courtyard. Two persons emerge from the vehicle's rear door. One is a very bulky man, and the other is Denise Handel.

Denise and her latest handler are met at the mansion's front door by an older woman who is clearly trying to look much younger. "Well, Missy," the woman declares to Denise through thin lips, "this is your last stop. Fuck up here, and you're toast." With a sly wink at the large man at Denise's side, the woman orders, "Bring her upstairs and put her in my room. She'll have to wait there until I can deal with her. I have to address the new waitstaff—we got another group in this morning."

Fred stands in front of the closed door at the end of the hallway and inhales deeply. Then he knocks and opens the door to a small, windowless office furnished with a couple of pieces of metal furniture. Overhead, a fluorescent light buzzes and flickers.

"Right on time," announces Rocco, who is sitting behind the desk, scratching himself. "Sit down. We have lots to talk about."

Fred takes a seat on a metal folding chair while Rocco stands, farts, and re-lights a soggy cigar.

"You have a fancy resume, and Rosenbaum wants you on his security staff," announces Rocco, puffing away on the cigar and eying Fred warily. "But I already have more men than I need, and there's already something about you I don't like."

Feeling's mutual, muses Fred.

"I did some checking around and found a better spot in the company for a man with your talents. I talked to Mr. Rosenbaum and he agreed with my recommendation." Opening a folder, Rocco grabs a piece of paper and hands it to Fred. "That's the address. They expect you there bright and early Monday morning. Ask for Mr. Cardone, and tell him Rocco sent you. If you don't have a suit, I suggest you get one. Now, get the fuck out of here."

Fred looks at the address and folds the paper neatly, placing it in his pocket. Then he leaves the office without having said a word.

As Fred walks back down the long hallway, he mulls over recent events and decides to drive directly to the police station to speak with Lieutenant Jeffers. He also intends to Google the address he was just given.

That Rocco character seemed awfully hot to get me to that Boynton Beach address. Wonder what the hell's going on over there.

Detective William Ballard and Associate D.A. Kevin Ingram stop at the fourth-floor nurse's station on the way to Mei Lan's room. Down the corridor they see a uniformed officer sitting on a folding chair.

"I'm Detective Ballard with FLPD, and this is Attorney Ingram from the D.A.'s office," says Will, displaying his badge to the nurse on duty. "We're here to see Ms. Zhao. How's she doing this morning?"

"She's fine," responds the nurse, not looking up from her computer screen. "But due to the attempted suicide, we'll have to keep her here for seventy-two hours. She's having breakfast now, so you can go in."

As the two men approach Mei Lan's room, the officer outside stands to block them. "Can I see some ID, please?" he asks. After inspecting Fred's ID, he nods and steps aside.

Inside the room, Mei Lan is poking glumly at the cold pancakes on her breakfast tray. However, when she sees her date from the night before, she perks up. "Will Ballard!" she cries. "They make me stay here! Why do they keep me? I am okay!"

"It's standard," replies Will kindly. "You tried to kill yourself, remember? They want to make sure you don't try it again." Gesturing to the assistant D.A., he declares, "Mei Lan, this is Kevin Ingram. He wants to ask you some questions about Eral Rosenbaum, and what you do for him."

At the mention of Rosenbaum's name, Mei Lan stiffens and stares at Will with woeful eyes. Rubbing her bandaged wrist, she declares in a subdued voice, "They will kill me. I am afraid."

Will removes a digital recorder from inside his suit jacket and places it on the tray table in front of the frightened girl. As he turns it on, he announces, "Don't be afraid. We'll protect you and put you in a safe place so he won't be able to hurt you. Anything you can tell us will help us put Eral Rosenbaum in prison." Will's assurances seem to calm Mei Lan, so he continues. "We're going to record this conversation now. Do you understand?"

Mei Lan nods, but she is not sure that she'll be able to find the courage to reveal what she knows.

"Okay, good," says Will. "Now please tell us how you came to the United States."

But Mei Lan doesn't answer. Instead, she stares down at her hands and picks at her bandages. Will is just about to ask her again when she says in a quavering voice, "A man we do not know come to our village and say I get good job in America if my family send me here. He say to my father she can send money home for mother, father, brothers. The man say he will give my family money if I go with him on next ship. My family very poor, so they say yes. They have no choice."

"We understand," says Kevin Ingram quietly. "But what that man said wasn't true, was it?"

"No. I come on ship with many others. Some, like me, were sold to the man by their families. Others come from the street. I am so ashamed!" cries Mei Lan, hanging her head so low that her chin almost touches her chest.

"We know that this is painful for you," murmurs Kevin. "What can you tell us about Mr. Rosenbaum?"

Mei Lan sighs deeply. "He is a bad man. Many girls work for him. We live together in a large house near the ocean."

"Can you tell me where the house is?"

"I hear them say, 'Horiwood.' You understand?"

"Yes, I think you mean Hollywood. It's a city in this area. What kind of work do you do for Mr. Rosenbaum?"

"Ha! It is not work for money that the man tell my parents! I work with other girls. He tell us be friendly to powerful people."

"What do you do when you're with those powerful people?"

Mei Lan begins to cry. "We go on dates, like I do with Will. There are parties... We are passed to all guests. It is so terrible! If my father knew...! Some girls try to leave, but they are caught. We never see them again."

"Does Mr. Rosenbaum go to the parties, too?

Does he threaten any of you?" asks Will.

"Oh, Mr. Rosenbaum give us English tutor. He not go to parties, but a man called Rocco yell at us very much. He make us do...things...with clients."

"I know this is hard," says Will, "but we need to know. Are you being forced to have sex with Mr. Rosenbaum's clients?"

"Yes!" cries Mei Lan. "Rocco beat us if we do not have sex with them! I do not want to do that! That man is very bad!"

"How old are you, Ms. Zhao?" asks Kevin.

Mei Lan turns her head to stare out of the window. "I am eighteen."

Kevin studies the girl before him. "Ms. Zhao, you are not under oath today, but you will be soon. Now, I need you to be honest. Would you like to change what you just told us in any way?"

Mei Lan glances at Will with tears in her eyes. "No. It is truth. I come here when I am sixteen. I am in Florida two years."

Will winces at the understanding that his "date" is only eighteen years old and that she has been forced into a life of sexual slavery in the United States. With images of Calista filling his mind, he asks, "How old are the other girls who are kept in that house by Mr. Rosenbaum?"

Ashamed, Mei Lan lowers her head again. "I am the oldest."

Will turns his head sharply toward Kevin. "I need to give this information to Jeffers, ASAP. Do you need me for anything else right now?"

Kevin shakes his head. "Let me have that recorder. I'll get her statement typed up so she can sign it. I'll also try to get the address of that house."

Will turns to Mei Lan. "I want you to talk to a police illustrator. Tell him what Rocco looks like so he can make a drawing of his face. I'll leave a guard outside of your room for as long as you're here. After you're released, other people who work with me will take you to a safe place." Will smiles at Mei Lan and squeezes her hand. "I'll come back to see you before you leave the hospital. Mr. Ingram will take good care of you; I promise."

Although Mei Lan seems more composed, she still grips Will's hand tightly. "Please hurry back," she pleads.

Will nods, easing his hand from Mei Lan's grasp. Pulling Kevin aside, he whispers, "I need to speak with you outside."

In the hallway, Will and Kevin have a hushed conversation a few paces away from the policeman stationed outside Mei Lan's door. Will warns, "Those girls are here illegally, so Immigration is gonna get involved, too. We need to protect every one of them from those bastards."

Kevin nods. "I'll do my best. I can give Mei Lan a new identity for testifying, but I don't know about others yet. This is going to get ugly."

CHAPTER TEN

Fred is on his way to the Boynton Beach address Rocco gave him. He turns south on State Road A1A, then begins to look for the house number. When he finds it, he is not surprised at what he sees. His destination in this exclusive section of the city is set behind high stone walls, invisible from the street.

Coasting his car down a short drive, Fred stops in front of a pair of ornate gates that block his path. By Fred's estimation, the wrought iron barrier topped by bronze lions is at least fifteen feet high. *That's a little excessive, even for this exclusive area,* Fred proposes, *and those walls are pretty high as well. It'll be interesting to see what's behind them.*

Alongside Fred's car is a small communications box that reminds him of the ordering system at a fast food restaurant, except for the surveillance camera he knows is watching his every move.

Rolling down his window, Fred leans out and presses a black button. "I'm Fred Staten," he declares. Rocco sent me; he's with Mr. Rosenbaum."

Releasing the button, Fred waits for a response while he listens to the sounds of seagulls and peacocks squawking in the distance.

After what seems like an eternity, a stern voice

crackles through the speaker. "Park near the garage and walk around to the left, Mr. Staten. Enter through the side entrance."

An electronic buzzer announces the opening of the gate. As the barrier swings inward, it seems to invite Fred to enter at his own risk.

As Fred drives down a winding brick driveway through swaying palm trees and tall sea grape bushes, he looks around and mumbles, *Where the hell is the house?*

"It's a very good morning!" Detective Will Ballard calls out cheerfully when he enters his boss' office. "We got Rosenbaum, and he's dead to rights!"

Jeffers looks up from his work. "Yeah, I spoke to Handel. It's great that the girl talked. Handel's going to present Mei Lan's testimony to a grand jury, and she'll probably get subpoenaed. He's also getting a warrant to raid the house where Mei Lan lives in Hollywood." Jeffers picks up a pen and twirls it in his fingers. "Sergeant Staten also called. He met with a guy named Rocco who works for Rosenbaum. The guy sent Fred to a house in Boynton. Handel wants us to find out if Rosenbaum is affiliated with the place in Boynton, along with the homeless shelter in Fort Lauderdale. He also wants us to keep an eye on this Rocco character and question the residents of the shelter. We may have discovered something more sinister than sex trafficking."

"This case is growing by the minute," declares

Will.

"Yeah. We need to talk to a woman named Lorinda Vitale. She works at the shelter. Make up some bullshit so she'll come in for questioning."

Denise Handel is deep in thought. She's been sitting on the bed of her newest jail cell on the top floor of the Boynton Beach brothel for a while now. Suddenly, an idea comes to her and she walks over to the window. "Well, fuck," she murmurs as she gazes out at the crashing surf just two hundred feet away. "It's a heck of a lot warmer here than in Colorado, and it's way closer to my dad. But I still need to get away from these people, and I will do it, one way or another." Turning away from the window, she scrutinizes the room's furnishings, which she believes make it look as if she's in a little girl's dollhouse. "Just call me Hooker Barbie," she mutters miserably."

Fred parks his faded green Dodge Dart where he was told to, but he feels uncomfortable. His early model car seems very much out of place next to the gleaming white Bentley in front of the four-car garage, and he hopes that the owners of this house won't tow his car away in disgust. *Maybe they'll think it's abandoned and junk it,* he worries.

To get to the entrance he was directed to, he follows a path of high-quality travertine paver stones around one side of the house, occasionally taking a moment to glance up at the upper stories of the luxurious home. When he reaches a single door set under an archway, he finds another security camera watching him.

Fred presses the doorbell and hears a muffled ring, then the buzz of the door's automatic lock. Leaning on the handle, he pushes the heavy door open and steps into an ornate hallway adorned with marble floors and elaborate base and crown molding. Inside, waiting for Fred is a muscular man in a well-cut black suit. With one look at the man, Fred understands that he's going to get a pat down, so without being told, he spreads apart his arms and legs. When Fred passes the guard's test, he gestures to Fred, and Fred follows him down the hall.

What is it with the long hallways? Fred wonders as he walks behind the man, peeking into every room he passes. When the guard stops in front of a set of closed double doors, he nods in the direction of the room and orders Fred to enter.

The room is a vast, oval-shaped expanse furnished with richly-patterned Oriental rugs, high-quality tables and chairs, and an imposing mahogany and teak desk that dominates at one end. The walls encircling the room are covered with expensive, tufted fabric, and a crystal chandelier casts a soft glow over everything. Fred can't help but think that the luxurious surroundings make it look as if he's in a mini-palace.

Gazing around in awe, Fred wonders what the hell he has crawled into. There is no one else in the room, so he openly gapes at everything.

After he's been in the room for a while and no one else has joined him, he decides to take a seat in one of the sumptuously-upholstered chairs in front of the mahogany desk. When more solitary minutes pass, Fred begins to wonder whether anyone but the man who patted him down knows that he's there.

After another interminably long wait, the double doors finally open and a woman dressed to the nines enters. Behind her, the Sasquatch from the hallway closes the large doors quietly behind her.

Fred jumps to his feet at the woman's entrance. Struck by her deportment, he reflexively observes that she is probably older than she is trying to appear, but he dismisses that thought as one of the many things women do to feel attractive.

Striding purposefully toward Fred, the woman reaches out her hand in greeting. "Welcome, Mr. Staten. I'm Debra Connelly, the manager of this house, and I'm very interested in getting to know you better. Mr. Despirito gave you a fabulous recommendation."

Psychologist Lorinda Vitale is interrupted from her routine paperwork by a knock at her office door. "Yes?" she questions the unfamiliar face. "Can I help you?"

"Miss Vitale," announces Will, walking toward her with badge and ID in hand, "I'm Detective William Ballard with Fort Lauderdale Police."

With her brows shooting up in surprise, Lorinda

hesitates a moment and then gives Will's credentials a cursory inspection. "Okaaay," she says, still uncertain. "What can I do for you?"

"We've received numerous complaints from local businesses about this shelter and some of its residents, so I need to ask you to come down to my office to address those issues. I understand that this may be an inconvenience, but it's procedure. Certain forms will need to be filled out, and then I'm sure we'll be able to dismiss the accusations. It shouldn't take more than an hour of your time."

"Oh, my," replies Lorinda. "I had no idea that we were causing concerns in the community. I'll be happy to go with you to clear this up immediately. Have a seat, please, while I inform my assistant that I'll be out of the building for a while. I'll be right back."

When Lorinda leaves the room, Will mutters, "Damn, I should write a book about all the things I have to do on this job!"

Lu Tang and the other children are now in a small room near the commercial kitchen in the Boynton beachfront mansion. They have been told to choose a seat at one of the study desks arranged in the room in neat rows.

All of the youths are nervous, but they have learned over the course of their recent travels to wait patiently, so they are quiet but alert.

Lu is especially edgy after the experiences she

suffered on the Essex. To calm herself, she allows her mind to wander back to pleasant memories of her parent's farm, but her happy thoughts are endlessly interrupted by images of the nightmares on the ship.

After a lengthy wait, an older Chinese woman enters the room and takes her place at the front of her newest 'class'. The woman is wearing a plain blue housedress and sensible white shoes. She starts by speaking to the children in Mandarin.

"You have all been brought here to work as domestic housekeepers," she says. "You will begin your duties only when I feel you are ready. Your first task is to improve your English language skills. Fail your English lessons, and you will not be needed in this household. Your new life depends on how well you do in this class, so let's get started."

While the frightened children begin English lessons at one end of the Boynton mansion, Fred is quietly watching Debra Connelly in the ornate room at the other end. She has been going through paperwork on her desk for a long time, and the silence is becoming awkward.

Squirming in his chair, Fred decides to speak his mind to his new employer. "Excuse me," he says, "I've been shuffled around today like an old fruitcake, with no details about what I'm supposed to be doing. I was told that I had to rush up here for a new job, but I've been sitting in this room for almost forty-five minutes, and I still have no idea what's going on. I assume that you've already read my file, so you must know my skills and areas of expertise. Excuse my French, but it's time to shit, or get off the pot!" Debra hears Fred, but she pays him no outward attention. Exasperated, Fred shakes his head and rises from his chair. "Okay, fine," he declares in a huff. "I'm done here."

When Fred takes a step toward the door, Debra finally looks up. "Mr. Staten," she proclaims regally, "I appreciate your aggressiveness. You have passed my test. Please sit down; we have a lot to discuss."

Surprised, Fred reluctantly reclaims his seat. "The ball is now in your court," he growls. "Dribble, or call time out."

Debra smiles at Fred's second cliché as she walks around her desk with her fingers tracing a pattern on the highly polished wood. Stopping in front of Fred, she perches on the edge of the desk and crosses her legs in a motion that causes her skirt to ride up her thighs. Following Fred's line of sight, Debra is happy that he notices and licks her lips seductively.

"Now that I have your attention," she murmurs in a low, sultry voice, "I shall proceed. I run an exclusive club here. We host private parties and elegant dinner events for very influential people. I need to make sure that our clientele is always safe and that their privacy is protected. That's where you come in. If Rocco is right about you, you'll become an integral part of my security team. Your main job will be to create a sense of well-being at all times, among our guests, and our staff."

"Hmm, it seems that Mr. Rosenbaum has some interesting things going on here," comments Fred.

Debra's hearty laugh makes Fred wonder if he said something wrong. "Mr. Rosenbaum does not own this club," she grins. "He is one of our sponsors, however, and we welcome and respect his input. But let's not talk about Mr. Rosenbaum; we need to concentrate on you. First, let's get you some new attire. Bargain store, off-the-rack clothing won't do in your new position. Our clients will entrust you with their safety and confidentiality; therefore, you must project an air of respect and competency. You will be working two six-day shifts with a week off after each shift. You will be housed here during each shift, and when you are working, you will be on call 24/7."

Debra stands and sashays back around her desk, but doesn't sit down in her comfortable chair. Instead, she bends over and presses a button under the desktop, making sure that Fred notices what's inside her low-cut blouse.

Responding to the call button, a different dark-suited man walks into the room, and stands silently behind Fred.

"Mr. Staten," says Debra, "Vincent Cardone, the head of our security team has just joined us. He will show you to your quarters and get you outfitted in more appropriate attire. He will also answer any questions you may have."

"Okay," says Fred, "but I need to ask something of you, if you don't mind. What compensation will I receive as a member of your security staff?"

"Your salary will begin at $75K a year, and all the clothing we supply you will be deducted from your wages. Good day, Fred, and welcome aboard. If you need anything at all, my door is always open."

Behind Fred, Vincent Cardone orders, "Let's go,

slick."

At the police station, William guides Lorinda through the organized confusion that typifies everyday life at his workplace. The place is loud and confusing—phones ring while victims give statements and alleged perpetrators are led to who knows where.

"We'll have more privacy if we speak with Lieutenant Jeffers in his office," offers Fred by way of apology.

As the pair enters Jeffers' office, Will can't help but notice that a sheet of plywood is affixed to the door where a pane of glass should be. "What happened, Lieutenant?" he asks.

Looking up from an open file, Jeffers answers with a frown. "Oh, that? Detective Hopkins got upset with the D.A. and slammed the door. Hard."

"Ha! That hasn't happened since Stenhouse left!" laughs Will.

"Yeah, well, such is life at the nuthouse. This must be Miss Vitale. Come in, please."

Lorinda sits in one of the chairs Jeffers points her to. "Can you tell me why I'm here?" she asks nervously. "Is the shelter in trouble?"

"That's what we're trying to find out," responds the lieutenant. "Miss Vitale, we've received reports from some of the shelter's former residents that people have been disappearing from your facility during the night. They've told us that members of the security staff, directed by a Mr. Rocco Despirito, are somehow involved in their disappearance. Do you have any knowledge of this?"

Lorinda attempts to keep a neutral expression on her face, but fails. She is stunned, and her face turns white.

"Miss Vitale, are you okay?" asks Jeffers.

To recover from the shock, Lorinda takes a deep breath and lets it out in a steady stream. "I had no idea," she asserts. "Um, disruptive people do come in from time to time, and our security team always deals with them. We ask those residents to leave, and I process their discharge paperwork. But those things happen during the day or early evening. Um, Immigration and Customs Enforcement comes in one in a while to remove residents, but they always identify themselves when they're there."

Will locks eyes with Lorinda. "We contacted ICE in Miami, and they told us that they've never been to your facility."

Lorinda's face becomes even more pale than before.

"We need a list of the residents you say have been asked to leave," says Will. "We also need a copy of Rocco Despirito's personnel records."

Lorinda swallows hard. "I can give you everything, except for the information on Rocco. He's a part-time associate who was assigned to the shelter by Eral Rosenbaum. You'll have to contact Mr. Rosenbaum to get information on Rocco."

Will and Lieutenant Jeffers exchange meaningful glances. Then Will says, “Lieutenant, I’ll accompany Miss Vitale back to the shelter to get that list of residents.”

“Okay, good. There’s nothing more we need to ask you at this time, Miss. However, we may want to talk to you again, after we speak to Mr. Rosenbaum.”

Jeffers reaches over the desk to shake Lorinda’s hand. “I appreciate your cooperation; we’ll be in touch. Please don’t tell anyone about our meeting. Let's just keep it to ourselves for now.”

CHAPTER ELEVEN

Harriet Tarsey didn't waste any time assigning Tara Smith to a foster home. Tara's mother wasn't able to complete the classes she needed to take in order to keep Tara at home, so now Tara is just another young child in the state's overburdened foster care system.

Evelyn Sawchuck, Tara's foster parent, is an overweight woman in her late forties. Her feeble attempts to disguise her age with too much makeup, penciled-in eyebrows, and fashions that are more suitable for younger women, aren't working. Years of hard living have hardened this state-certified caregiver, but she has become adept at hiding her sentiments from the system's higher-ups. Unbeknownst to the state's social services agency, the only reason Evelyn Sawchuck is taking in foster children is so she can use the state's reimbursement payments to buy herself liquor and sex toys. Tara isn't the only child in this home, however. Evelyn has a biological daughter named Hailey, and neither one of them likes Tara.

This morning, Tara is upstairs taking a shower while Hailey watches TV in the family room before school, and Evelyn cleans up the breakfast dishes in the kitchen. Suddenly, Evelyn glances at the kitchen clock and shouts to her daughter. "Hailey! Shut the damned TV and find out why Tara isn't down yet! She's going to be late for the damn bus!"

"Why do I have to go upstairs? She's always late!" moans Hailey from the next room.

Irked that her daughter is complaining once again, Evelyn storms into the family room and smacks Hailey in the back of the head. "Get upstairs now, before I take out the wooden spoon!" she snarls.

Fearing the frequent beatings that she receives from her mother's preferred method of discipline, Hailey rushes out of the room and bounds up the stairs two-by-two. Cursing as she goes, she sounds more like a sailor than an eight-year-old child.

At the top of the stairs, a thought suddenly comes to Hailey and she skids to a halt in front of the bathroom door. Adopting a devilish grin, she resolves, *I'll fix this fucking tramp. She's always getting me in trouble.* Curling her fingers into a ball, Hailey pounds on the closed door, and shouts to be heard over the sound of running water. "My mom said to hurry up and get downstairs!" she declares forcefully. When the water stops, Hailey waits for Tara's response.

"I'll be down as soon as I dry off and put on my makeup," says Tara.

Knowing that she doesn't have much time to put her plan into action, Hailey rushes into Tara's bedroom and opens Tara's makeup case. As quickly as she can, she smashes every container she sees and mixes the contents together, destroying all of it. Happy with her work, she runs her dirty hands all over Tara's mirror and leaves the room.

The morning promises to be a bright and sunny Tuesday, and as luck would have it, the Grand Jury in Fort Lauderdale meets on Tuesdays.

Darren Handel is ready. He has carefully prepared all the information he uncovered about Eral Rosenbaum, including the written statement from Mei Lan. She won't be released from the hospital for another twenty-four hours, so he hopes the grand jury won't want to question her in person.

Since it's a nice day, Darren decides to walk the two blocks from his office to the courthouse. On the way, he stops at a small coffee shop, where he waits in line with others who are also on their way to work.

Darren is feeling good about the case and cannot wait until the hearing begins. He's sure that it will become another feather in his cap; a plus to his career.

Dressed, and with her hair slightly damp, Tara rushes out of the bathroom to finish her preparations for school. But she comes to a complete standstill in her bedroom doorway when she sees the state of her makeup case and the wild colors smeared all over her mirror. Gasping in shock at the extent of the carnage, Tara charges over to her nightstand and lets loose a scream followed by a loud verb and pronoun that are heard all the way downstairs. Knowing who's responsible, she bolts down the stairs to confront Hailey, but she finds the girl calmly watching TV as if nothing happened. Enraged by the monster child, she grabs Hailey by the front of her shirt and pulls her off the sofa. "You fucking little bitch!" Tara screams at the top of her lungs.

Hearing the commotion, Evelyn flies into the room and pulls Tara off Hailey. With a hard slap across Tara's face, the foster mother shrieks, "Touch my daughter again, and I'll kick your ass! Get out of this house before I do something drastic! Get to the damn school bus!"

Tara flinches but stands firm, not budging in the face of the woman's wrath. Working hard to hold back her tears, she wipes away a trickle of blood from her lips. "She ruined all my makeup!" Tara informs Evelyn angrily, as if her explanation would mean anything to Evelyn. "If she doesn't stop ruining my things, I'll knock out every one of her teeth!" Turning on her heels, Tara runs up the stairs and grabs her backpack. Bag in hand, she races back downstairs and storms out of the door, making sure that she slams it as hard as she can.

On the way to the bus stop, Tara dissolves into tears. But when she catches sight of her fellow riders, she wipes her eyes and stakes out a place a few paces away from them. She doesn't want to talk to any of them this morning.

The trip to school is a quiet one for Tara. All she thinks about is the unfairness of her situation. The only thing she wants is to be back with her own family again.

Tara was able to keep her feelings somewhat in check for most of the morning, but when she stands in front of her locker, she loses her composure and slumps onto the floor. Feeling as if she's all alone in the world, she sobs openly, no longer caring that someone may see her crying. As if to reinforce her feelings of loneliness, most of her classmates pass her by without comment. However, Mandy Goldman notices, and stops.

"What happened?" asks Mandy, dropping down next to Tara. "Why are you crying?"

"It's my foster mother and her fucking little daughter," cries Tara. "They both hate me! The little cunt ruined all my makeup this morning. And when I confronted her, her fucking mother slapped me!"

Mandy puts a comforting arm around Tara. "Look, I'll take care of you. You can be part of my posse, but you can't go around like this all day. Get a grip on yourself. I'll let you use some of my makeup now, and after school, I'll take you shopping to get you re-stocked—my treat. Us girls need to look good, right?"

Lu Tang is once again sitting at a desk in the Boynton mansion's makeshift classroom. However, instead of listening to today's lesson, she is daydreaming about home. The Chinese teacher at the front of the room knows that Lu is not paying attention, so she throws a pen at her. When it hits Lu on the shoulder, the thump jerks Lu back to reality.

Pleased that she got the reaction she wanted, the teacher snickers, "So glad you can join us this morning, Lu Tang." Then, with a clap of her hands, she commands the attention of the rest of the class. "We are almost done with your training. Three of you will be assigned to work at a gala event this weekend in the city of Hollywood. A wealthy client is interested in adding people to his house staff, so those of you who are sent to the event will be observed very carefully. Remember, you must fulfill all of the guests' requests, or you will no longer work for us. At best, you will be sent home, but at worst, you will never be heard from again. Lu Tang, remain after class. I have some news for you."

Dressed in a new suit and shoes, Fred looks at himself in a long mirror while a tailor makes chalk marks on his suit. The tailor asks, "Which side do you hang, left or right? And which side do you carry your firearm?"

"Left, then right, please."

The tailor grabs Fred's crotch and makes more chalk marks. "Your suit will be ready later today."

Vincent Cardone, Fred's new boss, looks on as Fred removes his new outfit. Cardone is a tall, dark-skinned man with a head as smooth and bare as a cue ball and hooded eyes that peer over a nose that looks as if it's been broken several times.

"Okay, slick," Cardone says, "you need to wear this suit and the others we'll order for you whenever you're on the job. You'll work six days a week for two weeks, with one week off after that. Go home now. Grab some personal stuff and return here by five. When you get back, I'll show you to your quarters. You're going to bed down with five others. There's a communal shower, but you'll have a private closet for your things. Oh, don't bring your cell phone back with you. No phones are allowed in the house while you're here. Your suit will be ready when you return, and you'll be given a brief orientation after you tour the dorm. Any questions so far?"

"Yeah," says Fred as he slips back into his jeans. "What about food and personal time?"

Vincent glares at his newest employee with a cold, sniper stare. "We supply your food. While you're here, there is no personal time; you are on call 24/7. But you and the rest of the security team are allowed to use the private beach and rec-room to unwind if there are no events scheduled. When you're off duty and away from the house, you must say nothing about this place. We have too many influential clients who need to be protected. Is that clear?"

Fred nods. "Crystal."

Before they leave the tailor, Vincent grabs Fred's shoulder. "Look, as soon as you get some money under your belt, get rid of that POS car you're driving. Ms. Connelly can help you with that."

Nodding again, Fred parts company with his boss and heads outside to start up the old Dart sedan that Rosenbaum gave him. Pointing the car toward his apartment, he pulls into the first gas station he sees.

Parking in an out-of-the-way area behind the building, he pulls out his cell phone and clicks on Detective Ballard's name in his contact list. "Will," he says when the connection is made, "meet me at my new place in an hour."

As instructed, Lu Tang waits in her seat while the rest of the class files out of the room. After the last person has left, the teacher walks over to Lu and stands in front of her desk. "I have good news for you," says the old woman. "You have been selected to work as a house servant for a prominent judge. He will meet you at the grand event this weekend. Pack up your things and take them with you when you report to work. You know, you were my best student. Your English still needs improvement, but you will learn more at your job. Go now. You have some time for yourself until you leave for the party. Use the pool or go to the beach. Enjoy the Florida sunshine."

Fred has packed up his casual clothes and personal items and is ready to go back to the mansion. Sitting restlessly on his couch, he checks his Timex for the tenth time and wonders where Ballard is. It's getting late, and he needs to report back by five.

At the sound of a knock on his door, Fred jumps up from the couch and primes himself to give his police buddy a mock tongue lashing for being late. However, when he swings the door open, his mouth drops, and his eyes widen in disbelief.

"Better close your mouth before you choke on a fly," smiles Lorinda. "I was in the neighborhood, and I hoped I'd catch you at home. Can I come in?"

Fred doesn't know what to do. He doesn't have much time, and he expects Will to arrive any moment. "Wow, ah, sure," he stammers, "but I've been assigned to a new job in Boynton Beach, and I'm already late."

Lorinda enters the apartment with a puzzled look on her face. "New job?"

Before Fred closes the door, he hears a noise in the hallway and pokes his head out. Seeing Will coming toward him, he holds up his hand and motions for the detective to wait. Then, he closes the door and faces Lorinda.

"Yeah," Fred says in response to Lorinda's question. "It's a security job, and I'll be part of a team that has to remain on site at all times. I'll be on duty 24/7. We work two six-day shifts, and then we're off for a week. Thanks for stopping by, but I need to rush. I have to attend orientation."

Without a word, Lorinda grabs Fred and kisses him passionately. "Call me in two weeks, and I'll make you dinner and breakfast," she whispers in his ear. Then, she opens the door and walks out of the apartment, leaving Fred standing in his living room in dumbfounded silence.

In the hallway, Lorinda walks past Will, but he keeps his face turned away from her and stands in front of a door, appearing to wait for entry. Oblivious to the stranger the hall, Lorinda walks down the stairs and leaves the apartment complex without noticing him.

Exhaling the breath he was holding, Will waits a few minutes and then knocks on Fred's door. "I see you got a new girlfriend," he comments dryly when Fred bids him enter. “This case must be giving you some great benefits.”

Fred smirks. “Yeah, more complications in my life; just what I need. Look, I gotta make this quick. I’m gonna be working at a mansion in Boynton Beach, and I think it’s a high-class brothel. I’ll be part of their security team, working six days on and one week off, with no cell phone. Rosenbaum recommended me, but I don’t know if he’s involved in the place or not.”

“Yeah? Well, it looks like we got that bastard. Handel is developing a case to present to the grand jury. If it goes well, we’re going to shut Rosenbaum’s operation. We’re planning to raid his office, his condo, and a house in Hollywood where we think he’s stashing some girls. Go to the job and stay undercover. We’ll inform Boynton PD about your assignment there. I wouldn’t be surprised if that place is connected to the rest of this mess.”

CHAPTER TWELVE

It's still dark, but Eral Rosenbaum has begun to wake up in his posh penthouse condo on the beach. Sleeping next to him is his latest "toy," a Filipino girl not much older than sixteen. Hoping for some early morning delight, Eral takes a tiny blue pill off his nightstand and gulps it down with a drink of water. Then he walks into the shower while he waits for the tablet to help him jumpstart his day.

Not far away, the SWAT teams from local police, the FBI, and ICE are about to converge on three locations—Eral Rosenbaum's penthouse, his financial planning office on Las Olas Boulevard, and the large home on the Intracoastal Waterway in Hollywood where Mei Lan lives.

As the sun peeks over the horizon, the sounds of the first raid of the day disrupt the early morning quiet on Las Olas Boulevard. The door to Eral's financial planning business is forced open and the agents surprise several young women who are already on the premises.

Wisely, the girls don't put up a fuss. They cooperate with the authorities and answer basic questions. As they are being escorted into waiting squad cars, FBI agents walk around the office unplugging computers and boxing files.

Nearby, on an exclusive street near the ocean, the second raid of the day begins. Blue lights dance in the morning light as law enforcement officers retrieve an elevator passkey from a security guard in the lobby of Rosenbaum's high-class condo building. When the officers storm into Eral's unit, they catch him standing at attention in his shower while his young companion cowers in his bed, naked and in tears.

"Mr. Rosenbaum," intones Will, "you are under arrest for human trafficking and endangerment to minors. Would you like to wave your rights and make a statement?"

Scowling, Eral shakes his head. "I need to speak to my attorney."

The officers allow Eral and the girl some time to dress, and then they lead them out of the condo. On the way to the elevator, the young girl cries, and Eral finds it hard to walk.

Although Eral is angered by the raid and what it could mean to his business, his major concern at the moment is his reputation. Eral is a man who has carefully cultivated an image of culture and refinement around himself, so he is extremely anxious about being seen in handcuffs by the other occupants of his building. His unit is the only one on the top floor, so he hopes that none of the residents heard anything during the raid.

Unfortunately for Eral, several early risers are milling about the marble lobby this morning. When Eral exits the elevator surrounded by a group of law enforcement officers, his acquaintances notice him immediately and are shocked at seeing him in such a compromising position. Eral tries to hide his face from their whispers and sneers, but he knows that they have seen him.

The morning's final raid is at the mansion in Hollywood. Amid swaying palm trees and majestic sea grape bushes, the setting of this large home is tranquil and picturesque, suggesting an easy mission. However, this raid doesn't go off as smoothly as the others.

A locked, wrought iron gate set into an eight-foot-high concrete wall has stalled law enforcement's easy entrance into the compound. Prepared for such a problem, the SWAT team places small charges of plastic explosives around the main access point. However, the team should have considered the possibility of another problem, one caused by nature.

The grounds of this mansion are home to several peacocks and all of them have noticed the morning's unusual activity. The birds' screeches and squawks are loudly announcing the officers' presence, forcing them to speed up their task. Cursing the unwelcome noise, they hope that no one inside the house notices the birds' agitation.

When the explosives do their job, the team goes into action. Slowly and cautiously, they drive their MRAP vehicles up the winding driveway, still hoping to surprise the home's occupants. Instead, as soon as the mansion comes into view, a volley of small and large-caliber projectiles stops their forward march.

Leading the raid, FBI Field Agent Josiah Hawkins communicates with his team via radio transmissions through their bulletproof headgear. "Code eight! Taking fire from the compound!" he transmits to a marine unit positioned on the Intracoastal. "Proceed with caution!"

Flying overhead, a police drone relays the locations of the shooters to a computer screen inside the lead vehicle.

At Josiah's command, armed officers swarm the compound from land and sea like flies on shit. Although some are hit by well-aimed gunfire, their Kevlar and armor-plated protective gear do their jobs, and they soon rejoin the fight. As for the mansion itself, its bulletproof windows remain intact under the incoming fire, in contrast to its stucco façade, which crumbles easily. Altogether, the firefight lasts only a few minutes and then all is quiet—except for the still-shrieking peacocks.

When the bullets stop flying, law enforcement personnel surround and disarm the home's surviving security guards. Without further incident, the fighters kneel compliantly with their hands clasped behind their heads and passively submit to being handcuffed and led to a staging area near the front gate. The casualty count of the mansion's security staff is high, and EMT vehicles are called in to tend to the injured.

When the teams are confident that the outside security staff has been disabled and there is no fire from inside the house, Agent Hawkins and officers from ICE cautiously enter the mansion. With no time to gawk at the sumptuous surroundings, they swarm through the house and round up the mansion's occupants—all of them young girls aged thirteen to eighteen, from almost every corner of the globe.

While the girls are being questioned, District Attorney Darren Handel arrives on the scene and parks his BMW near the bullet-riddled portico. He doesn't exit his vehicle right away, however. Darren is nervous about seeing so many of the girls who ply the trade he is so intimately familiar with together in one place, so he remains in his car, hopefully out of sight, until he can study each of their faces. When none of them look familiar, he steps out of the car and walks past them quickly.

Although Darren is sure that he doesn't recognize any of these young women, he is still worried that one or more of them may remember him as a client. So when he passes them by without hearing any comments, he lets out a huge sigh of relief.

Nearby, Agent Josiah Hawkins has been watching Darren curiously. He became interested when D.A. Handel didn't leave his car right away, so he kept an eye on him. When Darren approaches, Hawkins asks, "District Attorney Handel, are you looking for someone?"

"Oh," responds Darren with a start. "Um, my daughter... I won't ever stop looking for her. Thankfully, she's not here." Eager to change the subject, Darren says, "You did good work today, Hawkins. Any of your men hurt?"

Narrowing his eyes, Hawkins wonders if Handel is telling him the entire story, but he decides to file that notion away for another day. "Some of my guys took fire, but no one is badly injured. There may be some bruised or broken ribs, though. All in all, it's a bad day for the bad guys."

Several towns north of the Hollywood raid, Judge Nick Handel is alone in his chambers when his cell phone rings. A quick glance at the screen causes him to answer the call with a puzzled, "Katzoff? What's up?"

"They got Rosenbaum!" shouts a frantic voice.

When Fred arrives back at the Boynton Beach house, he put his belongings away in the closet near his bunk and sits on the edge of his bed, wondering what would come next. Before long, a fellow security guard appears and instructs him to walk with him to Vincent Cardone's office. Wearing a casual T-shirt and jeans, Fred follows the well-dressed guard through the large building to meet with their boss.

When the men arrive at Cardone's office door, the guard whispers a hushed welcome to his new co-worker and leaves Fred to wait until the boss gets off the phone.

At the conclusion of Vincent's call, the security chief looks over at Fred and tilts his head to study him better. "You made good time getting here in your shitty POS car," he says. "But that thing still needs to go."

"I'll take care of it when I get some money behind me," replies Fred.

Cardone leans back in his leather chair and purses his lips. "Like I told you before, just knock on Ms. Connelly's door. She'll take care of it for you."

"Yeah, I bet she will," smirks Fred.

Vincent's laugh is hearty, but he quickly becomes serious. "Sit down. You need to know what we expect of you."

Fred takes a seat and then watches Vincent retrieve a fully loaded Ruger SR45 and three spare magazines from a safe behind his desk. He places them on his desk and then opens a drawer and pulls out a leather under-the-shoulder holster, which he sets alongside the firearm and ammo.

"These are your tools," says Cardone. "You'll also get a Kevlar vest when you pick up your new suit, which is ready. Now, for the rules. As a member of the security detail at this compound, you will not mingle with or socialize with any of our female staff, except for our boss. You will monitor the areas around the beach and the pool daily, and you will be assigned other special duties as needed. We schedule social events here two or three times a month, and your attendance is required at every event that is held when you're on shift. Aside from protecting our clients at all times, your presence at each event will assure our guests that they're being well taken care of. Many of them are well-known, highly-influential people from the tri-county area, and they are skittish about their privacy. Again, you will not engage with or converse with the female members of our staff, or any of our guests. If a guest disrespects one of our staff members, or vice versa, you will notify me and intervene to end the conflict as directed by instructions through your earpiece. I will assign that device to you before your first assignment. Any questions?"

Fred gives Cardone his best sniper stare. "Have there been any conflicts that have required deadly force? I want to get a read on what I'm allowed to do here."

"I like the way you think," grins Vincent. "But to answer your question, no, we haven't had to use deadly force. However, that option is not off the table. Any other thoughts?"

"Just one. When do I get paid?"

Vincent laughs aloud and pushes his chair away from his desk. Before rising, he watches Fred lean over the desk to grab his work tools.

"You don't mess around," notes Vincent. "I can see that you know what you're doing. Well, come on. Let's get you over to the tailor to pick up your clothes. After that's squared away, you can negotiate with Ms. Connelly about a salary advance. She'll let you know how she wants you to pay it back."

Fred tucks the .45 under his belt and walks behind Cardone, thinking, *How she wants me to pay it back? That's an interesting thing to say.*

Sitting alone in a police interrogation room, Eral stares into a two-way mirror while he waits for his lawyer. He looks out of place in his expensive jeans and overpriced polo shirt, the only clothes the raiding agents allowed him to dress into before they took him away from his penthouse condo.

On their side of the mirror, Detective Ballard,

Lieutenant Jeffers, and District Attorney Handel watch their suspect while they also wait for his lawyer.

After long moments of silent observation, Darren shakes his head. "This is bullshit," he complains, exasperated by having to follow strict procedures. "I got his ass. The trial will be an open and shut case, so I hope he gets nervous and implicates others. Maybe he'll ask for a plea. I got a feeling this is just the tip of the iceberg."

"If this is just the tip," considers Jeffers, "he ain't gonna say shit. His life won't be worth a damn if he offers us anything. Prepare for a trial."

Turning back toward the mirror, the men watch as one of the country's premier defense attorneys joins Rosenbaum.

"Aw, fuck," comments Will.

Lu Tang was surprised by her teacher's unexpected invitation to enjoy the sun. Donning a bikini she found in her closet, she has lathered herself up in SPF 50 sunscreen and made herself comfortable in a lounge chair near the mansion's pool. She is trying not to look at the other girls who are also sunning themselves around the pool, as they are all in various stages of undress.

Lying next to Lu Tang is Denise Handel, who is wearing only the bottom half of a yellow string bikini. Several of the other girls nearby are either completely naked or as bare-breasted as Denise. These girls are the brothel's prized, experienced harem, and they no longer have any sense of shame.

When Denise turns in her chair to offer a different part of her body to the sun, she takes a peek at Lu and remembers that many years ago, she was just like her. "Hi," she says with a wave, "I'm Denise. You must be one of the newbies. Glad to be working with ya."

Horrified by Denise's assumption that she is anything like her, Lu vigorously disputes her assessment. "Oh, no, I not work here," Lu stammers. "I going... Sorry, my English no good. Um... I will be house servant for judge. I leave soon."

Denise shrugs her shoulders and closes her eyes. *This girl doesn't know what she's in for,* she reflects inwardly. *I wish I could leave with her. I wonder if that judge knows my dad or grandpa. Fuck! I really have to get out of here!*

Once again, Fred is staring into the full-length mirror in the tailor's workshop at one end of the Boynton mansion. His new Armani suit and shiny black shoes make him look great, even though he's still wearing his T-shirt under the jacket.

"Here are your dress shirts, silk ties, underwear, and socks, says the tailor. "This is your Kevlar vest. Take off your T-shirt and put on one of the shirts and ties with the vest and holster, including your firearm. I made adjustments for your accessories, and I need to check my work."

Fred takes the clothes from the tailor's outstretched arms and proceeds to re-dress, putting his vest on first. Within minutes, he is in full gear.

"Everything looks good," nods the tailor as he examines every seam. "Are you comfortable with the vest and firearm? How about your crotch? All good?"

"It looks good from my angle," comments Debra Connelly, who has just walked into the dressing area.

Turning in her direction, Fred strikes a pose, which makes Debra laugh. "I hear that we need to get you a proper vehicle," she says with a grin. "Let's go to my office. I think I can make you an offer you can't refuse. You can go on duty later, when you report back to Vincent."

Not waiting for a response from Fred, Debra struts out of the fitting room as quickly as she arrived, her short and very tight skirt accentuating every swing of her hips.

Knowing that Fred is enjoying the sight of the sashaying woman, the old tailor standing beside him clears his voice loudly to re-capture Fred's attention. "My job is done," says the man when Fred's eyes finally fall on him, "but it looks like yours is just beginning. Better hurry. You don't want to keep her waiting."

CHAPTER THIRTEEN

Lisa Berg, well known in police circles as a defense attorney who never loses, draws groans from the other side of the two-way mirror. A pleasant-looking woman in her mid-forties, she cuts an imposing figure in a tailored, pinstripe suit.

Lisa takes a seat next to Eral, with only a cursory glance at the mirror. "Say nothing, do nothing, reveal nothing," she whispers to her client. "We'll beat this if you do as I say. I don't care if you're guilty or not." Then, she tilts her head, stares openly at the mirror and waves her hand to beckon the officers on the other side to join them.

Will is worried by Lisa's confidence, so he looks over at Darren to gauge the D.A.'s response to her invitation. "Fuck," groans Handel. "That broad is as tough as nails. Okay, let's get this over with." Will follows Darren out of the room while Lieutenant Jeffers remains behind to observe the procedure.

Always maneuvering for the upper hand, Lisa Berg begins speaking before Darren and Will are seated. "Everything you have can be refuted," she asserts. "It's all circumstantial, all hearsay. I'm petitioning the court for no bail, and I will contest the charges and request dismissal. There's no reason for us to remain here any longer, so we're going to leave now. I will accompany Mr. Rosenbaum when he's booked and brought before the court." Turning to Eral, she orders in a firm voice, "Come on; let's go."

Without having uttered a single word, the two officers of the court accompany the attorney and her client into the hallway, where they stare dejectedly at their suspect's retreating back.

"This is going to be a tough fight," growls Darren through gritted teeth, "but I know we have it in the bag."

"Oh, yeah?" frowns Will. "That's what they said about O.J."

Fred has followed the tailor's directions to Debra's office and is now watching her cross and uncross her legs in a mesmerizing dance that Fred cannot look away from. *What's with all the women in this place?* he wonders, not for the first time.

Perched on the edge of her desk, Debra's tight leather skirt is now three-quarters of the way up her thighs, and she notices that Fred notices. Licking her lips, she looks at Fred seductively. "Mr. Staten, we must project a certain image here, and that faded green car of yours does not fit that image. We have arrangements with certain dealers in this city to take care of the needs of our staff, so you can get yourself a new Camaro or a BMW on a no-money-down, sign-and-drive lease. The dealers will waive your first month's payment, and we will pay the dealer fees and any other incidental charges."

With some effort, Fred forces himself to look away from Debra's legs. Staring into her eyes, he asks, "Will I have to repay those fees?"

In response to the question, Debra slides off the desk, pulls up her skirt, and sits on Fred's lap. "Yes you do, and you can make your first payment right now," she declares in a low voice. "But I suggest that you remove your new suit first. You don't want to get it wrinkled, do you?"

Judge Handel disconnects from Rabbi Katzoff's panic-stricken phone call. Thinking through his options, he chooses the soundest one and picks up the desk phone to instruct his clerk to postpone the next case on the day's docket. Then, he sheds his judge's robe and stampedes out of the building, intent on meeting Katzoff at his temple, located only a few blocks away from the courthouse.

As the judge drives through the familiar streets, his lets his imagination run through various consequences of Rosenbaum's arrest—none of them good.

Parking his shiny Bentley Continental GT a little too close to the curb, Judge Handel jumps out and walks straight into the building next to Rabbi Katzoff's synagogue. Not stopping for his usual chat with the rabbi's secretary, he rushes past the woman and barges into the rabbi's office, slamming the door behind him.

Katzoff looks up with an annoyed scowl. "Hey, at

least knock first, will ya?"

Handel glares back at his friend. "What?! You were almost hysterical when you called me! What the hell happened with that fat fuck Rosenbaum?"

"Your fucking son is paving his way to the governor's mansion with Rosenbaum's blood, that's what happened! Let's hope the fat fuck doesn't decide to do any talking. We can have Rocco pay him a visit if we have to."

Handel plops down in the closest chair with a thud and rubs his temples wearily. "Rosenbaum won't talk; he likes to breathe. I'll schmooze my son to see what I can find out. If this goes south, we're all in deep shit."

"That's an understatement," glowers Katzoff. "But listen, after I called you, I got to thinking. Maybe we're jumping the gun on this. It may turn out okay, so whaddya say we release some tension? We just got some new meat in. You want a taste? Let's go take a look."

Fred zips up his pants while Debra is in her private bathroom. "Well," he mutters under his breath, "undercover work sure has its perks. I'll bet this lounge chair can tell quite a story."

Debra exits the bathroom refreshed and satisfied—for now—and saunters over to her desk. Picking up the phone, she dials a number. "Mr. Cardone, I'm going to take Mr. Staten out for a new car. He'll report back to you as soon as I'm done with him." Placing the handset back in the cradle, she gives her afternoon hook-up a meaningful glance. "Round three, coming soon!"

Attorney Lisa Berg's newest client climbs into the back of her black Maybach wearing an electronic ankle monitor under his fashionable jeans, courtesy of the criminal justice system. Lisa slides in after him and taps her driver on the shoulder. "Take us to the W Hotel. I booked a room there for Mr. Rosenbaum."

When the Maybach pulls out into traffic, Lisa turns to her client. "Eral, you're fucked on this deal. I'll do my best to keep you out of jail, but they have a case against you that's almost airtight. Be prepared; I'm going to have to negotiate a plea agreement."

"Fuck that!" shouts Eral. "If I talk, I'm dead, and if I make a plea, I'll need a new identity and a new life!"

"I'll do whatever I have to," soothes Lisa. "Just show up for the trial looking like a legitimate businessman. None of your fancy clothes, understand? Don't say anything to anyone—no statements to the press, no posts on social media, no phone calls, and no visitors-—male or female. You will stay in your hotel room and wait. You will not leave that room for anything. Do not go to the pool, do not go to the restaurant, do not go anywhere. To be safe, I'll have an armed guard stay there with you. My sources tell me that Handel is fast-tracking your trial. He wants to become governor, and he's going to use your case to ingratiate himself with the voters. Now, we still have a couple of days left. The pretrial hearing isn't until Monday, and my little birdie told me that the D.A. wants to go to trial by Wednesday."

Eral closes his eyes with a moan and sinks into the Maybach's thick leather seat, cradling his head in his hands.

Fred is a happy man. Although he knows he won't be able to keep his newly-purchased white Camaro SS after the case is over, he has vowed to enjoy it for as long as he can.

When he turns into the long driveway of the Boynton Beach mansion, Debra hums contentedly in the seat next to him. It is now late afternoon, and Fred is pretty sure that he won't be reporting for his first day of guard duty today. Not if Debra can help it, anyway.

Following Debra's instructions, he stops the sports car in front of a bank of garage doors and idles the engine while she pulls a remote from her purse.

When one of the five doors begins to open, Debra points at the bay. "Put it inside," she orders. "You need to protect it from the sun." Accelerating slowly, Fred does as he's told. Once they're inside the garage, he turns off the car's engine and waits for Debra to get out of the car. When she doesn't make a move, he shrugs imperceptibly and entertains himself by watching the door descend behind them in the rearview mirror.

When the door clangs shut, Debra leans over and

unzips Fred's pants. "Ready for round three?" she asks huskily, and Fred knows that it's more of a command than a question.

Morning comes too soon for Fred. He rolls out of bed slowly, tired and tender in certain areas.

As he lathers up in the communal shower, the other guards snicker among themselves and give him knowing looks. Fred endures their taunts silently until one of the guards pats him on the back. "Looks like you made it through your first test," he grins. "How ya feelin', stud?"

Fred winces and lowers his head into a stream of hot water. "I feel like I was rode hard and put away wet. When's breakfast?"

While the other guards continue to trade lewd remarks, the friendly guard grabs towels for himself and Fred. "Breakfast is good and hot, and there's plenty of it. Go get your shit together. You need to see Cardone after you eat. He has a special assignment for you today. Oh, and don't make any eye contact with Connelly. Well, not unless you want your pipes cleaned again."

Recalling the previous day's antics, Fred moans softly. "Oh, God, no. I can't do that again! Not today!"

Darren's morning routine is interrupted by the shrill bleating of his cell phone. To make it stop, he grabs the object roughly and studies the caller ID. Puzzled by the number, he connects to the call and activates the speaker. With the phone on the counter, he pours a cup of coffee and speaks loud enough to be heard. "Judge? What's up? You never call; especially not this early in the morning."

"Oh, come on, can't a father call his son to celebrate his achievement? Have you seen the morning paper? You're on the front page! But that article was quite a shock. What's going on with Rosenbaum?"

Darren rolls his eyes. His father never gave a shit about his career before, so he takes a minute to decide how to respond. "Look, Dad," he finally says. "I can't talk right now. I'm late for my press conference. I know you'll be at the dinner party for UNOS on Saturday, so maybe we can talk then. Gotta go. Bye." Disgusted by his father's weak attempt to seem interested in him, Darren disconnects from the call and finishes his coffee.

Judge Handel is not surprised by his son's reaction. "That fucking kid is becoming more like me every day," he grumbles.

Suited up in his Kevlar vest with his .45 holstered under his arm, Fred stands in front of Vincent Cardone's desk while the man finishes a phone call. After the call ends, Vincent looks at Fred and bursts out laughing. "That was Connelly," he says. "Damn, you must really know how to impress! She wants to see you again this morning, but I told her you were unavailable. You are unavailable, aren't you?"

"Oh, yeah!" agrees Fred.

With a nod, Vincent grabs a personal communications system off his desk and tosses it to Fred. "Put that on. Tuck the power supply and transmitter into your jacket pocket, and clip the microphone under your lapel. I got a job for you. Three of our newer recruits are needed at a party tomorrow night in Hollywood, and you're going to transport them there today. You will join the security detail at that party, so get yourself acquainted with the surroundings. The recruits are waiting for you in the garage. Take the Suburban; you can drive your new ride tomorrow. Any questions?"

"Just one," grins Fred. "You got any morphine?"

Fred shares a laugh with Cardone about their boss lady and then opens the door to leave, but bumps right into Debra. "Oops!" he exclaims. "Ah, good morning, Ms. Connelly."

Today, Debra is dressed in more business-like attire, instead of the previous day's leather miniskirt, but that doesn't prevent her from reaching out and grabbing Fred's crotch in an overly friendly way. "Ready for round five?" she whispers.

Fred pulls away from the sex-crazed woman. "Sorry; I can't," he replies in what he hopes is a tactful manner. "I've been given a job today. How about after I return?"

Debra chuckles. "No, that will be too late. By that time, I will have reached my goal for the day. I'll be in touch, though." With a wink and a lick of her lips, she turns and slinks her way into Cardone's office, closing the door behind her.

Fred shakes his head at the woman's brazenness and heads for the garage.

Inside the dark Boynton garage, Lu Tang and two other Chinese nationals are waiting for their driver. The little group is sitting on the floor with their overnight bags packed with essentials for tomorrow night's party. Their belongings are few, so their bags are small.

When Fred opens the interior door, he fumbles along the wall to locate the switch for the overhead lights, and when they click on, he is surprised by the three faces looking back at him. *These are the recruits for the party?* he asks himself. *They're so young!*

As the oldest of the three, Lu Tang feels the need to speak for them. "I am Lu Tang," she states dispassionately. "My companions speak little English. I will…ah, um… So sorry. My English is not good."

Fred smiles kindly and places a comforting hand on Lu's arm. The young girl's skin is soft, and she smells like Jasmine. "I understand," he says. "Let's get into the car now. I need to bring you to your assignment for tomorrow night." The forty-eight minute drive down I-95 to an exclusive neighborhood on the water is a quiet one.

Fred's mood darkens when he pulls the Suburban into the driveway of the address his boss gave him. The two large lions at the entrance give him the creeps; he gets the uneasy feeling that they're watching the SUV. The uncomfortable feeling continues when he spots a stunning, peach-colored house rising high above the water beyond it. Surrounded by tall coconut palms and towering cypress trees, the home's red-tiled roof peeks alluringly through the gently swaying foliage, but Fred isn't impressed. He's concerned for the kids in his back seat.

Continuing past a four-car garage, Fred parks the car under a nearby portico and exits the vehicle. Nearby, two armed security guards appear from under the archway and watch him warily. Stepping up to them, Fred announces, "Cardone sent me with new staff. I'm also assigned to the security team for tomorrow's event, so I need to acquaint myself with the layout."

Without comment, one of the guards speaks quietly into his wrist. Then, he orders Fred to drive around the house to the servant's quarters. "We'll meet you there," he says.

On the way back to the car, Fred turns around to take another look at the men, but they have vanished like a bad thought. Shrugging his shoulders, he climbs into the Suburban and drives toward a 1200-square foot building a short distance from the main house. Waiting at the door is an older Oriental woman flanked by the same two guards.

While the woman ushers the youths inside, Fred approaches the larger of the guards. "Name's Fred Staten," he says, looking up into sunglass-shielded eyes. "I'll be working your event tomorrow, so I need to get the lay of the land before I leave today."

The guard reveals his Asian heritage when he removes his mirrored shades to get a better look at Fred. And when he extends a rather large hand in greeting,

Fred braces for a hand-crushing. *This guy is huge!* he cringes. *He must have been a sumo wrestler or something!* But Fred is pleasantly surprised when the hulking man's handshake is quite gentle.

"My name is Ken Okito," says the guard. "I'm chief of security at this complex. Ms. Connelly spoke very highly of you. I'll give you a quick tour, and then you can get back to whatever you do for her." With a sly smile, Okito points Fred toward the back of the house.

"Geez," marvels Fred. *Seems like everyone in this organization has sampled Connelly.*

"Eral," says attorney Lisa Berg, "I'm going to make this short and to the point. We know that Handel wants to be governor. He's railroaded you to trial, and his case seems solid. I'll argue that everything they have is unconfirmed, but that probably won't resonate with a judge or a jury. I'll do my best to have the case dismissed, but you need to know that that probably won't happen."

As Lisa watches, Eral sighs and paces his hotel room. Several tense minutes later, he stops in front of his attorney. "I know a lotta shit about important people in this state," he frowns. "If I make any kind of deal, my life will be in danger, and I'll have to go to into the witness protection program. I'll leave it up to you to decide if I need to spill what I know or not. I do NOT want jail time. Is that clear?"

"Yes, I hear you, Eral, but don't get your hopes up. I'm good, but you're in very deep trouble."

Lu Tang keeps her head down while she studies the Oriental woman who ushered her and the other two youths into the Hollywood mansion. The woman has told Lu to wait apart from the others, and they are peeved. It appears that Lu is receiving special treatment once again. The youths curse Lu loudly when they file past her to their quarters, not bothering to hide their disdain. Lu has become used to the behavior of her companions, but it still hurts.

After the children leave, Lu catches the eye of the weathered Oriental woman. "You are not liked by the others. Why is this so?" she asks.

With her eyes still on the ground, Lu says, "I was favored on the ship. I was made to do things I am not proud of."

Ming Li, the mansion's cook, clucks her tongue sympathetically and places her arm on Lu Tang's shoulder. She knows what things Lu had to do to survive her trip to this country, and she also knows that this girl will have to keep doing them here.

"Lu Tang," the woman says, "I work for Judge Handel, the man you and the others have been sent to help at the party. Do not worry about those two. They will go back to the house in Boynton Beach after the party, but you will stay here. You work for Judge Handel now. I will explain your job and help you with your English. Be prepared to do whatever you need to do to survive, just as you have been doing so far. The judge will have special tasks for you. Keep him happy, and you will remain safe. Make him angry, and you will disappear. Do you understand?"

Lu nods her head sadly and wishes that she never came to America. Grabbing her small bag, she follows Ming Li to a bedroom in the servants' quarters.

Fred is touring the main house with Security Chief Ken Okito. He is listening closely as the man rattles off details about the massive structure.

"This house is one of the larger ones in the neighborhood," Ken says. "It occupies 30,000-square feet and contains seven bedrooms and ten baths. We are now entering the grand ballroom, the largest room in the house. It spans 5,000 square feet, and its floor-to-ceiling windows are fifteen-feet-high. Each window provides a view of the Olympic-sized pool and the Intracoastal Waterway." Stopping in front of one of the windows, Ken points to a one-hundred-foot yacht moored to a dock beyond the pool. "The owner likes to entertain," he says.

Fred is awestruck by the size of the house and the luxurious furnishings he's seen in every room. Gazing out of one of the ballroom's windows, he admires the elaborate gardens bordered by royal palms and coconut palms swaying in the breeze.

"That small enclosure off the pool houses an 18,000-watt generator for backup power," comments Fred's guide.

"What's upstairs?" asks Fred, remembering the

ornate staircase they passed near the front doors.

"Oh, don't worry about that; you won't be going up there," answers Ken. "Your main job tomorrow night will be to secure the outside perimeter with the rest of our team. Now, all of the windows in the house are hurricane-resistant, except for the ones in this room. These are bulletproof."

Fred's eyes open wide. He looks over at the square-jawed man in his mid-twenties who has been showing him around. "All of these enormous windows are bulletproof?" he asks. "That must have cost a fortune! Who the hell owns this place, and what the hell does he do for a living?"

The guard laughs at Fred's reaction. "If I told you, you wouldn't believe me. Come on; let's take a walk outside. I'll introduce you to the rest of the guys you'll be working with at the party."

While Calista is holed up in her room, Will polishes his shoes for the big party tomorrow night. He doesn't know where it's going to be held yet; all he knows is that the D.A. asked him to attend. He doesn't want to go, but his sixth sense keeps haunting him to turn up.

Glancing at his watch, Will realizes that it is now midafternoon and Fred Staten still hasn't called in. Sighing for at least the twentieth time, he returns to polishing his shoes, and when his phone finally rings, he hurries to answer the call. "Talk to me," he commands.

"I'm gonna work with the security detail at a big benefit party tomorrow night for UNOS," says Fred. "It's going to be in a fancy neighborhood in Hollywood at one of the largest houses I've ever seen."

"Hot damn!" exclaims Will. "I'm going to that same party with the D.A.! Where will you be stationed?"

"I'm assigned to the outside perimeter, but they may move me around. That place is like a fortress, Will. And get this... I'm driving a new Camaro! This job has the kind of perks you won't believe!" Fred allows himself some brief images of his latest on-the-job encounters, then reluctantly shelves those thoughts. "I'll tell you about them some other time," he says. "I'm not sure who's in charge of all this, but I'll bet my salary it's all connected."

"Yeah, it sounds like a big operation," agrees Will. "Hey, text me the address of the party, will ya? Handel didn't give it to me."

"Okay. See ya tomorrow night."

When Will receives Fred's text, he sits down at his computer and searches for the address on the property appraiser's website. Seconds later, he purses his lips at the screen.

"Katzoff!" he growls menacingly.

CHAPTER FOURTEEN

The next evening, the ballroom of the Hollywood house hums with animated chatter under the soft light cast by several enormous crystal chandeliers that does wonders to enhance the festive atmosphere. The party's well-dressed guests are happily sampling endless trays of drinks and delicacies offered by attractive, youthful servers amid the delectable aromas of caviar, wild salmon, and designer fragrances.

Outside the house, Fred Staten is now on duty. He's walking the grounds near the pool and dock, trying not to be obvious as he takes occasional peeks into the floor-to-ceiling windows of the crowded ballroom. Fred doesn't know what he's looking for, but all his senses are on high alert. It is also a hot evening, and Fred's Kevlar vest is making him and the other guards very uncomfortable. Whenever a slight breeze blows off the water, each of them breathes deep sighs of relief.

Inside the house, Ming Li very busy. As head cook in charge of the sous chefs and waitstaff, she is acutely aware that the success of the evening's event hinges directly on her. If the exacting guests are not kept happy with trays and trays of hot and cold hors-d'oeuvres and endless drinks, she knows too well that she is the one who will be held to blame. So when Judge Nick Handel walks unexpectedly into the kitchen in an unpleasant mood, Ming Li is worried.

"Where's my new house servant?" the judge questions her gruffly. "I need to become acquainted with her as soon as possible!"

Pulling away from overseeing the preparation of smoked trout blinis, Ming Li signals anxiously to Lu Tang and motions her over. "Lu Tang," says the cook, "this is Judge Handel. He is your new employer."

Although Lu is dressed tonight in the typical server's uniform of plain white blouse, black bow tie, and black slacks, the judge appraises his newest acquisition as if she were wearing nothing at all. Like a wolf with x-ray vision, his eyes travel up and down, eventually settling on Lu's breasts, which the judicial official notes with approval are pushing against the buttons of the one-size-too-small blouse he requires of all his female staff. Lu keeps her head bowed while the judge stares at her.

"Judge Handel," interjects Ming Li, "this one knows little English. With your permission, I will teach her."

"Yes, and so will I. Lu Tang, come with me. Your lessons begin tonight." Holding a manicured hand on Lu's buttocks, the judge guides Lu purposefully out of the kitchen.

Ming Li knows where the judge is taking the young girl, but she can't do anything about it. So she does the only thing she can do—she curses the despicable man under her breath in her native Mandarin Chinese, and returns to work.

Sometime later, District Attorney Darren Handel and Detective William Ballard arrive at the party. Along with other guests, they hand their invitations to a man seated at a table inside the marbled foyer and wait to be admitted. While their invitations are checked against the guest list, Darren scours the faces of the people milling about the ballroom's entranceway. The many years he has spent searching for his daughter have trained him to scrutinize all the faces he sees.

When they finally make it through the security check, Darren stops in his tracks when he sees a beautiful young girl walking down the marble staircase. He stares at Lu Tang with such focus that he barely acknowledges Will when the detective tells him that he's going to try to find Sergeant Staten.

Lu notices Darren staring at her, so when she passes him by, she smiles at him demurely, and that captures Darren's heart. He is pleased that the attractive girl noticed him, so he returns the smile and follows Lu with his eyes until she is out of sight.

Watching from the upper landing, Nick Handel scowls at his son's reaction to his new toy. "I'm going to have to watch that boy," he gripes as he adjusts his slacks and strolls down the staircase.

A short time later, Lu emerges from the kitchen holding a silver tray topped by crystal glasses filled with expensive champagne. As she walks through the crowd, she stops to offer each guest a glass, and eventually reaches Darren. With another smile that mesmerizes him, she asks, "Champagne?"

Darren nods and reaches for a glass, but can't

stop looking at Lu's face. "Thank you," he manages to say. "You're very beautiful. What's your name?"

Lu bows her head demurely, blushing at the compliment. "So sorry," she whispers. "Know little English."

Darren points to his chest. "My name is Darren." Then, he points at Lu and hopes she understands.

"I... Lu Tang," she responds, and quickly backs away to serve the other guests.

Darren would be happy to watch Lu all night, but Mr. and Mrs. Aaron Goldman, members of the city's elite social scene see the young D.A. and meander over to engage him in conversation. When they approach, Lisa Goldman quickly becomes aware that the young district attorney is staring at one of the servers, so she clears her throat to capture his attention.

"I cannot thank you enough for representing the state with your pending case," she gushes when Darren focuses on her. "We saw your press conference the other day. Sex trafficking is so cruel! How can anyone do that to another human being?"

Darren is miffed that his fantasy has been interrupted, so he replies to Mrs. Goldman as briefly as possible to try to get them to move along. "They treat people as chattel and move them around wherever they want. They don't care about their victims, as long as they bring in the money."

Unperturbed, Lisa Goldman smiles prettily as she fingers the diamond necklace that lies across her ample bosom. She has calculated her action to show off her jewels and to point out exactly where they are placed above her low-cut gown.

Knowing what his wife is up to, Mr. Goldman interrupts the show. "That's why we're flying out to Paris tomorrow," he interjects, "so we can help with the fight there. It's a huge problem in some of the European countries."

Once again, one of Darren's fantasies is interrupted, and he struggles to move his eyes from Lisa to her husband. "Yes," he maintains, "it's great to have allies in the cause that has hit so close to my home. Please remember, though, that trafficking is a large problem here as well."

Aaron Goldman looks from Darren to his young wife, who is still fingering her necklace alluringly. "Counselor," he says, "you know that we're very sorry about your daughter. Lisa and I are happy to help you end this scourge. Please keep our children in this country safe while we try to help the children overseas." As soon as he ends his comment, he takes firm hold of his wife's arm and moves her away from Darren to socialize with the rest of the county's rich and famous.

In another part of the ballroom, a large dolphin ice sculpture is the backdrop for a tense conversation between Judge Kathleen Rose, a mature Chinese woman, and Randal Levy, the guidance counselor at the school attended by the Goldmans' daughter.

"Mr. Levy, I cannot discuss the details of that pending case," chastises Judge Rose. "Perhaps you should speak with the D.A."

Randal has been testing the waters to see if he could learn anything useful from the judge. Taking a step back, he pauses before responding to her accusation. "Judge Rose, I'm not trying to pry. I'm just saying that the most common types of trafficking are prostitution, domestic servitude, and forced labor. I'm sorry if you took my question the wrong way."

"You're quite right, Randal, and the top three countries those children are recruited from are Mexico, Honduras, and Guatemala, followed by the countries of the Far East."

Fortunately, the pair's conversation is interrupted by Lu Tang, who has walked over to them with a tray of champagne. Accepting a glass, the judge thanks Lu in Mandarin.

Happy that one of the VIPs speaks her language, Lu is about to respond when Rabbi Katzoff approaches and motions for her to resume her job. Disappointed, Lu turns away with her head bowed, and the rabbi enters the conversation between Judge Rose and Randal. "It's a pleasure to see you out of the courthouse, your Honor," gushes Katzoff. "Who is this fine young gentleman who has captured your ear this evening?"

In another part of the room, Will still hasn't caught a glimpse of Fred Staten, so when he sees Darren talking with several people in front of the room's large windows, he walks over while continuing to scan his surroundings. He is relieved when he finally spots the sergeant walking around the pool outside.

After a while, the people Darren has been talking to move away to chat with others, leaving an opening for Will to talk to the D.A. for the first time since they arrived. "It's great that the rabbi is holding this event for UNOS," Will comments. "It's important to bring attention to organ donation, don't you agree?" Darren is not paying attention to Will, however. "Darren? You seem distracted," observes Will. "Is there a problem?"

Darren doesn't want to seem as if he's ignoring the detective, so he reluctantly participates in the conversation. "Ah, Will. It's nothing, really. Someone caught my eye, that's all. Yes, I agree with what you said. It's a shame that so many people have to wait on long lists for suitable organs." Darren's attention is once again diverted by the sight of Lu Tang, who is exiting the ballroom.

At that moment, a UNOS doctor joins the two men. "I overheard your comment," the doctor says to Darren. "Some of those patients wait decades for an organ, and a majority of them don't survive the wait. We have over 800,000 patients on our lists worldwide, and we fervently hope that we can help them all. In fact, if you really want to help, the best thing you can do is to become an organ donor yourself."

While Darren and Will nod their heads in agreement, Herb Katzoff joins the discussion. "Ah, I see that our UNOS physician has met our distinguished District Attorney and his companion, one of Fort Lauderdale's finest detectives," he grins effusively.

Nearby, Lu passes close to the foursome with another tray of food and smiles at Darren, which causes the D.A. to once again lose interest in the people around him.

Noticing the subtle exchange between Darren and the server, Will jumps in to cover for Darren's inattention. "Rabbi Katzoff, it's so wonderful of you to host an event dedicated to such a great cause," he interjects quickly. "And to top it off, the food is spectacular!"

Rabbi Katzoff puffs out his chest at the compliments. "I appreciate your kindness," he says, "but your thanks must also be extended to Judge Handel for lending me his superb kitchen staff. Did the good doctor explain that over 800,000 people are waiting for an organ transplant?"

Will is not interested in continuing the conversation, so when he spots Mr. and Mrs. Goldman across the floor, he excuses himself and wends his way toward them through a collection of high-quality designer clothing and expensive jewelry.

Will is unconcerned that he is dressed in off-the-rack clothing amid this elegant crowd. Approaching the Goldmans, he says pleasantly, "Excuse me. I'm happy to see that you like to support causes other than law enforcement's charity events. How is your daughter?" Will knows Mandy through her past encounters with the juvenile detention system.

At the mention of her stepdaughter, Mrs. Goldman raises her brows and looks questioningly at her husband.

"Hello, Detective," responds Aaron Goldman coolly. "Mandy is still adjusting to the charter school. She's doing as well as can be expected."

"Well, I wouldn't worry too much," responds Will with a wave of his hand. "She's probably just going through a rebellious stage. "I know a little something about that. My daughter, Calista, goes to her school.

They may know each other."

Never one to keep her opinions to herself, Mrs. Goldman jumps into the conversation. "Detective, my husband is an upstanding person. He didn't raise Mandy to do the things she's done. We're confident that she'll soon learn to become a model citizen."

Will knows all about Mandy and her high school crew, so he hides a biting comment behind a smile. "High school can be hell," he says. "Just sayin'."

Mr. Goldman laughs uneasily at Will's comment while his wife glares at him for not defending Mandy.

"Will, you were always the class clown," grins Goldman behind gritted teeth. "No one ever expected you to become a cop."

Bristling at the veiled insult, Will forces himself to be polite. "We prefer to be called police officers, Aaron. Or, you can just call me Detective."

Sensing that the conversation is about to become tense, Goldman's wife takes her husband's arm and gives Will a dazzling smile. "Detective Ballard, we're leaving for Paris in the morning, and we'll be gone for a few weeks. Would you be able to keep an eye on Mandy while we're away? A relative of ours will be caring for her at our house, but we're nervous about leaving her for so long. We heard about the creep the D.A. indicted. I hope a conviction in that case will put a stop to crimes against the young people in this area."

"I'll do my best," says Will, graciously shelving his resentment for his old classmate and promising to try to check on Mandy through Calista. Then, he excuses himself with a comment about wanting to take a walk around the pool.

Upset by their conversation with the detective, the Goldmans grab glasses of champagne and plates of hors-d'oeuvres from passing waiters and munch on their delicacies in uneasy silence.

Spotting the couple standing by themselves, Rabbi Katzoff sidles over to strike up a conversation with his congregants. “How is Mandy getting along at her new... Well, how is she adjusting?” asks the rabbi.

Dismayed that her stepdaughter is known to be a troubled child by more than one person in the room, Lisa Goldman attempts to appear as if she is in control of the situation but fails miserably. With a heavy sigh, she says wearily, “We go through house staff on a weekly basis, Rabbi. She’s too demanding. We’re trying to encourage her to be more respectful, but the more we try, the more she rebels.”

This piques the rabbi's interest. As nefarious scenarios run through his mind, he urges the couple to send Mandy to him for counseling. “We offer programs that encourage good social behavior,” he advises. “I promise that we can help her become a new person.”

Across the room, Darren watches with disgust as his father grabs Lu’s elbow and begins to escort her out of the room. Moving quickly, he intercepts the pair before they reach the staircase to the second floor. “How’s the case with Jennifer Smith going, Dad?” he asks impulsively.

Annoyed that his plan for the rest of the evening will have to wait, Nick Handel motions for Lu to go into the kitchen. “I was just going to review some of the household policies with my new employee," he says testily. "As for Mrs. Smith, it's all up to her now; I ordered her to complete a parenting course. But as long as we're talking, Darren, how are you doing with Eral Rosenbaum? Do you expect to get an indictment?" The judge can't help but notice that Darren isn't looking at him. His son is still following Lu as she walks away.

When Lu is out of sight, Darren directs his full attention to his father. "You know I can't say anything about an ongoing trial," he responds icily. "Why do you care, anyway?"

As if offended by Darren's question, the judge sighs deeply. "He helped me with investments, Darren. I was taken aback by his arrest."

"Hmpf," mumbles Darren, who turns away from his father and walks toward the kitchen. On the way, he catches glimpses of Randal Levy standing in a corner texting, and Detective Ballard speaking with Sergeant Staten outside, near the pool.

Inside the ballroom, Doctor Ethan Waterford, CEO of UNOS, taps on a champagne glass in front of one of the microphones near the string quartet. "Attention, everyone!" he shouts. "I want to thank you all for attending this gala to support UNOS! I also want to offer my deep appreciation to Rabbi Katzoff and Judge Handel for making this night so memorable. Our goal is to provide an organ for everyone who needs one, so there is no longer a waiting list. For those of you who are already registered donors, I thank you. For those of you who are not yet donors, please see me or any of our associates milling about the room. Have a great evening!"

Inside the kitchen, Darren looks around for Lu as the partygoers in the other room erupt in applause. When he finds her, she is at the opposite end of the room, crying and talking with an older woman. Striding purposefully toward them, Darren asks the woman, "Do you speak English?"

When she responds in the affirmative, Darren says, "I know this new life must be overwhelming for her," indicating Lu. "Tell her that I'm available for support... If she wants it."

Lu's eyes widen as the cook translates Darren's comments in low whispers. Then, she jumps up and puts her arms around Darren.

Surprised, but pleased, Darren holds the young girl against him and gently strokes her hair.

Looking on, the world-weary cook is rendered speechless by the mystifying scene before her. She knows that Lu is very young and that she craves normalcy in her life, but she has severe misgivings about Darren's intentions. She knows Darren—he is Judge Handel's son, after all—and as far as she is concerned, he cannot be trusted. With a roll of her eyes and a shake of her head, she walks away and vows to talk some sense into Lu at a later time.

CHAPTER FIFTEEN

Monday morning appears to be another sunny day on Florida's Gold Coast, but Darren is oblivious to its promise. Absorbed by his preparations for the pretrial hearing later that day, he has been hard at work in his office for several hours, so he raises his head in surprise at a knock on his office door.

"Detective Ballard?" asks Darren. "You're up early today."

"Yeah, I know. I was hoping to catch you before the hearing."

"Oh? What's so important? Does it involve what you talked to Staten about at the party?"

Will closes the door and sits down. "Yeah. I thought you might like to know what Fred told me."

"Yeah, I do," responds Darren.

"Well, to begin with, Fred was only at that house in Hollywood for the party. He's actually working at an exclusive gentlemen's club run out of an upscale home in Boynton Beach. Rosenbaum sent him to work at the club."

"So Rosenbaum may have some connections there," says Darren thoughtfully. "That's good to know."

"Fred also found out that some of the men who work at Rosenbaum's shelter also work for Rabbi Katzoff, the same guy who hosted the party for UNOS. Fred's going to try to get more info on that, but it looks like there may also be a connection between Rosenbaum and Katzoff. I thought you might need this info as well."

Darren sits back in his chair and stares blankly at the far wall. He knows that his father is working with Katzoff, but he doesn't share that fact with Will.

"Hmm, that's interesting," says Darren. "Let me know if Staten digs up anything else I can use. Look, I still have a lot to do, so I'm going to have to ask you to leave now. Thanks for stopping by, Detective."

Darren rises from his chair to end the conversation but then remembers something. Reaching into his inner suit pocket, he removes a folded piece of paper and hands it to Will. "As long as we're exchanging information, I thought you might want this. Mei Lan will be released from the hospital today. The address on that paper is the safe house where she'll stay during the trial. I've got to run, so my assistant will show you out." Apologizing for having to leave Will alone, Darren excuses himself and abruptly exits the office.

Still seated, Will studies the paper and mulls over his conversation with the D.A. *I got a weird vibe from Darren when I mentioned Katzoff. He seemed nervous. Is it possible that he's hiding something?*

A few miles away, a middle-aged married couple

is sitting before a large mahogany desk. The husband glances at his wife and then turns to the person behind the desk. “You promised us,” the man pleads desperately. “You promised that you would help our son get a new liver, so here is your check, our final payment of ten thousand dollars.”

Rabbi Katzoff takes the check and places it in his pocket. “Very good,” he says. “Our team will now start working on your request.”

“How long is this going to take?” asks the wife. “Our son doesn’t have much more time to wait.”

Rabbi Katzoff walks around his desk to place a comforting hand on the woman’s shoulder. “Don’t worry,” he says soothingly. “I’ll make it a priority. We should have results within forty-eight hours. We recently expanded our database with UNOS, so your son will be fine. I’m sure of that.”

Nodding with renewed hope, the couple stands and wipes tears from their eyes.

Katzoff ushers the couple from the room and waits a few minutes to make sure they’re gone. Then, he presses a button under his desk. Seconds later, a large man enters.

“I have a new target for you,” says Katzoff indifferently. “His name is Samuel Cummings, and his DNA matches a liver we need. Your team has less than twenty-four hours. Here’s the file.”

Gabriella Handel Hoffman is looking vacantly

out of the car window while her second husband drives their SUV to a meeting she hastily arranged with Rabbi Katzoff. But she becomes highly agitated when she sees several young children playing on the sidewalk without adult supervision.

"I would never let my Abby play outside like that!" Gabriella asserts. "Not after losing Denise! Those parents don't know anything about the dangers out there! We still don't know what happened to her, or even if she's still alive!"

"I know," says Ted Hoffman soothingly as he stops his car to let a middle-aged couple's vehicle leave Rabbi Katzoff's driveway. When the couple's car passes by, he turns into the same driveway.

"Are we ready for this?" asks Gabriella with hope in her eyes.

Nervous and anxious, the couple walks up to the portico and rings the doorbell. Soon, a professionally-dressed woman opens the door. "Welcome, Mr. and Mrs. Hoffman," she says, "you're right on time. Come in; the rabbi is expecting you.

Gabriella takes hold of her husband's hand as they follow the woman through a large room decorated with exquisite marble, custom-made furniture, and fine art. Gabriella leans toward Ted. "The rabbi seems to live very comfortably," she whispers.

The small group eventually arrives at an office containing a finely-wrought mahogany desk and several tufted leather chairs. "Please have a seat," says their guide. "Rabbi Katzoff will be with you shortly."

No sooner do they sit down than Herbert

Katzoff exits an adjoining room and claims the chair behind his desk with a sigh. "Hello, Gabriella. Ted. How can I help you today?"

"It's my daughter," Gabby begins, choking back tears. "She needs a heart transplant, and she's been on the waiting list for a long time. If she doesn't get one soon..." Gabriella dissolves into sobs, which Katzoff tries to assuage with a box of tissues.

"That's it," voices the rabbi, "let it out. The Almighty understands your grief, and he always provides. We have been very successful in resolving these types of issues."

Gabriella dabs at her eyes with the tissue, careful not to smudge her makeup. "How long will the process take?" she asks. "Abby's specialist told us that it wouldn't be long before her problems become more severe."

Rabbi Katzoff folds one hand under his chin. "I can assure you that there will be a rapid response once you fulfill your end of the agreement your ex-husband discussed with me."

Ted knows how Gabriella feels about Darren, so he responds for her. "We're prepared to live up to our end, Rabbi, and we thank you for getting our Abby a new heart."

"We are helping each other," replies Katzoff, "more than you can imagine." Holding the couple's eyes with his own, he presses the intercom button. Instantly, the door opens, and the professionally-dressed woman stands expectantly in the doorway.

Understanding that the rabbi has concluded the

meeting, Ted stands and hands a bulging envelope to Katzoff.

"Thank you, Mr. Hoffman. Your daughter is in good hands. Mrs. Ehrlich, our guests are ready to leave now."

As soon as Mrs. Ehrlich closes the door behind the Hoffmans, Katzoff stuffs the envelope into his jacket pocket and grabs his ringing cell phone. "Oh, that's right... I'll be there in a minute," he says. "And by the way, we have two new clients. One for a heart, and one for a liver."

Stuffing the phone into another pocket, Katzoff rushes through the house to a separate wing on the far side that contains a rudimentary hospital. Inside a small room, he encounters the surgeon who placed the call.

The physician is standing over an operating table where an attractive and heavily sedated girl in her late teens is being prepped for surgery. When Katzoff arrives, the doctor props the girl up so the rabbi can take a look at her.

Grabbing the girl by the chin, Katzoff studies her from head to toe, stopping his gaze at all the places where dirty old men's eyes linger.

"Doctor," Katzoff announces after his inspection, "I think she's too weak for harvesting. Send her down to the subfloor. We'll perk her up for other special duties."

The next day, the usual morning rush-hour crowd is milling about a local coffeehouse, impatiently awaiting their orders of coffee, scones, and muffins. One of the patrons, Samuel Cummings, a forty-year-old GenX wannabe, considers himself lucky to have already received his morning fix—a White Chocolate Macchiato mixed with half soy milk and half almond milk.

On the way out of the store, Samuel receives an important call on his ever-present iPhone and stops to answer it. With his favorite drink in one hand, he stands in front of his late model Beemer and presses the phone to his ear with the other to converse with his broker.

Chatting away about a trade he wants the broker to execute this morning, Sam places his coffee cup on the roof so he can unlock the car. Then, he climbs behind the wheel and carefully places the beverage concoction into the center console cup holder while he continues his conversation.

When Samuel ends the call, he reaches over to insert his key into the ignition, but a gun suddenly pressed to the back of his head freezes him in mid-motion.

"Just drive," orders a voice from the back seat, "and don't fucking turn around. Go where I tell you to."

Sam begins to say something, but when the intruder jams the barrel of a suppressed semi-automatic weapon even harder into the base of his skull, he closes his mouth in fright.

"Don't say a word," says the voice. "Pull out of the parking lot onto Pine Island Road. Then, go south to Sunrise. Drive west on Sunrise, or your day ends right here, right now. Got it?"

Terrified, Sam nods his assent and backs his car out of the parking space as his fellow wannabes exit the coffeehouse with their intricate breakfast beverages.

One hundred yards out from the Boca Raton Inlet, the surface of the ocean sparkles like diamonds as a blue and white Azimut 50 bobs gently up and down under a group of seagulls that are circling it and laughing.

Huddled inside the luxury yacht's cabin are Christian Garcia, a weathered Mexican national, and his fifteen-year-old son, Jesus. Dressed in faded jeans and torn T-shirts, the pair is anxiously watching a third man prepare two sets of documents.

Every few minutes, the illegals steal nervous glances at each other. *"¿Qué está pasando, papá?"* asks Jesus.

"Practice English, *mi hijo,*" urges Christian. "We are in America now. Everything will be okay."

"Okay, Christian," says Rocco, looking up from his small desk. "I need another five thousand dollars."

Opening his mouth in shock, Christian pleads, "You say we have deal to get to America!" Rocco laughs heartily while holding up the pair's phony papers. "These are American waters, *amigo.* Do you still want these papers, or are you very good swimmers?"

Christian is angry and scared but tries to force the deal he made. "I already give you the money you want when we board the boat," he asserts. "You say you have work for me."

"Ha, I do," Rocco says, narrowing his eyes at young Jesus. "But the money you gave me only got you to here, among the fish."

Christian continues to plead his case, hoping that his captor has a heart. "But *Señor,* I have no more to give!"

"You do have something else, though," says Rocco, pointing a tanned finger at Jesus.

"NO!" shouts Christian, grabbing hold of his son while the boat sways gently and the gulls laugh louder. "Not *mi hijo!* Take me! Use *me*!"

Rocco cricks his neck with indifference. "Your son is more valuable than you. *Comprende?"*

"No! Please, I work hard, you will see. I give you me. Me, for my son!"

Rocco studies Christian anew, and after what seems like an eternity to the man and his son, takes a deep breath and says, "Fine, then."

Rising from the desk, Rocco yells up the stairwell. "Get us going and pull her in!" In obedience, the engines come to life, and the yacht lunges forward.

As the craft heads into the inlet, Rocco turns to his passengers, his eyes sparkling at the prospect of new meat. "Welcome to the United States!" he hoots. The loud cackling laughter that follows overpowers the shrieks of the gulls and the drone of the engines.

Ming Li and Lu Tang have been up for a while. Ming Li has been tutoring Lu in Judge Handel's stainless steel commercial kitchen for several days now, and the lessons are going well.

On his way out of the house, the judge passes the room and overhears the women talking, so he stops in the hallway to listen to one of the lessons.

Very slowly and deliberately, Lu reads aloud, "See...Jane...run. Run, Jane, run." Ming Li stands over her and follows along.

"You are doing well," Ming Li says in Mandarin. "You are learning English very quickly."

From the hallway, the judge calls out, "Teach her well, Ming Li. She has a lot to learn!" The judge sniggers heartily and leaves the house. He doesn't see the mournful look that Ming Li gives to Lu.

As Judge Handel drives away, he catches a glimpse of his son's car passing him in the opposite direction. Looking into his rearview mirror, he is not surprised when the car turns into his driveway. With a knowing laugh for his son's behavior, he continues on to his breakfast meeting.

Darren Handel saw his father's car pass him and is glad that he's no longer at home. He didn't want to have to explain why he was there this morning.

Ming Li is still coaching Lu when a young female staff member interrupts them. "Miss Li," the young girl says softly with her head bowed and her hands clasped demurely in front of her, "an American gentleman is here to see Lu Tang."

Surprised, Lu says something to her teacher in Mandarin but stops when she sees the woman's stern gaze. "Sorry," Lu says in English. "I not know who this is."

Turning to the staffer, Ming Li orders, "Do not keep the man waiting. Send him in."

Outside the house, Darren has been anxiously willing the large double doors to open. When they do, he follows the maid eagerly into his father's 7,000-square-foot palace.

"Mr. Darren Handel?" says Ming Li over Lu's shoulder. "What business do you have with Lu Tang?" Lu smiles broadly at the sight of Darren standing in the kitchen entryway.

"Well," begins Darren, "I was hoping that you would allow Lu to take a break for a couple of hours. I have some free time today, and I want to introduce her to Fort Lauderdale and our beautiful beach, and maybe take her out for a quick lunch. Is that okay with you, Ming Li? And of course, only if it's okay with Miss Tang."

Ming Li switches to Mandarin to question Lu. "He wants to take you to lunch. Did you understand? Do you want to go with him? It's okay, as long as you are back by one o'clock."

Li nods and turns her attention to Darren. "That okay, sir."

"Mr. Darren," interjects Ming Li, "Lu needs to be

home by one o'clock. She speaks very little English, so be patient with her."

"Yes, I understand. One o'clock is no problem. I have a hearing at three. I'll wait in the foyer while she changes out of her uniform." Looking back at Lu, he urges, "Please call me Darren."

Lu blushes and bows her head. "Okay...Darren. I am ready soon."

Ming Li watches Darren's eyes as they eagerly follow Lu out of the kitchen. Seeing Darren's father, the Judge, in them, she grimaces and grits her teeth. "Mr. Darren, she is fragile. She has been through a lot. Please take good care of her."

Darren nods and heads for the foyer.

Alone in the kitchen, Ming Li sighs and mumbles in Mandarin, "Just like father."

With the day off from school today, two close friends, both barely fifteen years old, are practicing their dance routine. Abby Handel waits for the music on her iPhone to start playing and grins at her friend, Calista Ballard. "Okay, five, six, seven, eight," she counts when the music begins. Abby continues the count as the girls step into their routine.

"I love this dance!" shouts Calista. "We're going to win the show for sure!"

Happily moving to the beat, the girls twirl and kick their heels until Abby stops and grabs her chest. Gasping for air, she crumbles to the floor and writhes in pain.

"Abby! Abby!" yells Calista. "Mrs. Hoffman, come quick!"

Breathing heavily, Abby lies on the floor and looks up at Calista with an annoyed expression. "I'm okay," she wheezes, "don't call my mom."

Gabriella is already on her way, however. Barging into the room, she sinks to the floor and cradles her daughter in her arms. "Abby! Oh, my baby!" she whimpers.

A few minutes later, Abby is almost back to normal, and she is pretty upset—not at her mother or Calista, but at her delicate health. "Gee, Mom," she protests. "I'm okay. Really, I'm fine. It's just another one of those stupid attacks."

But Gabriella knows better. She strokes Abby's hair while Calista sits on the bed and watches. "Honey," soothes Gabby, "you need to take it easy until you get your new heart."

Pushing her mother's hands away, Abby sits up with some effort. "Ugh, yeah. Dad promised me a new heart, and I hope it comes soon. This is so lame! Mom, can you get me a glass of water, please?"

Gabriella rises from the floor. "Yes, I'll get you that water. Then, I'll fix you both some lunch. I want you to relax for the rest of the day."

When Gabriella leaves the room, Abby joins Calista on the bed. Leaning over, she takes a look at the text her friend's typing. "Okay," says Abby, breathing more easily now, "now that my mom is gone, you have to tell me about that guy."

Calista shows Abby the screen. "Look at his profile pic."

"Wow! He's really cute!"

"Yeah," glows Calista. "He even has his own car—a Mustang!"

"So he can take us anywhere we want?" giggles Abby.

"Hey, girlfriend, he's all mine, ya know!" objects Calista.

Abby rolls her eyes and pouts. "Aw, relax," she chides her friend. "He may be yours, but that doesn't mean he can't take us both shopping!"

"That would be fun for us, but he'd probably hate that!" laughs Calista.

Abby grabs Calista's phone and studies the boy's photo again. "Have you met him? Ya know, in person?"

Calista takes her phone back. "No, not yet, but soon. I can't wait!"

When Gabriella returns to the room with Abby's drink, both of the girls are laughing and giggling together. "Okay," questions Gabby, "what are you two plotting?"

Instead of responding, the girls poke at each other and laugh even more. Their cheerfulness releases Gabriella's tension, and she laughs along with them.

CHAPTER SIXTEEN

The next time Eral Rosenbaum meets with Lisa Berg, he is not wearing his usual tailored clothing. Today, he is dressed in a plain black suit with a bargain-priced shirt and a tie that was on the sale rack. Ms. Berg, however, is dressed in an expensive power suit.

Attorney Berg has been pacing the room for the last ten minutes. When she finally comes to a decision, she stops in front of Eral and looks down on him sitting on the sofa. "This is a preliminary hearing," she states. "I know we went over this before, but it's well worth repeating. I'm going to try my very best to have the charges dismissed. However, as I've already said, that probably won't happen. District Attorney Handel wants a speedy trial, and he wants it to end before the election. He believes that a high-profile conviction will look good on his record when he runs for governor. Eral, you need to keep the possibility of a plea agreement in the back of your mind. If the worst happens and I can't convince the judge and jury that the charges are hearsay and circumstantial, well, you're probably going to have to spend the rest of your life in prison. And I can assure you that if you do go prison, the remainder of your life will be pretty short."

Eral has been staring at the floor while his attorney was speaking. When she is finished, he looks up and says, "I'm not worried. I have information that will rock this county, and I'll let it out if I have to."

Tara is smiling at her image in the mirror as she dresses for school. The makeup items Mandy bought to replace the ones Hailey ruined is helping to ease her sorrow over losing her freedom to the court system. As she brushes her long blonde hair away from her face, she looks longingly at a photograph of her mother on the table next to her bed. Stretching out an arm, she lifts the photo and holds it close to her heart. "I want you back, Mom," she says achingly. "Please don't mess things up again."

Tara replaces the photo on the table and looks for her school report, but it's not where she left it. Confused, she scours the room and eventually finds it under her bed, shredded into little pieces.

Shocked, Tara sinks down to the floor to consider her options. The report is a significant part of her grade, and it is due today.

Hearing a noise, she looks up to see Hailey in the doorway sporting a grin like the cat that ate the canary. "How's your fucking homework?" asks the girl, with malice in her dark eyes.

Tara's eyes narrow in disbelief. She cannot understand this little monster. "Hailey!" she wails, waving a piece of her torn report. "Why the hell...? How could you?! This is due today! What the hell am I gonna do now?"

Hailey only expands her spiteful smirk. "Your homework needed my fine touch! I don't care what you do now! I can't wait till you go to court, and get the hell out of my house! Nobody here likes you, anyway!"

Turning around with a flourish, Hailey skips down the hallway, leaving Tara sobbing as she gathers together the torn bits of her hard work.

With tears streaming from her eyes, Tara looks again at her mother's photo and whispers, "I miss you so much, Mom!" Then, she raises her eyes toward the ceiling and prays, "Please, God! Don't let them keep my mom away from me! Please!"

Fort Lauderdale Beach is busy today. Tourists, locals, and parents toting children on their day off from school are frolicking together on the famous beach. Some are splashing in the water while others are lounging on the sand.

Darren and Lu are also at the beach, but they are not on the sand. They are sitting on a low wall that marks the boundary between the beach and the sidewalk along State Road A1A.

As Lu looks out at the rolling waves of the Atlantic Ocean, she recalls her ocean voyage from China and contrasts it with the carefree people she sees in front of her. Lu's thoughts are dominated by fantasies of the freedom she so desperately longs for, and she hopes that the man sitting beside her will help her to attain that freedom.

But Darren's thoughts are not as noble as Lu's. Acutely aware of the strikingly beautiful girl by his side, Darren is busy formulating a strategy for the fastest way to become more personal with her.

Neither of the two has said much to the other; they're just enjoying the sun, the sand, and each other's company.

After a while, Darren glances at his watch and realizes that the afternoon's interlude must end—for now. He places his arm around Lu's waist and draws her close. "You might not understand me," he says, "but we have to leave now. I have to go to court."

Lu watches Darren tapping his watch. "You...go to work? Me, too."

"We'll meet again tonight for dinner, okay?" Darren asks, not knowing if he's being understood. To clarify, he mimes putting something into his mouth.

Lu laughs at Darren's attempt at an explanation. "Good, yes. Okay," she says.

On the way back to Darren's car, Lu looks out at the ocean one more time, hoping to sear the beautiful sight into her memory. Instead, she shudders and turns away abruptly. In the distance, a container ship sailing toward Port Everglades has brought back a flood of bad memories, ruining the scene for her.

Oblivious to the beautiful weather outside, a masked surgeon in a blood-splattered gown removes his rubber gloves while a nurse hands him a clean pair.

"Get him out of here," the surgeon orders. "We have a liver to harvest."

Christian Garcia, the illegal Mexican immigrant, is lying on the surgical gurney that is being wheeled out of the makeshift operating room. Just coming to, he opens his eyes a crack and sees his son sitting in the hallway on a folding chair.

Jesus jumps up and runs over to his father, forcing the nurse to stop the bed's forward motion. "*Papá, Papá!*" Jesus calls. "Are you awake?"

"What day is today?" asks Christian, groggy and in pain.

Taking hold of one of his father's hands, Jesus replies, "*Lunes,* ah, Monday."

Happy that his son spoke English, Christian squeezes Jesus' hand. "Very good," he says approvingly, and attempts to sit up. "We must go now."

"No, *Papá!*" says Jesus, glancing at the bloody bandages under his father's street clothes. "Rest now! You need rest."

Christian shakes his head and attempts to button his shirt while his son tries to get him to stop.

Unnoticed by father or son, a rather large orderly suddenly looms above them at the head of the gurney and shoos the nurse away.

Christian continues to try to make himself presentable but the stitches that mark the place where his left kidney once resided hinder his movements and send waves of excruciating pain through his body, nearly causing him to black out. Understanding the older man's distress, the orderly lends Christian a helping hand.

"He'll be okay," the man says to Jesus as he buttons Christian's shirt. "But both of you need to leave now." Without waiting for a response, the orderly places one arm under the man's shoulder and helps Christian off the table. Neither patient nor child questions why they have to leave so quickly.

With Jesus supporting Christian's other arm, the three walk haltingly down the short hallway. "You are a good boy, *mi hijo,*" Christian says between moans of pain.

At the rear of the rabbi's house, the trio exits into a secluded area where Rocco is waiting in the hot sun. Taking over from the orderly, Rocco helps Christian into the back of his van. "Your contribution is accepted," he whispers to Christian. "I'll take you to your job now. Your debt has been paid." Pointing at Jesus, Rocco motions for him to join his father inside the box-like vehicle.

When Tara climbs down from the school bus, she enters the noisy schoolyard holding her torn and crumpled papers in her fist. Trying to remain calm, she walks across the yard toward her friend, Mandy Goldman.

"What the hell is that pile of shit?" Mandy asks, eyeing Tara's hand.

"My foster mother's daughter tore up the report

that was due today."

Disgusted by her friend's situation, Mandy lashes out in anger. "I can't believe that little shit did that to you! I would've clocked the bitch!" she hollers. "But Tara, that pile of papers looks like crap! If you want to hang with me, you can't be holding garbage!"

Reaching out, Mandy smacks Tara's hands, causing the torn papers to fly into the air and scatter in the breeze.

"Why did you do that?" cries Tara, shocked by Mandy's thoughtlessness. "That was the only proof I had of all the work I did! What the hell am I gonna do now?"

"You're with me, remember?" declares Mandy as she places her arm protectively around Tara's shoulder. "I got you. Those two nerds in our class did my report for me. They both think I'm gonna give them head, the fools. You can have my extra one." Reaching into her backpack, Mandy hands Tara a typed and bound report. "Look, your makeup is running," she says. "Let's go to the ladies room. I'll fix it up for ya."

Although Tara initially accepted the report, she is now having second thoughts. "Mandy," she says nervously, "this isn't right. I didn't write this."

With a roll of her eyes, Mandy urges Tara forward. "Our teacher is an idiot! She'll never know!"

Tara shakes her head. "You already got me into trouble with Mr. Levy when you made me cut school. In fact, my Mom has to go back to court because of the trouble I got into."

Ignoring Tara's protests, Mandy pushes her into the bathroom and chases out a girl who was washing her hands at the sink. "What they don't know won't hurt 'em!" she advises with a finger pointed at Tara. "Besides, all you did was skip school; you didn't kill anyone. You want my help or not?"

Tara sighs. "Yeah, I guess you're right. Thanks for helping me, Mandy. I really hate my foster family. I just want my mother back."

Digging into her backpack, Mandy takes out a well-used makeup bag and grabs hold of Tara's chin, turning her friend's face toward her. "My dad says that everything will be all right if you just go to counseling."

When the repair job is complete, Tara approves of her reflection and gives her friend a half-smile. "I hope your dad's right," she says wistfully. "But please don't ask me to cut class again."

Mandy shakes her head. "FINE!" she retorts. "Gee, you are so lame!"

CHAPTER SEVENTEEN

The unmarked van pulls up to a house in an upper-class community on Fort Lauderdale's New River. While Jesus helps his father out of the vehicle, Rocco rings the doorbell.

"Good morning, Mrs. Hoffman," Rocco utters in his most polite voice. "I brought Christian Garcia, your new groundskeeper, and his son, Jesus. Christian is not feeling well today, but he'll be able to start his duties in the morning. We've made arrangements for Jesus to go to your daughter's school."

Gabriella looks past Rocco at her new employee. "Welcome, ah, *buenos días,*" she says. "Come in. I have a room for both of you at the back of the house."

With a lopsided grin, Jesus considers that his new life in this strange country may not be so bad after all. *If this lady's daughter is as pretty as she is, I don't think I'm going to mind living here,* he muses happily. His father, on the other hand, hasn't paid much attention to Mrs. Hoffman. He is spending all of his energy trying to mask his pain and discomfort.

After her visit to the beach, Lu went directly to

her room inside the mansion. She knows that she has to change into her uniform and report back to work, but she can't help thinking about the beach and the promise of dinner with Darren later that evening.

Sitting on the edge of her bed with her uniform in one hand, Lu is enjoying pleasant thoughts until a knock on the door startles her. Holding her breath, she makes no response, but the door bursts open and Judge Handel barges into the room.

Lu instinctively scrambles to cover herself up, but the judge moves quickly. Grabbing her hands, he leers, "There's no need for that. It's time for another private lesson."

Lu wants to struggle against the tight hold the judge has on her, but she knows that if she protests she may be hit again, so she succumbs to the judge's advances. Aware of what the judge prefers, she undresses quietly.

With a contented sigh, the judge assumes his favorite position like the dog he is, and Lu braces for what is to come. Closing her eyes tightly, she cries as silently as she can and attempts to block out the sounds of the judge's loud grunts and heavy breathing by concentrating on the beach and her father's farm. By now, she has learned how to absorb the unwanted blows and bodily insults that have come to her on the road to the new life that was promised to her father. She tries hard not to think of what her father would do if he knew what that new life was really like.

A few miles away, Fred Staten is once again on a shift at the Boynton Beach mansion and he's trying to lay low so he won't run into Debra. More sex is not what he needs or wants. In mid-afternoon, the day has become hot and humid and Fred and the other guards are preparing for their afternoon posts at the pool.

"Hey, good news!" announces Vincent Cardone as he walks into the bunk area. "You don't have to wear your jackets outside today; it's too damn hot!" Their boss' proclamation elicits rounds of applause and shouts of "Best news I've heard yet!" from several of the men. Acknowledging the positive reactions, he adds, "You can wear a T-shirt under your shoulder holster, but you still gotta wear your dress slacks and shoes." When he hears groans, he explains, "Look, I'm working on getting you guys some light, casual clothes that you can wear outside when no events are planned, but I don't have approval for them yet. Staten," he says when he spots Fred, "Connelly's asking about you again."

When the rest of the guards snicker and pump their fists in a crude gesture, Fred stands and takes a bow. Then, he shouts to be heard above the men's loud, guffawing laughter. "But seriously, Boss, can you help me out here?"

Laughing even louder, the guards file out of the bunk area for afternoon duty. As they pass Fred, they throw some playful comments his way. "Need some help, Fred?" asks one. "Can't do it alone?" asks another. "We'll chip in for some ice when she's finished with you!" says a third. Vincent joins in the laughter, but motions for Fred to remain behind. "Look," he says after the last man leaves, "I know what you're going through; we've all been there a time or two ourselves. But damn, she's been on you like white on rice! I'll do what I can to handle it today, but take some vitamins or something. You're gonna need them."

Fred shrugs his shoulders. "Thanks, Boss. I owe you one."

When Fred steps out of the air-conditioned coolness to join his coworkers, the hot air hits him like a freight train, and he notes with despair that there doesn't seem to be even a tiny breeze. With a groan, he hopes the girls won't be staying outside too long. Moving toward the rear of the house, he enters the pool area where the guards are already stationed at each corner of the screened enclosure.

The day is brutally hot, and although the sun is beating down mercilessly through the fiberglass enclosure, the two girls in the water and the others sunning themselves on lounge chairs are as naked as jaybirds, oblivious to the heat. Trying not to ogle them, Fred takes up his assigned position.

"Hey!" calls Denise, holding out a tube to Fred. "Can you put sunscreen on my back?"

Hoping for guidance from his fellow guards, Fred turns his mirrored aviators toward each of them in turn and receives a negative head shake from all of them. Understanding their message, Fred ignores Denise's request and stares impassively across the pool.

"Hey, I'm talking to you!" pouts Denise, rising to

a sitting position and showing off the enhanced assets that were forced upon her. "Don't you hear me?" she shouts. "Hey! Don't you see me? Don't you like this?" she yells loudly, waving her hand over her curvaceous body.

Out of the corner of his eye, Fred notices Debra Connelly walking out of the house in a tiny, two-piece bathing suit. *Oh, fuck! Vinnie didn't do shit!* he groans, assuming that the woman is looking for him.

It's quite the opposite, however. Debra has heard the drama unfolding between Fred and Denise and is strutting over to Denise. Perching on the edge of Denise's lounge chair, she looks at Fred, who is standing nearby, stoic and silent. Knowing that her latest plaything is paying attention even if it looks like he isn't, Debra takes the tube out of Denise's hand and caresses Denise's face. Purring suggestively, she speaks in a voice loud enough for Fred to hear. "Oh, Sweetie, it looks like you need someone to help you get all lathered up." Leaning over the young girl, Debra kisses her on the lips, grabs her hand, and leads her into the house.

Fred continues to stare out across the pool, but is stunned by the woman's behavior. *That woman is a real piece of work! But it looks like I'm off the hook for now,* he adds gratefully.

"To the judicial system and the downfall of Eral Rosenbaum!" toasts Darren, raising his bourbon on the rocks to Will Ballard in his fifth-floor office at the Broward County courthouse.

The two men sip their drinks in silence until Darren remembers his schedule for the week. "Jury selection is tomorrow and the trial begins on Wednesday. This is going to be an epic takedown of a first-class bastard!"

Will considers Darren's high expectations while he absentmindedly stirs his drink with a forefinger. "Watch out for the guy's lawyer," he warns. "She almost got the case thrown out."

Darren chuckles at the thought. "Not this time," he asserts. "I got the press on my side and the judge in my pocket. I have a feeling he's going to try for a plea. There are more people involved in this shit—Rabbi Katzoff, for one."

Surprised at hearing the prominent rabbi's name attached to Rosenbaum, Will snorts his drink and nearly chokes when the bourbon goes up his nose. "You need to be sure about that one!" he says, coughing loudly to clear his throat. "That guy has powerful people behind him. He even knows your father."

Darren downs the rest of his drink in one gulp. "My dad is only involved with Katzoff's organ transplants and UNOS, so if Fred Staten comes through with more info and Eral decides to squeal, we got Katzoff, too." With a peek at his watch, Darren says, "Hey, Will, I have to cut this celebration short. I have a hot date tonight."

Will has his suspicions about who Darren's date may be, but he chooses to keep that to himself for the time being. "Yeah," he answers with a suppressed smile, "you and me both. I promised Calista a pizza and an early movie."

Darren reaches out for Will's glass and looks Fred in the eye to make sure he has his colleague's attention. "You'll be called to testify," he advises, "so watch your back, Detective."

For the second time that day, Darren pulls into the driveway of his father's mansion. As he walks up to the house, he becomes aware of a growing sense of excitement in anticipation of the encounter he hopes will come later that evening with the young girl in his father's employ.

Intensely focused on that objective above all else, Darren doesn't see his father peering down at him from an upstairs window. "Hmpf!" mutters Judge Handel, holding the curtain aside to get a good look at his son. "I bet I know what that boy's up to."

While Darren fidgets in the foyer, the judge hides in an inconspicuous place at the top of the stairs to eavesdrop on the gathering downstairs. Before long, Ming Li appears trailed by Lu, who is wearing a cocktail dress that Ming Li lent her.

Darren almost falls into a trance at the sight of the stunning beauty. With his roving eyes, he takes in her youthful curves and her long black hair, gracefully falling over one shoulder.

Recovering his composure, Darren recalls the words he rehearsed earlier and speaks haltingly in Mandarin. Surprised, the women chuckle while Darren flushes with embarrassment. "Did I say something wrong?" he asks.

"You said the sky is beautiful," grins Ming Li. "But Lu Tang knows what you mean."

With a triumphant glance at Ming Li, the girl takes Darren's arm and they head for the door.

Upstairs, Judge Handel scrambles to resume his position at the window. He remains there until the pair is out of sight, all the while chuckling at his son's behavior.

Tonight, Darren Handel is a happy man. Not only is he anticipating an easy win in court that will do wonders for his career, but he's also drunk on the possibility of enjoying a fulfilling evening with a beautiful girl, even though he knows she's too young for him. Eager for the evening to begin, he drives a little too fast for his unsophisticated date.

Sitting beside Darren, Lu is nervous in the fast-moving car. Holding onto her seat with both hands, she suspects where they are going, and becomes worried. She thought Darren said they were going out to eat, but it looks like he's bringing her to a hotel.

Darren notices Lu's distress and tries to make her feel comfortable. "It's such a nice evening that I thought we would walk to the restaurant. It's across the river from my apartment; not far. Understand?"

Lu understood only a few words of what Darren said. Still concerned, she asks in a hushed tone, "We walk? Where?"

When Darren stops at a light, he uses hand motions to explain. "Over the bridge, to the restaurant. It's near the river."

"Ah," laughs Lu, "we walk to eat. I so sorry. Please forgive m..."

Darren stops Lu by placing two fingers over her lips. "I'm sorry," he says. "I know you don't understand much. It's okay."

Minutes later, Darren parks his car in the garage of his apartment building and shuts off the engine. Motioning for Lu to remain seated, he walks around the car and opens her door. Then, he takes her by the hand and leads her out of the parking garage toward the walkway over the Andrews Avenue Bridge.

Lu is enthralled. She is not used to being treated well by a man, and the large yachts anchored along the riverbank, and the cars and trucks whizzing by on the roadway almost make her dizzy. When she turns to Darren in delight, he detects both peace and deep sadness in her eyes, and he shudders. He knows that the young girl has probably gone through terrible circumstances on her journey to America, so he puts a protective arm around her shoulder and pulls her close. This makes Lu feels warm and safe for the first time in this new place, and she places her head against Darren's chest with a happy sigh.

Cuddling close, the couple walks over the bridge, oblivious to passing drivers who are eyeing the lovebirds with varied opinions about their greatly mismatched ages.

While Will finishes his third slice of pizza in a neighborhood restaurant, his daughter, Calista, reaches into her purse to remove her cell phone. Annoyed by Calista's constant attention to the inanimate object, Will reaches out and covers the hand holding the phone. "Come on, girl," he pleads, "not tonight. No phones, remember? Just the two of us."

With an exaggerated sigh full of drama, Calista reluctantly puts her phone away. "I want to see that new superhero movie," she pouts. "Can we please see it, Dad?"

"I thought I was your superhero," winks Will.

When Calista rolls her eyes at her father's attempt at levity, he says, "Okay, but we need to leave soon. That movie is popular, so I don't know if we'll get any seats if we wait too long."

"Well, hurry up, then. And pay the check fast!" orders Calista.

"Okay, okay!" laughs Will, motioning to their waiter.

Will waits for the bill, Calista becomes restless. "I need to use the bathroom," she announces, and leaves the table for the ladies room—not to use the facilities, but to text her new boyfriend.

"How can such a small person eat so much?" asks

Darren as he sips his coffee and watches Lu devour her dessert.

Lu laughs heartily, pleased that she understood Darren's question. It's been a long time since she had a good laugh, and she is thoroughly enjoying the sensation. Lu likes Darren. He seems like a kind man, and she hopes he likes her as well. "I am hungry," she responds. "It is very good. You not hungry?"

Actually, Darren is very hungry, but not for food. "Lu, let's take a walk along the river," he replies. "I want to show you where I live."

Lu wants a real relationship in this new world, and she likes Darren. "Okay," she answers, "but I need to pee."

Throwing his head back, Darren laughs loudly. He is amused by the coarse term Lu used and wonders whether she thinks the terminology is proper. Filing away a future English lesson, he calls the waitress over for the check and asks her to point out the location of the restrooms.

When Lu returns to the table, Darren is ready. He grabs Lu's hand and leads her out of the restaurant, toward his apartment.

The walk along the river is pleasant, but Darren wants it to end quickly, so he picks up the pace. Lu doesn't mind; she is also feeling a sense of urgency.

When the door closes on the apartment, Darren can no longer wait. With passionate kisses he undresses Lu feverishly, and Lu responds in kind. There is no time to head to the bedroom for these two—the sofa works just as well. And this time, when Lu envelopes her lover, she enjoys his attention.

That same evening, an exclusive and very private cocktail party is being held at the Boynton Beach house, and Fred is once again on duty. This time, he is stationed near the large French doors in the grand ballroom which are opened wide to invite the guests to stroll around the grounds near the canal and the Olympic-sized swimming pool.

The night is dark and moonless—perfect conditions for horny high-society members and oversexed politicians to mingle with the mansion's "employees" in the same fevered romp that has been taking place since time immemorial.

As Denise and the rest of the harem begin their "duties," Fred keeps his eyes narrowed on them in laser-like focus. He watches as each of the girls displays their wares enticingly before they sidle up to the person they've chosen for the evening. Although Judge Handel has already been claimed, Fred observes with disgust that the unsavory public servant is continuing to openly appraise each of the other girls' attributes.

As the judge hands his "date" a glass of champagne, he spots Denise in the crowd and briefly wonders whether he knows her. Shrugging off the thought, he whispers in the ear of this evening's tart, a newly-acquired dark-haired beauty not more than seventeen or eighteen years old. Laughing obligingly, the girl takes Judge Handel's arm and leads him out of the room.

On the way, the pair passes Rabbi Katzoff, who

glares at the judge in unrestrained annoyance. Handel knows why Katzoff is irritated, so to goad his friend on, he shrugs his shoulders in feigned indifference as he heads toward the stairs. Now even more peeved, Rabbi Katzoff stomps off to the bar for another glass of champagne. "Fuck that pervert!" he mumbles crossly. "He's always sure to be the first to sample all the new ones! He'd screw a snake if someone would just hold its head down!"

Standing sentry at the doors, Fred has watched the entire drama unfold. Filing away mental notes, he resolves to report the scene as accurately as possible, and hopes that the evening will go smoothly. But when Debra Connelly enters the room wearing a form-fitting, lace cocktail dress with no undergarments, he slips into the backyard to try to avoid his flagrantly nymphomaniacal boss.

Unfortunately, his boss saw him leaving.

Determined to avoid another narcissistic session of tickle and grab, Fred speed-walks around the pool to try to get as far away from Debra as possible. But Debra doesn't give up easily. She follows Fred as quickly as she can, but when she realizes that she won't be able to catch up to him in the fancy shoes she's wearing, she stops in her tracks and puts her hands on her hips in frustrated anger. "Fred Staten! Stop this instant!" she howls into the darkness.

Exasperated, Fred stops and turns around slowly.

Framed by the lights from the ballroom, Debra's dress becomes transparent and it appears as if she's naked. Enticed by the vision, Fred stares at his demanding boss until his better judgment takes hold. "Ms. Connelly," he says wearily, "I'm on duty. I need to check the yacht and the dock."

Standing nose-to-nose with her newest employee, Debra pokes her finger into Fred's chest. "You are on duty because I have chosen you to be on duty," she declares haughtily. "Rosenbaum sent you here, but that's irrelevant now. You have no friends in this house, so you will do what I want. You like this job, right? Your new car, your fancy clothes? Do as I say, and you will enjoy this gig. If you ignore me again, I will boot your ass out of here faster than you can run. Do you understand me, Staten?"

Fred holds back his temper because his investigation is not over. However, one more incident like this, and he will lose it. To calm himself, he inhales deeply through his nose and exhales through his mouth. "I'm sorry," he says contritely. "I got hung up with my security duties. I guess it comes from my military training. How may I help you, Ms. Connelly? By the way, you look ravishing tonight."

Debra exhales noisily. She can't remain angry; her inner passions won't allow it. "Let's check that yacht out together, shall we?" she commands coquettishly. "I'm sure we'll find something inside it that will pique your interest. Oh, and ditch that Ms. Connelly stuff. Call me Debra."

The pair disappears into the darkness as the warm breeze carries the sounds of music and laughter over the shimmering waters around the gently swaying yacht.

Will and Calista return home after the movie. Because tomorrow is a school day, Will kisses Calista goodnight and assumes she will soon be asleep behind her closed bedroom door. Calista will turn off the light to appease her father, but she will remain awake for hours, texting her new boyfriend. So far, Will knows nothing about the crush she has recently developed online.

With Calista in her room, Will grabs a beer from the fridge and walks into the living room to watch TV. However, after he picks up the remote control, he remembers the note Handel gave him. Unfolding the paper, he looks at it and reaches for the phone.

"Hello?" says Will. "This is Detective Ballard with FLPD. I need to speak with Mei Lan."

"Oh, yes, Detective," replies an unfamiliar voice. "Please wait while I get her for you."

There is a lengthy pause, and then Will hears Mei Lan on the line. "Hello, William Ballard!" she gushes enthusiastically. "I am so happy you call me! Are you well?"

Will smiles into the phone. "I'm fine, Mei Lan, but I need to speak with you. I'd like to bring you some breakfast tomorrow so we can talk. Say, nine o'clock?"

"Oh, that is wonderful!" replies Mei Lan. "But I must ask Officer Olivia if it okay."

When Mei Lan returns to the phone, she says, "She say it okay. But she want...fresh fruity? From...I-

HOP? Is this good English?"

"Yes, that's okay, no problem," laughs Will. "I'll see you both tomorrow."

CHAPTER EIGHTEEN

As the sun rises off the ocean, it greets the Florida coastline as it has every day since time began. Many who are awake at this early hour are trying to earn a living while others are just coasting through life, not knowing or caring what is happening around them.

As dawn breaks, Christian and Jesus emerge from the bedroom of their new home dressed and ready to tackle the day. Not sure about where to meet their new employer, they wander around the house until they encounter Mrs. Hoffman in the foyer. "Good morning," she says pleasantly. "Jesus, you will be going to school with Abby. I drive her there every morning and pick her up every day."

Jesus' father listens intently to the exchange but makes no comment. He is still in almost constant pain after the crude surgery that removed his kidney. Jesus knows that his father is trying to disguise his discomfort, so he bites his lip to prevent himself from saying something that will make his father's condition known to Mrs. Hoffman.

"Mom," calls Abby, stopping halfway down the steps, "I forgot my report. I'll be right back." Turning around, she scampers up the stairs.

Gabriella checks her watch. "Hurry up, Honey!

We'll wait in the car!" she shouts back, beckoning to Jesus. "Let's go. She'll be down soon. I'll stop at Burger King to get you both some breakfast. We usually eat at home, but we're getting a late start today."

On the way out of the door, Jesus turns to look back at his father and is distressed to see him slumped in a chair in the hallway, examining his wet and oozing bandages. The sight of his father's wounds frightens him. "*Papá,* that is not good!" he calls out.

Surprised, Christian looks up. "*Mi hijo,* I am okay," he says with a weak smile, "but I cannot do much; I will rest today. Have a good day at school." Heaving himself out of the chair, he heads back to their room to lie down.

Just then, Abby comes running down the stairs. When she hits the landing, she grabs Jesus' hand and pulls him out of the house. "Come on!" she frets, "Let's go, or we'll be late!"

Jesus stares back at his father before Abby closes the door behind them. He is worried that his father is not telling him the entire truth and that something may be very wrong.

Breakfast time in the Goldman household is not turning out well—Mandy is once again flexing her muscles.

The television in the kitchen is droning on and a reporter is asking, "Well, do you think the jury will reject the prosecution's accusations and acquit Rosenbaum?" however, no one in the kitchen is listening. Mandy is intently watching the cook as he very carefully sets down a cup of coffee on the table in front of the irritable child.

When the cook retreats, Mandy makes a show of inspecting the beverage and decides that she doesn't like it. "I wanted the foam under my coffee, you brainless ass!" she screams at the hapless man. Then, she grabs the hot cup and flings the liquid at the cook, burning his arm and staining his clean white jacket.

Gasping in alarm at the pain on his arm, the cook backs away from his employer's daughter but doesn't criticize her; he needs this new job. Instead, he bows his head and utters the beginnings of an apology, which is cut short by the household's nanny.

The stern nanny has been with the family since Mandy was born and she knows the child well. Stepping between the two, she declares, "Mandy Goldman! You must stop demanding things that are impossible! Your parents cannot keep replacing staff! If your mother were here, she would say the same thing!"

Mandy is still furious and doesn't want to hear anything the nanny says. "That person is not my mother!" she yells at the woman. "I don't listen to her, and I don't care what she says! Anyway, how do you know what she would say?"

"She does not like it when you treat us that way. We are human beings, just like you."

Mandy laughs uproariously at the nanny, as if she has just told a joke. "People?" she snickers. "You're not people; you just work here! I'm your boss, and there's no one like me! I'm one of a kind!" she adds proudly.

"Well, I certainly hope so," smirks the woman. "Now, you've wasted so much time that there's no time left for breakfast. Get your things. It's time to leave for school."

"I am not going to that school!" Mandy pouts, trying to stand firm. "I *hate* that charter school! The teachers there are stupid!"

The nanny also stands firm. "Well, if you didn't get yourself kicked out of your private school, you'd still be there with your friends. Nevertheless, you *are* going to school today."

Mandy knows that she's fighting a losing battle, so she gives in—this time. With a frown at the floor, she mumbles, "Shit. Okay, fine! Let's go."

It's only eight thirty in the morning, but it's already hot. Every day, it seems the weather in South Florida becomes more and more unbearable.

As the sun rises higher in the sky, Gabriella anticipates the increasing heat and turns up the air conditioner inside her car. She is impatiently waiting for the car door to close after dropping Abby and Jesus off at school.

Released onto the sidewalk with Abby, Jesus follows her every move. He is ill at ease among this crowd of unfamiliar English-speakers and is determined to remain close to the only person with whom he is acquainted, even though they just met.

Abby knows that the son of the family's new gardener is following her, and she also knows that he's sticking out like a sore thumb. His clothes are two sizes too large, and several years out of style. Still, she only shrugs at Calista when Calista raises her brows in a silent question about the boy trailing behind them on the way to the school's open-air courtyard.

When they enter the courtyard, Mandy, the class bully, and her pal, Tara, materialize out of the crowd unbidden and unwelcome, stopping the trio's forward march. Always eager to make a scene, Mandy gears up for one of her many daily confrontations. Dramatically placing her hand against her forehead, she swoons mockingly and inquires, "Ooh, Abby, darling, whooooo is the new guy? Is he your *boyfriend*?"

Abby grimaces at her tormentor but replies as politely as she can to try to avoid a problem. "That's Jesus," she says, walking around Mandy.

Although Mandy allows Abby and Calista to pass her, she stops Jesus. Placing an arm around his waist, she pulls the boy close. "Jesus," she says with syrupy sweetness, "you should step up in the world and hang out with us instead of that heartless little bitch."

Standing nearby, Calista watches Mandy's dramatic display with growing distaste. "Hey!" she shouts, "The only bitch around here is you!"

Tara has also been watching the confrontation and is equally uncomfortable with the turn of events. "Hey, Mandy, cool it down!" she advises. "You don't want to get in trouble again, do you?" But Mandy is not listening. She is still perturbed by her morning tiff with the cook and the nanny, so she pays little attention to her friend's advice.

Defiant as always, Mandy gets Abby's attention and thumps her chest in rhythm with her heartbeat. "I am not cooling it down!" she yells. "I don't have to worry about getting upset! *My* heart works just fine! Isn't that right, dear Abby?"

"Leave me alone!" whines Abby. "Leave us all alone!"

Jesus tries to follow Abby as she walks away, but Mandy holds him fast. "Get your hands off him!" shouts Calista, observing Jesus' distress. "He doesn't need a 'ho like you!"

But Mandy only chuckles at Calista's attempt to offend her; she's heard that insult and many others before. Looking Calista in the eye, she bellows in a voice loud enough for the other students around them to hear, "But I can teach him some things that you two can only dream about!"

Hearing Mandy's rant, Abby stomps back to defend Jesus and face her bully. "You don't need a girl like that!" she shouts at Jesus. "She's a liar and a tramp!"

"You calling me a liar, you sick little freak?" Mandy screams as she slams her hand into Abby's chest and pushes her to the ground.

Standing in defiance over Abby, Mandy seethes with anger while a crowd gathers around, shouting, "Fight! Fight!"

Surrounded by students, Abby remains on the ground, holding her chest and moaning in intense pain.

"Mandy! Come on! Let's go!" urges Tara, trying to pull her pal away from Abby. But Mandy is still in a rage. She pushes Tara away and attacks Abby as she attempts to get to her feet. Flailing wildly, several of Mandy's punches land on Abby's chest and cause her to collapse back onto the ground.

Horrified by the unprovoked attack on her defenseless friend, Calista joins the fray. She grabs Mandy by the hair and yells, "Try me, bitch!" and instantly, an all-out brawl breaks out with Calista and Mandy rolling around on the ground, pulling and tugging at each other. With the crowd cheering them on, Tara tries to pull them apart, but a teacher finally arrives and separates them.

While the teacher grips Calista, Tara keeps a firm hold on Mandy. "What's going on here?" demands the teacher, shouting to be heard above the crowd of onlookers.

"That slut attacked Abby!" shrieks Calista, still full of piss and vinegar as she pulls against the teacher's grip to get another shot at Mandy.

Mandy suspects that she may be outdone by the crowd, so she turns on the waterworks in a bid for sympathy. "They were bullying me!" she cries with quivering lips.

"Bullshit!" yells Calista. "You punched Abby in the heart, you bitch!"

"I was just trying to be friends," sobs Mandy, increasing her tears.

Left on the sidelines during the altercation, Jesus approaches Abby and helps her off the ground.

"You are no friend!" he responds in loud opposition to Mandy's declaration.

"Okay, that's enough!" declares the teacher, not knowing who is lying and who is telling the truth. "All of you can tell your stories to the school counselor in detention!"

"Mr. Phillips, you can't be serious!" cries Calista, outraged that she and Abby will be punished along with Mandy. "She started it!"

Exasperated, Mr. Phillips considers each of the troublemakers individually and then directs his attention toward Calista. "Mr. Levy will iron this out," he states. "And Miss, if you keep this up, I'll have you suspended. All of you, follow me." Looking out at the crowd, he adds, "Everyone else, get to class!"

As the teacher helps Abby into the building, the others trail along behind them and the onlookers scatter in various directions.

Behind Mr. Phillips, Mandy clutches her chest dramatically and snickers mockingly, prompting Calista to smack her hard in the back of her head. When Mandy reacts with a loud, "Ow!" Mr. Phillips turns around sharply and looks from one person to the other to determine the cause. When he seems to settle on Calista, she responds with an innocent, "She was bothering me," and shrugs dismissively. "Just get inside and keep quiet," Mr. Phillips sighs between gritted teeth.

Inside his small office, Randal Levy is texting on his cell phone when Mr. Phillips enters with Abby, Calista, Jesus, Mandy, and Tara. The student counselor doesn't stop his cell phone activity even though there is now a crowd in front of his desk, so the teacher clears his throat to get his attention.

"Ah," says Randal when he finally raises his head. "How can I help you all?"

Pushing Mandy and Calista forward, Mr. Phillips declares, "These students decided that it would be a good idea to start the morning off with a fight."

"Oh, really?" says Randal. "Well, I'll take over now. Thanks."

Relieved to be rid of the disruptive students, Mr. Phillips leaves the office in a hurry.

Randal looks over the group for several moments and then says quietly, "Miss Goldman and Miss Smith. So nice to see you both again. Sit down, please."

"Mandy punched Abby in the heart!" interrupts Calista. "She needs to see the nurse!"

Observing Abby, Randal notes that she is holding her chest and seems to be in pain.

"I don't feel safe near Mandy," Abby states weakly.

Looking past the stricken girl, Randal is surprised to see an unfamiliar face in the room. "I haven't seen you in here before," he says. "What's your name, young man?"

Abby is not sure that Jesus understands, so she whispers a quick clarification.

"I am Jesus Garcia," Jesus responds.

"Okay, Jesus. Please escort Abby to the nurse's

office. The rest of you will remain here until you can get along with each other. If you don't learn that lesson today, you'll have to return every day for one hour after school until you do. Now sit down, all of you."

Tara and Calista sit down, but Mandy remains standing. "You can't do anything to me," she says boldly. "My father rules this place."

"Is that so?" says Randal. "Well, maybe Child Services can do something. Just ask Tara. Now do you want to sit down, or should I give them a call?"

Outmaneuvered, Mandy takes a seat next to Tara with a huff.

On the other side of Tara, Calista is still agitated and determined to make sure the counselor knows the truth. Leaning across Tara, she points an accusing finger at Mandy and snarls, "She punched Abby in the heart for no reason!"

"She called me a liar and a tramp!" Mandy growls back.

Sandwiched between the two feuding girls, Tara begins to cry as the girls yell back and forth across her.

Randal shouts to be heard above the din. "Shut up, you two! That's enough!"

Surprised by the outburst, Mandy and Calista stop yelling and turn expectantly to the school counselor.

Drumming his fingers on the desk, Randal considers his next move. "Calista," he says sternly, "I'm going to call your father. I'll let him decide your fate. You can go now."

Calista jumps out of her seat and storms out of the door, happy that she doesn't have to stay for the promised detention.

"Oh, that's just great!" protests Mandy. "You only let her go because her dad's a cop!"

"I told you to be quiet!" shouts Randal. "Aren't you tired of coming to my office, Mandy? I told you not to bully Abby! You'll have detention every day until I decide you no longer need it, or you're put into the system. Now, leave my office and come back after school. I want to speak to Tara alone."

Mandy rises but gives a warning look to Tara. "Don't rat me out, girl!" she cautions. "Got it?"

"Wait for me outside?" asks Tara hopefully.

"Yeah. I got you, girl."

Tara nods in appreciation but doesn't make eye contact with Mandy.

When the door closes, Randal opens a large folder. "Tell me your side of the story, Tara. What happened in the courtyard?"

Tara keeps her head down so she doesn't have to look at Randal. "Like Mandy said, I guess," she answers quietly.

Randal is aware that Tara has a troubled home life, so he probes further. "Tara, is everything okay?"

"I have a lot on my mind," she says.

Looking down at the folder, Randal pages through its contents. "You mean the court case with your mom?"

Startled, Tara looks up. "How the hell do you know about that?" she asks.

"I have your file right here," says Randal. "The court sent me a copy."

Tara is now alert, but nervous. "I'm really scared, Mr. Levy. They want to take my mother away from me—permanently. They gave her an impossible task to complete and she couldn't do it! She didn't do anything wrong, she just..." Tara stops speaking as gut-wrenching sobs overtake her. Controlling her grief, she continues haltingly, "She can't do it...and save her job! She has to go to counseling...there are supervised visitation hours...but they're during work! She works three jobs! If my dad didn't die..." Letting those words trail off, she bursts into tears again.

Randal reaches across the desk and hands Tara a box of tissues, which she uses to dab at her face. "It's all my fault!" Tara sobs. "I skipped school because of Mandy!"

Randal's brows shoot up at the revelation, but he remains silent.

Resuming her story more softly, Tara says, "The kids here bully and tease me. They call me Terrible Tara. And my foster mother is a witch! Her daughter ruined all my makeup and tore up my book report. Mandy got me new makeup and a new report. She's the only one who cares about me, besides my mom. I can't say no to her. Uh, oh. I shouldn't have said that."

Randal hands the box of tissues to Tara again, and she grabs more than one this time.

"Would you feel better if I come with you

when you go to court?" asks Randal after a moment's thought.

"I... Oh, yes, that would be great! Thank you!" says Tara, brightening at the idea.

"That's what I'm here for," replies Randal. "You can go now. There won't be any detention for you, either."

Rising from her seat, Tara looks back at Randal before she turns the doorknob. "I thought you were going to make me rat out Mandy," she confesses.

"Is there something about her that I don't already know?" smirks Randal.

"No" chuckles Tara.

When Tara leaves Randal's office she feels better than when she walked in, but when she passes the teacher who rounded up the group, she averts her eyes.

The teacher is on his way back to the counselor's office to give Randal some advice. Poking his head into the doorway, he says, "Mr. Levy, I want to caution you about how to treat Mandy. The Goldmans..."

"I don't give a damn about the Goldmans!" retorts Randal angrily. "Don't tell me how to do my job! Their money doesn't give them a free pass to act irresponsibly! That family can fund the U.S. government for all I care! Now is there anything I can assist you with today, or can I get back to work?"

Startled by the vehement rebuff, the teacher removes his head from the doorway and retraces his steps down the corridor, passing Mandy and Tara, who are hugging each other near Tara's locker.

"Did you rat me out?" Mandy asks.

"No, he wanted to talk about my court case."

"Why?"

Tara blows her nose. "I don't know, but he offered to come with me to court. He's the only person I'll have there on my side. You can't go; you're not eighteen, and my dad and his young-ass bride are in Europe."

Mandy puts her arm around her friend. "It's so lame that I can't be there. You're my girl, you know." Turning Tara's head toward her, she studies Tara's face and shakes her head disapprovingly. "Damn! Your makeup is ruined again! Come on, let's fix it up. You're too pretty to be crying." Leaning over, Mandy gives Tara a kiss, a long kiss, and Tara doesn't mind or resist.

Balancing several bags in his arms, Will is barely able to free one hand long enough to knock on the door of a small, two-bedroom house in Deerfield Beach. The home, typical of those built in this area in the early fifties, is currently being used as a law enforcement safe house. Will waits patiently in front of the door because he knows he's being checked out by the officer inside.

After a suitable amount of time, Police Officer Olivia Johnson cracks open the door to take a closer look at Will. When she determines that he isn't a threat to the person she's guarding, she opens the door wider.

Will and Officer Johnson have run into each other at police headquarters in the past, so they're not complete strangers. Even so, Will suspects that Olivia is about to ask him to see his badge, so he declares, "Oh, come on, Olivia. Don't just stand there. You can see that my hands are full! Take your breakfast, and let me in." Yielding to her colleague, Olivia removes one of the bags from Will's arms and steps aside.

When Will enters the house, he hears Mei Lan shouting his name. "Detective Ballard! Detective Ballard!"

Will places his breakfast treats on a small table and opens his arms to accept Mei Lan's enthusiastic hug. "I can't stay long," he says to the happy girl. "I have a meeting this morning." With a glance at Olivia, he asks, "Can I speak with Mei Lan alone?" Will knows that the only other rooms in the house are two bedrooms and a kitchen, so he lifts a questioning eyebrow at Olivia.

Understanding what Will wants, Olivia nods her head. "Yeah, well, I guess I can eat in my room. Thanks for breakfast."

Searching for her food, Mei Lan takes a seat and starts opening bags. As his witness eats, Will says, "Mei Lan, Immigration is reviewing your case. District Attorney Handel has connections in Washington, and he's asked them to grant you a temporary visa. I volunteered to vouch for you, so you can stay with me and my daughter, Calista, until you can get a job and a place of your own."

Overwhelmed by the detective's generosity, Mei Lan jumps up and hugs Will again.

Watching the pair from her bedroom, Olivia notes with surprise that Will has taken a kindly interest in the unfortunate girl. Hoping for the best, she trusts that Mei Lan may one day be able to put her tormented past behind her.

CHAPTER NINETEEN

Will has grounded Calista until further notice. Well, sort of. She can still practice her dance routine with Abby, but without permission from Will, she's not allowed to do anything else. That isn't stopping her from texting her new boyfriend, however.

Tara's involvement in the fight hasn't caused her any direct problems, but she isn't out of the woods yet. She's been on pins and needles while she waits for a chance to see her mother again. Even if it's only for a few minutes in court, Tara is desperately in need of that familial connection before she can return to some sense of normalcy.

As usual, Mandy is in the most trouble. She will remain in detention for as long as Mr. Levy sees fit, and if Mandy's past behavior is any indication, she may be in detention for a long time.

Sergeant Fred Staten is continuing his undercover job in Boynton Beach. Although the perks of his assignment are numerous and by no means boring, he's looking forward to ending his role at the brothel. Fred's mission to determine whether there's a connection between several disturbing events in his town is involving him in some of the more upsetting parts of the seedy side of life in sunny South Florida, and he's becoming increasingly bothered by what he's seeing.

A major player in those disturbing events is Eral Rosenbaum. He and his attorney have been meeting in Eral's hotel room every night since the trial began, and Attorney Berg has begun to predict that the case will be handed over to the jury any day now.

"Eral, you must know that the trial hasn't been going in your favor. It's so blatantly obvious that Handel has the jury, the press, and the judge in his pocket that I'm going to have to warn you once again. Be prepared for a plea agreement. I'm going to try to get the case dismissed again tomorrow, but if that doesn't work, remember that we can still enter a plea after the jury receives the case. That must be done before they reach a verdict, however."

Eral turns his head sharply to try to relieve pressure in his neck. He's been stiffening up a lot lately, and pain is something that he doesn't need right now. When he hears the familiar crack, he exhales in relief. "Don't worry," he says to Lisa, "I know what I'm gonna do. They're gonna be shocked at what I have to offer, and I probably won't get any jail time because of it." Eral pauses while he gives Lisa the once-over. "Ya know," he says thoughtfully, "I've been wanting to tell you that you're not bad looking—for a lawyer."

With an indignant "Hmph," Lisa stands and smooths her skirt. "You can't afford me," she states crossly, highly annoyed by her depraved client's comment. "Good night, Mr. Rosenbaum. By the way, jail time IS in your future."

The next day, before going to court, Judge Nicholas Handel stops at his ex-daughter-in-law's house unannounced. He intends to maintain a connection to his granddaughter, even though his son has divorced her mother.

Sitting at the breakfast bar with Abby and Jesus, the judge studies Abby over a cup of black coffee. "You're going to get that new heart soon," he states definitively. "You can trust me on that. I am a judge, you know."

Abby looks at her grandfather but doesn't feel a great connection to him. "I trust my dad; he promised me." Looking away, she says, "Hey, Mom, don't forget-—Calista is sleeping over again tomorrow. We need to practice." Then, as if they were both on the same wavelength, Abby and Jesus slide off their chairs and rush into the living room to gather their things for school.

Abandoned at the breakfast bar, Judge Handel looks at Jesus. "How's that new gardener working out?" he asks Gabby while she cleans up the kitchen.

Gabriella stops what she's doing to respond to her ex-father-in-law. "He's doing fine," she answers. "My roses have never been healthier. He is rather slow, however. He said he had some surgery before he started and that it's slowing him down. Other than that, it looks like he'll work out well. His son is getting along well with Abby, so it's a win-win. Look, I need to drive the kids to school now. If you want to stay to finish your coffee, just lock up after you leave."

"No, thanks," says Handel. "I have a full caseload today. I'll leave with you."

As the group exits the house, the judge makes sure to walk behind Gabriella so he can take a long look at his daughter-in-law's shapely derriere.

It is now late morning, and Darren is once again standing before Judge Kathleen Rose's bench. This time, he's waiting for Will Ballard to get comfortable on the stand.

When Will stops fidgeting, Darren begins his line of questioning, knowing that everyone in the courtroom is focused on the detective.

"Please state your name for the record."

"William Ballard."

"What is your occupation, Mr. Ballard?"

"I'm the senior detective in charge of Vice at Fort Lauderdale's Police Department. I've been with FLPD for twenty years."

"Very good, Detective. Thank you for your service. Are you familiar with the defendant, Mr. Eral Rosenbaum?"

"Yes, I am. I was assigned to this case as an investigator. My department obtained search warrants to raid Mr. Rosenbaum's business, his condo, a home in Hollywood, and a rented house in Boynton Beach.

"What did you find when you searched those places?"

"When we arrived at Mr. Rosenbaum's condo, we found him living there with a young woman and several under-aged girls. At the Boynton rental, we found evidence of 112 missing persons and the bodies of three young girls. In Hollywood, we found a number of young girls who were being held there against their wills. They were being used as 'entertainment' for paying customers."

Darren turns to the jury. "Three dead, under-aged girls in Boynton, and others held against their wills in Hollywood?" Then, he turns back to Will. "What else did your search of the Boynton Beach location reveal?"

Will gives his response to the jury. "It revealed that Mr. Rosenbaum was buying male and female children, and trafficking them for sex."

Seeing the jurors' eyes widen in shock, Lisa Berg stands and declares loudly, "Your Honor, I object!"

"Sustained!" responds Judge Rose.

Darren continues with a barely concealed smirk. "Let me rephrase the question. Detective, what information did the evidence provide that led you to believe that various acts of sex trafficking were being committed at the rented home?"

"We found a journal that listed bank transfers of large sums of money. Every one of them referred to the sale of people—young people—for sex. Also, after examinations were performed on the victims we found there—both the living and deceased victims-—we found signs of physical and sexual abuse on all of them."

This information hits a nerve with the members of the jury. Most of them look uncomfortable, and some of them seem angry. Noting their reaction, Lisa Berg shouts again, "Your Honor, I object! This witness doesn't have the credentials to make medical determinations."

Before the judge can rule on the motion, Darren retrieves a large folder from his counsel table. Gripping it tightly, he approaches the bench. "Your Honor, here are certified medical records from the hospital and the medical examiner that will corroborate Detective Ballard's testimony."

Accepting the folder, Judge Rose reviews its documents slowly while the jury watches. Eventually, she hands the folder to her judicial assistant. "Mark this as Exhibit R. Counsel, you are overruled. State, please proceed."

Darren looks over his shoulder at Lisa and smiles at the jury as he approaches Will. "Detective, how old are the victims you found?"

"Some of them are as young as seven. The oldest was about twenty-five."

Darren looks at the jury. "Seven to twenty-five... Thank you, Detective. No further questions, your Honor."

Lisa rises in a hurry. "I would like to cross-examine this witness, your Honor." The attorney walks around her table to approach the witness stand. "Detective Ballard, you inferred that my client is involved with under-aged children at the rented house, but that is not correct. My client, Mr. Rosenbaum, was not at the house at the time you arrived. He was in his condo. He has already testified that he knew nothing about the children in Hollywood."

With a glare at Lisa, Will states, "There were under-aged girls at his condo, and..."

Lisa interrupts Will to keep him from saying anything else. "I have no further questions for this witness, your Honor. The Defense rests."

Judge Rose turns to Will. "You may step down, Detective Ballard." Then, because it has been a long day, she takes a moment to shift in her seat. When she's comfortable, she looks out at the members of the court. "The State may begin their closing statements."

Anticipating this moment with glee, Darren rises and tightens his tie on his approach to the jury box. "Your Honor and ladies and gentlemen of the jury, I have presented this court with multiple witnesses and concrete evidence that prove that Eral Rosenbaum..." Darren pauses for a moment to stare at Eral, and then continues, "...showed complete disregard for his fellow human beings by forcing young girls into a corrupt life of unwanted sex and servitude. Eral Rosenbaum is guilty of one hundred twelve cases of sex trafficking and endangerment of minors through the willful rape of children, teens, and young adults. In addition, seventy-eight of his victims were either murdered or left to die alone and unwanted. The people of the state of Florida ask for your quick conviction on all counts, and we recommend the death penalty."

At the conclusion of his closing statement, Darren returns to his counsel table and stares across the courtroom at Eral while Lisa Berg jumps to her feet and struts over to the jury box.

"Other than stating that there were indications that young people were being coerced into sex, the prosecution has not tied any of that activity to my client, Mr. Rosenbaum, and neither has he proven that my client had any knowledge of what was happening at the property in Hollywood. To remind the jury, that property does not belong to Mr. Rosenbaum. Your Honor, because there are no concrete links to my client, the defense rests and once again makes a motion that all charges be dismissed."

A profound silence overtakes the courtroom while everyone waits for Judge Rose to respond. "Motion denied," she finally declares. "This court will adjourn until such time as the jury reaches a verdict. Members of the jury, you will rule on the multiple charges that have been placed before you, which I summarized in my opening statement to you. You must only review the testimony that has been presented before you, and you must determine your verdict beyond any reasonable doubt. You are the sole judges of the facts and credibility of all the witnesses that have testified during this trial. You must base your decision on the evidence presented, and you must use your common sense, not your personal feelings or any statements that were given during opening and closing arguments. You will choose a jury foreperson, and that person will be the liaison between you and the Clerk of this Court. Members of the jury, if a verdict is not reached within normal business hours today or by early this evening, you will be sequestered at a local hotel for the night, and you will resume your deliberations in the jury room tomorrow morning. Bailiff, please escort these fine gentlemen and women to the jury room."

Judge Rose strikes her gavel while the members of the jury file out of the courtroom. "This court is now adjourned until a verdict is reached."

As an officer of the court calls out, "ALL RISE," the judge leaves the room, and some of the spectators clap.

Grabbing his attaché case, Darren frowns at Eral in disgust. On his way out of the courtroom, several spectators stop him to offer their congratulations on his handling of the case, but one of the spectators still hasn't left his seat. Randal Levy is in the back row, texting furiously.

At the defense table, Lisa tells Eral to remain seated. "We'll wait until the courtroom clears out and then we'll exit through the back to avoid the press. If they offer a plea agreement, we better jump at it."

When Darren exits the courtroom, he's immediately surrounded by a crowd of people who want to talk to him. He indulges them for a while and then manages to break away, but then he's stopped again, this time by Randal Levy.

"District Attorney Handel, how do you think it went in there?" Randal asks.

Impatient to leave, Darren glances at his watch and answers as quickly as possible. "It's a conviction for sure. But with a jury, anything is possible."

Randal shakes his head. “You know there are more offenders like him out there. Think you can get them all?”

Darren wants to walk away, but Randal is blocking his path. “I can try my best,” the D.A. responds.

“Well, as a youth counselor, I’d love to see you try,” says Randal. “We should grab a drink together sometime and talk.”

Darren’s phone conveniently rings at that moment, relieving him of the need for further conversation with this stranger. “Sometime, maybe,” he responds. “I have a very hectic schedule. Please excuse me.”

When Randal moves aside, Darren walks as quickly as he can toward the elevator to catch it before its doors close. Sliding inside, he brings his phone to his ear to answer his call and sees Randal still in the hallway, texting on his cell phone.

Because he’s in a crowded elevator, Darren keeps his call brief. When it ends, a man and woman behind him tap him on the shoulder. “Mr. District Attorney,” says the woman, “our daughter was one of the victims they found alive. We can’t thank you enough for what you’ve done. Is there any chance at all that that horrible man who nearly killed our daughter will go free?”

“I don’t believe so,” answers Darren, turning around slightly. “The evidence was overwhelming. How is your daughter doing now?”

“She’s recuperating, but it’s going to take some time,” sighs the man. “We’re afraid she may never be the same. If that man goes free, I swear, I’ll... Never mind.”

Darren closes his mind to thoughts of his own daughter, who is still missing. "I'm sure that your daughter will be able to recover, now that she's back in a loving environment. Let the courts handle Rosenbaum."

When the elevator door opens, Darren puts a comforting hand on the man's shoulder and heads toward the building's exit.

Outside the courthouse, the press has set up a podium crowded with microphones from multiple local and national news outlets. In front of it, several print and television reporters stand together with a small crowd of onlookers, all of whom are being held back by Fort Lauderdale's Finest.

Darren expected this; he's not surprised by all of the attention the case is getting from the media. Certain that the verdict will go his way, he takes his place confidently at the podium.

"The jury has received their charge," he states, "and we expect a full conviction. We requested the death penalty."

"What are the chances the jury will reject the evidence and acquit Mr. Rosenbaum?" asks a local journalist. "He's a wealthy man, and he's well-known in this community."

"Believe me, that is highly unlikely," responds Darren. "He may receive consecutive life sentences, but he is guilty. Now if you will excuse me, it's pretty hot out here, and we don't need to be standing in the sun any longer than necessary."

As Darren walks away, two police officers flank

him while journalists call out his name to try to get more information. When he doesn't respond, the crowd disperses.

In an attempt to avoid Judge Handel, Lu Tang has attached herself to Ming Li. While the older woman prepares the evening meal, Lu washes dishes and does whatever she can to make herself indispensable so she can remain out of sight for as long as possible.

The cook knows why Lu is there and feels sorry for her. Speaking in Mandarin, Ming Li tells her, "Don't worry; you can stay here with me as long as you want. The judge is a powerful and demanding man, and he is not good. He won't bother you as long as I am with you."

Lu stares into the sink, letting the hot water from the faucet rush over her hands. "I am so ashamed and afraid," she replies in her native tongue. "If only he were more like his son."

Ming Li shakes her head sadly, knowing firsthand about Darren and his desires. "Darren is just like any other man," she says with a sigh. "He is not the father and he seems to like you, but..."

"He loves me!"

Ming Li sighs again. "Be careful, little one. He comes from the same tree."

Darren's favorite Irish Pub is very busy and noisy tonight. The inside crowd stands shoulder to shoulder while all the tables outside are occupied. Even though this establishment is frequently crowded, Darren enjoys coming here—it's one of the preferred watering holes for downtown Fort Lauderdale's young and influential businesspersons.

Tonight, Darren is standing at the edge of the crowd with one hand over his ear. He's trying block some of the sounds from the testosterone- and estrogen-filled people around him so he can hear the speaker. Straining to listen, he spies William Ballard making his way through the throng and motions for him to go to the bar while he continues his call.

"Yeah, Dad, I got your call," he shouts into the phone. "I was in court today... Yes, I did bring Lu to the beach. What...? Yes, the case went to the jury; I think we got him. Another sex trafficking sleazebag is off the streets... Of course, it's worth it. If I can save one child like my daughter—your granddaughter—it's all worth it... What? Um, well, I can try. I'm at the pub right now with Detective Ballard."

When Darren ends the call, he heads to the bar to join Will. On the other end of the line, Judge Handel laughs as he pulls up his pants and stares down at Lu.

At the bar, Detective Ballard greets Darren with a broad smile and a beer. While sipping their drinks, they scan the room for an empty table and spot one that has just been vacated. Plowing their way through the chattering crowd, they arrive there before anyone else and sit down gratefully.

Safely ensconced in the spot they'll occupy for the rest of the night, the pair resumes the conversation they began at the bar.

"Well, it's up to the jury now," says Will. "You think they'll return a quick verdict?"

Darren savors his Guinness, letting it flow slowly down his throat. "Yeah, they should," he responds, "but I can't shake the feeling that we missed something... some other shit besides Rosenbaum's."

"Yeah," agrees Will. "Sergeant Staten is still knee deep in the hoopla in Boynton. There may be a connection to Rosenbaum there. But you seem more concerned than that."

"Come on, Will," says Darren as he sees someone he recognizes in the crowd. "Rosenbaum was a scapegoat, a sacrificial lamb. I think it goes deeper than him, and higher up as well."

Will follows Darren's gaze, wondering what has gotten his attention. "Well, at least he'll be out of commission for a long time," he says. You spot a friend of yours?"

Randal is at the far end of the bar, texting. Looking up at that moment, he makes eye contact with Darren and instantly recognizes the district attorney. With a frown, Darren realizes that Randal has spotted him and is now walking over to their table.

"Well, it looks like you're available for that drink after all," Randal says as he plops down into the chair next to Darren.

Will stares quizzically at Darren as the intruder stops a waitress. "Can you bring us three single-malt Scotch whiskeys?" asks Randal. "The sixty-five-year-old kind. Wait…make it four."

The barmaid smiles broadly, knowing that this order will bring a good tip. "Sure thing, Hon," she says. "Comin' right up."

"You have an expensive palate," comments Will.

"My pleasure," says Randal, looking down at his phone, now resting quietly on the table. "We need to celebrate our D.A.'s victory. Oh, and we should also congratulate you on the service you provide to the people of Fort Lauderdale, Officer Ballard. I work closely with kids, so this one hits close to home."

Will is about to ask Randal how he knows his name when the barmaid returns with the drinks. Opening his wallet, Randal hands her several large bills. The waitress is pleased and thanks him with a big smile.

Grabbing one of the glasses, Randal downs his drink in one gulp and grabs another to do the same. "So tell me how you did it," he says to Darren. "You know, how you built the case."

Darren takes a sip from the glass Randal passed to him. "It took a lot of investigation by Detective Ballard," he replies. "Why are you so interested in my approach to this case?"

Recognizing a familiar sound, Randal looks down at his phone to see a new text message pop up. "I told you," he replies, "I work with kids all the time.

I'm actually counseling a few of them now. I even counseled Calista," he says, looking directly at Will.

As Will's mouth pops open, Randal quickly adds, "Hey, it was great talking to you both, but I have to leave now. Good luck with your verdict, Mr. D.A."

The pair watches with unabashed curiosity as Randal thumbs a text message and weaves his way through the crowd. "I always attract the crazies," Darren comments sadly.

"I think I've seen that guy at Calista's school," says Will. "I'm gonna do a quick check. There's something odd about him."

Much later that night, when most of Fort Lauderdale is trying to sleep and the streets are lonely and silent, Randal is not one of those who are asleep. He on his computer, paging through Tara Smith's social media accounts.

As he waits for a photo of Tara print, he hears another ping from his phone and reads a new text message. Shrugging his shoulders, he shuts the phone off and lays it down. "No more tonight," he mumbles. Then, he grabs Tara's photo from the printer, writes her name at the bottom, and pins it to a cork board on the wall above his desk.

The photo of Tara Smith now rests among similar photos of Abby Handel, Calista Ballard, Jesus Garcia, Mandy Goldman, Mei Lan, and Lu Tang. Several other images on the board have red X's over them, while others are connected by a red ribbon.

Randal sits back at stares at the board, then looks at his phone. “Fuck it,” he mumbles. Turning the phone back on, he begins to text again. It is now three o’clock in the morning.

The occupants of an apartment across town are also awake at this early hour. Lu Tang and Darren Handel are lying next to each other in Darren’s bedroom.

This evening, Lu is enjoying her encounter with a member of the Handel family. The couple’s frequent gasps and moans are eclipsing the sounds of the chiming grandfather clock in the hallway as it announces three fifteen a.m.

CHAPTER TWENTY

By nine o'clock the next morning, Fort Lauderdale has been awake for quite some time, and several persons involved in Jennifer Smith's custody case have joined Judge Nick Handel at a large conference table in his chambers.

Jennifer is seated close to her daughter, Tara, and is holding her hand tightly. Across from them are Hilda Tarsey from Child Protective Services and Harriet Petrov, the agency's newest foster parent. Also in the room are the judge's judicial assistant and a court bailiff. The bailiff is there as a deterrent against unruly behavior, and to watch over the proceedings for the court.

As the judge begins his opening remarks, a quick knock at the door announces the arrival of one more person. "Sorry I'm late, your Honor," states Randal Levy apologetically.

Judge Handel is surprised. He does not know Levy and is upset by the disruption. Gesturing to the bailiff, he asks, "Who are you? This is a private case, sir."

"Oh, it's okay," pipes up Tara. "That's Mr. Levy, my counselor at school. I asked him to come today."

Nick peers at Tara and then at Hilda. He is not pleased, not at all. But he relents, albeit reluctantly, when he sees the hopeful expression on Tara's face. "Fine. Have a seat, Mr. Levy."

Randal slides into the empty seat next to Tara and pats her shoulder comfortingly. "Thank you for coming," whispers Tara.

"Are you two finished?" barks the judge. "May I proceed now?" Handel frowns in the silence that follows until he is satisfied that he has established dominance over the proceedings. Only then, does he begin his remarks. "I have called you here today for a final ruling in the case of the State of Florida vs. Mrs. Jennifer Smith regarding the neglect of her minor child, Tara Smith. Does the State wish to apprise me of the status of this case?"

Hilda adjusts her glasses and flips open Jenny's file. "Yes, your Honor. Mrs. Smith was recently provided with a plan of action by the court. She was to complete thirty counseling sessions, fifteen parenting classes, and forty supervised visitations within sixty days. When she did not complete the plan in sixty days, the court gave her an extension of fifteen days. However, she did not complete the plan within the extended time, either."

"Your Honor, I work three part-time jobs!" interrupts Jenny in her own defense. "The sessions were scheduled during my working hours, and I couldn't take..."

Judge Handel is not interested in Jenny's excuses. "Mrs. Smith, you are out of line. Another outburst like that, and I will charge you with contempt of court. State, please continue."

Tara looks at Randal hopefully while Hilda adjusts her glasses again and clears her throat. "The minor child has been living in a temporary foster home. She has attended school on a regular basis, except for one incident when she was caught skipping school. Her grades have improved since that event, and there have been no further problems. Overall, we feel that the foster home is a positive environment for the minor child, and we have determined that it has been a contributing factor in her improvement at school. Our recommendation is the termination of Mrs. Jennifer Smith's parental rights and permanent placement of her minor child into the state's foster care system."

Jenny and Tara gasp in horror as they hear Hilda Tarsey's harsh advice. "Your Honor, please!" pleads Jenny. "Don't take my baby away! I'm so sorry! I'll find a way to do whatever I have to! I'll try harder! I'll complete the plan! Please don't take Tara away from me!"

Tara also tries to plead her case. "It was my fault!" she declares. "I skipped school because I didn't want to be bullied!"

Judge Handel's mood changes from bad to worse as he watches the hysterics at the other end of the table. His disposition is not souring because of the heartbreaking circumstances of the mother and child before him, however. What is bothering the judge is that this proceeding is taking longer than expected, and that Jenny has spoken out again. "Bailiff! Remove Mrs. Smith from my chamber!" he declares firmly.

At the judge's order, the bailiff, a rather large man, jumps into action. He peels Jenny away from her daughter like the skin off a banana and drags her out of the room while she and Tara wail and cry out for each other. The unfortunate situation is beyond their control.

When the door closes on Jenny, Tara rests her head on Randal's shoulder and cries for her mother.

Watching Tara with noticeable distaste, Judge Handel declares, "At this time I will accept the recommendation of the State of Florida and terminate the parental rights of Mrs. Jennifer Smith. I hereby place the minor child, Tara Smith, into the temporary home overseen by Ms. Harriet Petrov until permanent arrangements can be made."

Judge Handel signs the transfer paperwork and hands it to the judicial assistant so she can make copies.

"Everything will be okay," whispers Randal to Tara. "I know people. I'll make some calls and try to resolve this. Just cooperate for now."

When the assistant returns with the duplicates, Harriet Petrov pulls Tara away from Randal and leads her out of the room. Disgusted by the turn of events, Randal rises from his seat and breaks out his phone. Texting furiously, he glares critically at the judge as he also leaves the room.

Although Darren is in his office sanctuary, he is restless. He has been going over the Rosenbaum case with a fine-toothed comb to see if there are any details he may have missed, but his thoughts keep returning to Lu Tang.

Abandoning the notion of getting any work done, Darren gives in to his urge to connect with the young girl and picks up his phone. Scrolling through the contact list, he finds a small photo of Lu Tang next to her phone number. Longing to hear the girl's voice, he is about to press the call button when he has second thoughts. In that short space of time, his cell phone rings, so he presses the answer button instead. "Detective Ballard?" he inquires.

The D.A. listens quietly to the voice on the other end of the phone. "I did a background check on Randal Levy, but I couldn't find anything on him except an employment record at Calista's school," states Will. "Other than that, the guy's a ghost; I found nothing else. No birth records, no driver's license, no Social Security number, and nothing on social media. Nothing at all."

Lost in thought, Darren gazes out of the window. "Who is this guy?" he asks rhetorically. "How can a school counselor afford four single-malt drinks, let alone one? Keep digging, and let me know if you find anything else on him. Anything at all."

Darren ends the call and broods over the photo of Lu Tang on his phone.

Several miles away, Lu is in distress. She is not feeling well at all. Once again she leans over the toilet, but this time, it is only dry heaves. Her stomach muscles are sore, and she is worried about soiling her uniform. She is thankful that so far, it has remained clean throughout this latest bout of nausea.

While Lu is still hunched over the bowl, Ming Li enters the unlocked staff lavatory.

Lu knows that her situation doesn't look good, but she can't help how she is feeling. Rising from the tiled floor, she avoids looking at the cook as she walks to the sink to wash her face.

Assessing Lu's condition rapidly, Ming Li grabs her by the hair and reproaches her in rapid Mandarin. "Don't try to pretend you are sick, little one! You are pregnant, I know it! Who is the father—the judge or his son?"

Lu pleads for understanding, but Ming Li is disgusted. Cursing loudly and angrily, she releases Lu's hair and storms out of the bathroom.

"Lisa, says Eral, "I decided to take your recommendation. I want to make a plea deal before that fucking jury fries my ass. Get in touch with the D.A. I got information on his daughter's whereabouts and some other info that will curl his toes." But Lisa has not responded to Eral's statement. She is studying her client with narrowed eyes as he tries to look up her skirt.

Fed up with her client's ogling, Lisa scowls and rises from the sofa. Walking over to the couch directly across from her, she leans over Eral and declares angrily, "Do that again, and I will neuter you right here, right now." Then, she rises to her full height and adds, "I will make that call for you, Eral. And I fervently hope that after that, I will be rid of you."

After school, Abby and Calista are giggling in Abby's room as Calista sends a text to the boy she met online.

"You're meeting him today?" asks Abby, wondering whether Calista is doing the right thing.

Calista smiles distractedly as she continues to send and receive messages. "Yeah, around five, before my curfew begins." She shows the phone's screen to Abby.

Hello, Angel. I'm excited to meet you.

Abby smiles at Calista but she is worried about her friend. "Any more photos?" she asks.

Calista nods and scrolls through her photo gallery. "Here, look," she says, turning her phone toward Abby. "He's hot, right?"

"Wow, he's gorgeous!"

"Hey! Watch it, girlfriend!" responds Calista with feigned indignation.

"Oh, don't worry," Abby assures her friend. "But can I come with you today?"

"No! He wants to meet me alone. I guess he's kinda shy."

Abby wants to ask for more details, but Calista changes the subject. "Enough about me," she says. "What's going on with you and Jesus? You looked awfully pissed when Mandy tried to steal him away from you the other day."

Abby blushes at Calista's deduction that she has a romantic interest in the gardener's son. "Oh, that," she says dismissively. "We just met and stuff. He's cute and kinda sweet. But I can't believe Mandy tried to pry him away as soon as she saw him! She always tries to take away everything I have."

Yeah, even your health, reflects Calista silently. To Abby, she says, "Listen, girl, just ignore her."

"Abby, come down and say hello to your grandfather!" calls Gabriella from the kitchen, prompting Abby to groan and roll her eyes.

"Look, you're busy, so I'll leave now," says Calista. "How do I look? Hair, teeth, breath?"

"Well, two outta three ain't bad," teases Abby.

Calista tries a self-test on her breath and frowns when Abby laughs. "Very funny," she says.

"You look fine," promises her friend. "Text me later. I want to know everything!"

Calista gives Abby a hug and then runs down the stairs, calling out a quick goodbye to Mrs. Hoffman.

Down the street, Randal Levy is parked a few houses away from the Hoffman home. He's monitoring the household's comings and goings while texting endlessly on his phone.

In her second-floor bedroom, Abby rises from her bed a little too quickly and feels light-headed, so she sits back down. When the feeling passes, she rises more slowly and makes her way downstairs. When she enters the kitchen, she gives her grandfather a stiff embrace.

"Abby, dear, how are you feeling today?" asks Nick Handel. "I just saw Calista rushing out the door. How's that dance routine coming along?"

"We're having fun with the routine. Sometimes I get a little tired and I have to rest, but I'm not going to give up."

"That's my granddaughter!" the judge beams at Gabriella. "She's just as stubborn as her father and me." Reaching out, he strokes Abby's cheek. "You'll have a healthy heart soon, I know it."

"You staying for dinner?" asks Abby to change the subject. She doesn't really care if her grandfather stays or not.

"No, I can't stay for dinner. I was on the way to a business meeting and I thought of you, so I decided to stop for a quick hello." Turning to his ex-daughter-in-law, he says, "Gotta run, Gabby. Oh, by the way, is that new gardener of yours getting any faster?"

Gabriella wonders why the judge cares about her gardener but she answers his question anyway. "Oh, he's doing fine. I think Abby has a crush on his son, though," she adds with a wink at her daughter.

"Mom, STOP!" protests Abby as Nick and Gabriella share a laugh.

"I'll take a raincheck on that dinner," Nick says as he plants a kiss on Abby's forehead.

Outside in his car, Randal watches intently as Judge Nick Handel walks out of the Hoffman home.

CHAPTER TWENTY-ONE

It's now five o'clock and Darren has spent the entire day alone in his office, catching up on paperwork. He told his secretary to hold all his calls so he'd be available for the jury's verdict, but since there has been no word yet, he decides to go home. As he gathers up his things, a tall woman in a pinstripe suit and stylish heels surprises him in the doorway.

"Lisa Berg? What brings you into the enemy's camp?"

Eral Rosenbaum's attorney saunters into the office, closing the door behind her. "My client has incriminating evidence that will help you indict many powerful people in this city. He wants a plea deal before the jury comes to a verdict. We can meet at his hotel room at eight tonight to discuss the specifics."

Darren grabs his attaché case with an air of smug indifference. "What can that man possibly offer me that I don't already know or suspect?"

Lisa sashays back toward the door with an equally unconcerned air. "He knows where your missing daughter is," she states casually over her shoulder. "See you tonight at the W Hotel, Room 513. We'll only plead to kidnapping and child endangerment. We also want a minimum security prison, and parole in two years."

Lisa disappears from the room like a bad dream, leaving Darren openmouthed and shaking. When his phone rings, he coughs to clear his throat, and answers with a hoarse, "Hello?"

"I need to see you!" wails Lu Tang. "You come tonight! It very important! Come to mansion!"

Darren is conflicted. He must meet with Eral tonight to learn the whereabouts of his daughter, yet Lu is obviously distressed. "What's wrong, Lu? Are you all right?" he asks. "I..."

"You come, please. Seven o'clock. Very important!"

Darren's mind is racing. *What to do? What to do?* As he locks his office door, he bumps squarely into Mandy Goldman, who's been walking the courthouse floors on a mission.

"Move, you jerk!" she shouts, until she gets a good look at Darren. "Oh, hey, wait a minute! You're the guy I'm looking for! I saw you on the news. You were talking about the trial of that pervert."

"Ahhh, you mean, I'm that district attorney guy?" Darren asks sarcastically. "How did you get up here?"

"Never mind that," Mandy says, poking at Darren's chest. "You help people, and my friend is in trouble! Her mother was taken away from her today, and my stupid, useless school counselor didn't do shit! You gotta do someth..."

"Wait, a minute, slow down and take a breath!"

says Darren. "First of all, what's your name?"

"Mandy."

Darren narrows his eyes at the blonde before him. "Mandy? Are you Mandy Goldman?"

Mandy shoots Darren a dirty look. "Yeah!" she says, with her hands on her hips. "How'd you know that?"

"Well, you look a lot like your father. I met your parents recently at a charity event. Now what happened with your counselor?"

"Not a fucking thing! Mr. Levy did nothing!"

Hearing another familiar name, Darren asks, "Do you mean Randal Levy?"

"Yeah, I guess. I don't really know," replies Mandy glumly. "Who cares about his stupid first name, anyway? He works at my school. He was at Tara's hearing, but they still took her mother away. You have to do something!"

"Hold on," Darren declares, trying to process the situation. "Who's Tara?"

Frustrated, Mandy punches the wall, but the action does nothing to soothe her. "Tara Smith!" she shouts. "How do you not know this? Isn't it your job to know about everything that happens in court? Holy shit!"

Darren exhales noisily while fumbling through his attaché case. When he finds a pad of paper, he hands it to Mandy with a Monte Blanc pen and instructs her to write her phone number down so he can call her after he looks into the situation.

Mandy complies and hands the pad back. "You better call me, or my daddy will make sure you don't have a job anymore," she says with a huff. Then, she turns on her heels and storms down the hallway.

Now, Darren is even more conflicted than he was before.

Dazed by his encounter with the young, volatile daughter of a wealthy philanthropist, Darren runs through his options for the evening. His first impulse is to put everything aside to meet with Eral Rosenbaum. He's been hoping to find Denise for years and doesn't want to waste another minute. If Eral has reliable information, he wants to act on it quickly. Then again, he also wants to find out why Lu Tang was so upset. And now, he's been thrust into a third situation that demands his urgent attention.

With a deep sigh, Darren reaches for his phone and dials the number Mandy gave him, hoping that it won't take long to find out what's going on with the girl's friend.

One thing at a time, he mutters as waits for his call to be answered.

At a quarter to five, Calista walks alone down a side street toward the local food mart. The fourteen-year-old knows she is disobeying her father's curfew, but she is so excited to be meeting her new boyfriend that she told herself that she wouldn't mind if her punishment is extended. For the umpteenth time, she looks at the boy's most recent text: *Pick u up in white van.*

As Calista walks, a van matching that description pulls up alongside her, so she stops.

That was a huge mistake.

Before Calista can grasp what's happening, two men rush out of the back and pull her into the van in a well-rehearsed ballet of savagery.

Inside the vehicle, one of the men covers Calista's mouth and shoves her to the floor, while the other pins her arms down so she can't squirm away. Calista struggles mightily but is soon resigned to the fact that she is powerless against the mens' strength.

Suddenly, Calista has a coughing fit, and when the man covering her mouth releases his grip, she turns her head and spots two other men in the van—one driving, and the other riding shotgun.

At a stoplight, the man in the passenger seat turns around and stares menacingly at Calista. "Hellooo, angel!" he shouts, straining to be heard above Calista's muffled coughs and screams. "After all of these weeks of texting, it's great to finally meet you in the flesh!"

Calista is stunned. When the man holding her down uncovers her mouth, she asks in disbelief, "It was you?"

"Well, not exactly," laughs Rocco. "But he told me everything I needed to know. Now stop squirming and be nice and quiet! You wouldn't want my two friends to mess you up, would you?" Rocco snickers ominously as the van dissolves into rush hour traffic.

After taking some time to weigh his options, Darren decides that he will talk to Lu Tang before meeting with Eral and Lisa. Reasoning that whatever is bothering Lu will be easy to fix and that it couldn't possibly be as important as getting information about Denise and negotiating an end to his critical trial, he leaves the courthouse and heads directly for his father's house.

When he is informed that he must wait for Lu in the kitchen, he is annoyed that she is not already waiting for him. Fidgeting in his chair, he checks his watch repeatedly, willing Lu to appear so he can be on his way.

When fifteen minutes pass and Lu has still not appeared, Darren considers leaving, but Lu finally enters the room. Accompanied by Ming Li, neither of them looks happy. Lu doesn't make eye contact with Darren, and it is apparent that she has been crying.

Concerned, Darren tries to cheer Lu up with a light kiss on the cheek, but she pulls away and sits down glumly at the table, with Ming Li right beside her.

Baffled, Darren pulls up a chair. "What's wrong," he asks. "Do you have to go back to China?"

Lu turns to Ming Li and says something in Mandarin, which Ming Li translates.

"Darren," says Ming Li, "Lu Tang says you are very special to her. She says she loves you, and she wants you to know something important." The cook hesitates for a moment, and then utters her next words with unmasked disapproval. "Darren, Lu Tang is pregnant."

The news of a pregnancy hits Darren like a two by four. Opening and closing his mouth in shock, he frowns and shakes his head firmly. Rising from his chair to think, he paces the floor for a while and then sits back down. "Look, Lu," he begins, "I want to be with you, I really do, but a baby? I can't deal with that right now. I mean, my career, my future... I can't have this happen, not now. I want to keep you close, but if you love me and want to be with me, you must end this pregnancy. Don't worry about anything; I'll take care of all the arrangements. Anyway," he adds, "how can it be mine? I mean, we only met a short time ago, and you were..." Darren stops himself before giving voice to unthinkable thoughts.

Ming Li is disgusted by Darren's comments and tries to make light of them in her translation, but Lu caught enough of what Darren said to know that the cook did not tell her everything. Lu begs the cook for a full translation, and when she hears it, she wails anew.

From Lu's reaction, Darren knows that there will be no reasoning with her tonight. "Look," he says, "I know this is upsetting, but I can't stay to talk about it. I have an urgent appointment that I can't miss. Call my office tomorrow, and I'll give you the address of the place you can go to for help. I'll also give you all the money you'll need to take care of this. Lu, please do it for me. For us."

After Ming Li translates, Darren gives Lu a tight smile and squeezes her shoulder. Then, he leaves the kitchen and exits the house, intent on keeping his next appointment.

Back in the kitchen, Lu is inconsolable. "Evil runs freely in this family," mumbles Ming Li loud enough for Lu to hear. "Father is the head and son is the heir."

Darren's mind is definitely not on his driving. His thoughts are wandering all over the place as he heads to his meeting with Lisa and Eral. On trendy Las Olas Boulevard, he doesn't notice that the light has turned red and he blows through the intersection, barely missing some tourists who had just started to cross the street.

Nearby, a police officer in his squad car saw the whole thing. He pulls his car behind Darren and flashes his lights as he follows the offending vehicle down a side street and into a public parking lot.

Unnerved by the incident, Darren brings his car to a stop and fumbles for his ID and registration with shaking hands. When he finds what he's looking for, he exits his car and waits for the patrol officer.

"Oh, District Attorney Handel, I didn't know it was you," says the officer as he reads Darren's license.

"Hello, Officer...Schaeffer," says Darren with a glance at the policeman's name tag."

"I'm sorry, Mr. Handel, but you did go through the light."

"Yeah, well, with a big case on my mind, I guess I just missed it. But, hey, I understand if you need to give me a ticket."

The young officer knows that he may need to interact with the D.A. on a legal issue sometime in the future, so he decides to tread lightly. "Mr. Handel, I'll only give you a warning today. Try to keep your cases in the office, not behind the wheel. Have a good day." With a nod at Darren, the officer climbs back into his squad car and drives away.

Exhaling deeply, Darren stares up at the sky in silent thanks. Careful to remain alert and under the speed limit this time, he heads back onto Las Olas Boulevard.

Twenty minutes later, Darren is standing in the hallway in front of Eral's private suite at a popular hotel on Fort Lauderdale Beach. Hoping for good news about Denise and a triumphant end to the most significant trial in his career, he knocks firmly on the door.

"You're late," rebukes Lisa crossly. "We were concerned that you weren't coming."

"I got hung up in traffic," replies Darren, slipping past Lisa into a large room that looks more like an expensive condominium than a hotel room. "Okay," he declares, "you called this dog and pony show, so impress me."

Eral is seated calmly at a table in the suite's dining area. "My lawyer has a flash drive that contains the names of individuals in this area who are profiting from child trafficking, prostitution, pedophilia, and organ harvesting. The list includes many well-known, influential men and women, and even the governor—you know, the man you want to replace? However, and this is very important, Mr. D.A., you won't get that flash drive unless we negotiate favorable terms for my future. Oh, and I also have a word of warning for you. Some of the names on that list are persons who are very close to you."

Eral waits smugly for a reaction from Darren, but when Darren doesn't reply, he concludes with what he hopes will seal a deal. "By the way, I know where your daughter is, but you won't get that little bit of information without a satisfactory deal. What I want is a new identity and little or no jail time. However, I'll consider a greatly reduced sentence at one of those fancy resort prisons."

Although Darren was listening to everything Eral said, the only thing that registered is that the man knows where his daughter is. "Fuck you! Where's Denise?" he shouts.

Eral leans back in his chair and smiles at Lisa with a self-satisfied, "I told you so."

"She's in a compound—a brothel in Boynton Beach," responds Lisa. "It's run by some of those influential people Eral named on the flash drive."

Darren's mind works overtime as he tries to process all the information he just received. However, try as he might, all of his thoughts keep returning to his daughter. Running his hand through his hair, he seethes at what she must have gone through all these years.

With considerable effort, he stops his runaway thoughts and turns to the lawyer. "Give me that flash drive and the address of the house, and you got a deal."

When the attorneys shake, Eral sneers at Darren.

"I'll bring the drive and the address to your office

tomorrow," says Lisa. "Enjoy your evening, Mr. Handel."

As usual, Judge Nicholas Handel is up to no good. Dressed to the nines, he is strolling casually down a dingy hallway in a seedy hourly motel, fully expecting that his instructions were followed to the letter. When he comes upon foster parent Harriet Petrov seated on a folding chair outside one of the rooms, he stops and looks at her expectantly.

"She's ready for you," declares Harriet.

Handel nods. "I knew she would be. And I'm ready for her."

"I'll wait out here," says Harriet. "You know, two's company, and all that."

"Yes, but three's a party," replies the judge with a suggestive wink.

Turning the doorknob, Nick Handel walks into a shabby room where Tara Smith is sitting stiffly on a wooden chair. The girl is wearing lots of makeup, but little else. Her red lace teddy is trying to cover her young body, but it's not doing a very good job.

Tara is shaking, and she eyes the judge warily. "Judge Handel? Why are you here? What's happening? Oh, what are you going to do?"

"What am I going to do?" the judge leers at his new plaything. "Oh, we're going to have some fun!" he declares with a smack of his lips.

Tara starts to cry and her heavily-applied mascara runs down her face in long, black streaks. In a high-pitched voice, she wails, "Let me out of here, you freak! Why did you take my mother away from me? Why, why, why?!"

But Nick Handel is indifferent to Tara's anguish. Ignoring her pleas, he lets his eyes wander slowly over her body. Then, he looks into her face with a thoughtful tilt of his head. "I have better plans for you," he says.

"Oh, I'm sure!" shouts Tara defiantly. "Like finding a 'forever family' for me as long as I play around with you?!"

Although the girl's impertinence angers the judge, his rage enhances his desire. "Yeah, that's right, you little bitch!" he growls menacingly. "A whole new family for you! Now stop talking, and come over here!"

"Go fuck yourself!" Tara shouts, spitting at the floor.

"I said, come here!!" bellows the judge, lunging at Tara. In an instant, Nick grabs Tara by the chin and smacks her across the face so hard that it throws her off the chair. Lunging again, he grabs a chunk of Tara's hair, which causes Tara to scream and twist wildly to get away from him. However, Nick Handel is too strong for the young teenager. Throwing Tara onto the bed, he climbs on top of her and sneers, "I'm going to break you like a wild mare!"

Still twisting, Tara tries her best to get away, but she is pinned under the judge's weight. "Oh my God! You're hurting me!" she yells, but to no avail.

Thrusting ever forward, Judge Nick Handel rapes Tara and pummels her around the head until she is subdued.

Throughout all of this commotion, Harriet has remained outside the door, nonchalantly reading a book on her tablet. When Tara finally quiets down, the foster parent chuckles to herself. *Another one bites the dust,* she mutters, and keeps on reading.

When Handel is finally sated, he rolls off Tara, leaving her whimpering and moaning. No longer concerned with the girl, Handel casually zips up his fly and smooths his hair. But when his cell phone rings shrilly, he snatches it out of his pocket and answers with an annoyed, "WHAT?"

"We got a match for your granddaughter's heart," says Rabbi Katzoff.

Suddenly interested, the judge sits down heavily at the foot of the bed while Tara curls up in a far corner. "Really, when?" he asks.

"We'll harvest it tomorrow. I heard you got a new toy."

Leaning over, the judge fondles Tara with his free hand. "Sure do," he replies, "and I'm playing with it right now. It's ready to be shared, and it's really cute. I may keep it for myself."

Hearing that, the rabbi is not pleased. "How are we going to make money if you keep them all for yourself, like your precious Lu Tang?"

Nick laughs and continues to fondle the trembling Tara. "My friend, there are plenty of fish in the sea for all of our needs."

It's close to midnight, and Calista is scared. She's sitting on the floor of a cold, dark room with her arms wrapped tightly around her knees to keep from shivering. She got a brief glimpse of the room when she was tossed in, but she hasn't been able to see much of anything since then. She remembers that the room seemed unfinished, though. She saw concrete walls and a lot of sand on the floor, which Rocco said was put there to absorb blood. The noises she's hearing in the darkness tell her that the room is full of kids, both boys and girls, and that all of them are frightened. Calista hugs herself and waits.

Sometime during the night, the children are alarmed when the door opens to admit another victim. In the light from the corridor, they see Harriet Tarsey pushing another girl into the room.

After the door bangs shut, Tara Smith stands immobile in the middle of the dark room. The day's events have frightened her into rigidity, and the darkness has blinded her. Not being able to see, she doesn't realize that there are others in the room and that someone she knows is also there.

"Tara? Is that you?" calls a familiar voice.

Tara turns toward the sound but can't see the person she connects with the voice.

Since her eyes have already adjusted to the dark, Calista rises from the floor and walks toward her schoolmate. "What the hell happened to you?" she probes, shocked by Tara's bruises.

Focusing on her chum, Tara dissolves when she sees the look on her face. "It was terrible!" she cries, clinging to Calista's shoulder. "It was horrible! He, he... raped me! He took my mother, and then he raped me!" Tara shudders uncontrollably and grips Calista's shoulder as if her life depended on it.

"He? Who?" asks Calista, shaking Tara to get her attention.

"The JUDGE!" shouts Tara finally, heaving great sobs.

Uncomprehending, Calista walks Tara over to an unoccupied corner of the room. "A judge raped you?" she inquires quietly.

Tara nods vigorously and crumbles to the floor with her hands covering her face. Frightened and embarrassed, she confides, "It was Judge Handel."

"What?!" exclaims Calista, astonished by Tara's revelation. "Abby's grandfather?" A moment later, Calista puts all the pieces together. "Oh, shit!" she hisses. "This is crazy! We have to get out of here! We have to get out of here right now!"

Tara laughs at what she considers to be a preposterous proposal. "Get out? Where are we gonna go? They're everywhere! They're connected to everything! He's a judge, for crying out loud!"

"Yeah, but we have to try!" urges Calista, and the two of them spend the rest of the night plotting an escape in quiet whispers while they try to stay warm.

CHAPTER TWENTY-TWO

Will is in panic mode—Calista did not come home last night. He called Gabriella first, hoping that Calista was with Abby, but she wasn't there. Then he called the school and drove around the malls and parks, but got nowhere. After a while, he headed back to his apartment hoping that she returned home, but she still wasn't there. Racking his brain, Will thinks of one more person who might have some information—the mysterious school counselor, Randal Levy.

Before leaving the apartment again, Will files a missing person's report, knowing all too well that the longer Calista is missing, the higher the chances are that she won't be found.

As soon as he arrived at the office the next morning, Darren notified Judge Rose of the pending deal with Eral Rosenbaum's attorney and the judge informed him that the jurors would be back in the jury room soon to continue their deliberations.

Facing another day of waiting, Darren swivels his chair around and faces the window. Staring outside, he sees nothing as he ponders the horrors he'll most likely hear from Denise when he sees her again. His mind is wandering around so much that when his secretary pokes her head into the open doorway, her voice seems as if it comes out of nowhere.

"Mr. Handel, Attorney Berg is here to see you."

"Oh! Yes, I'm expecting her. Um, please send her in."

The secretary steps aside just in time for Lisa to stroll past. "District Attorney Handel, I believe this is what you're looking for," Lisa says, holding out a small flash drive and a folded piece of paper. "I hope to hear from you by noon today."

Darren accepts the objects and stares at them without acknowledging Lisa's presence.

After a few minutes of silence, Lisa lifts her brows, shakes her head, and leaves the office as quickly as she arrived.

Minutes later, Darren's cell phone rings. "The wheels are in motion," states a voice. "We're ready. Thanks."

Darren ends the call and stares again at the objects in his hand.

Abby did not attend school today. She didn't feel well when she woke up, so her mother said she could stay home, and she drove Jesus to school as usual. Now, when the school day is over, Jesus is waiting for Gabriella to pick him up, but she still hasn't arrived.

Unfortunately, Mandy Goldman is also still at

school. Her almost perpetual detentions are keeping her there most afternoons. She's usually the only one leaving at this late hour, so when she sees Jesus standing at the curb, she brightens at the sight of the new guy. Behind her, Randal Levy waits in the doorway to make sure his student catches her ride.

"Hey, Jesus!" Mandy calls. "You wanna hang with me for a while? I can help you with your English. Besides, your precious Abby isn't here today."

Jesus holds his hand high to shield his eyes against the late afternoon sun and frowns at Mandy. "Why are you so mean to *mi amiga*...my friend?" he asks suspiciously.

"Oh, you don't have to worry about Abby," laughs Mandy. "She'll be gone soon. You can be my *amigo* now."

"Where does she go?" asks Jesus.

"She has a bad heart, you idiot. If she doesn't get a new one soon, she's gonna die. Now, I have a strong heart." To emphasize the point, Mandy grabs Jesus' hand and places it on her chest. "See?" she asks in as seductive a voice as she can muster. "You can feel it, right?"

Looking up from his phone, Randal sees the two students still at the curb. Walking toward them, he asks sternly, "Where are your rides? Don't you know what's going on?"

"No, what's going on?" asks Mandy innocently.

"Calista Ballard has been missing since yesterday. It's not safe for you to be out here. Call your parents and go home, both of you."

"Why should we believe you after what you did to Tara?" asks Mandy with a look of disgust. "Jesus, come with me. My driver is on the way; he can take you home. It doesn't look like Abby's mother is coming for you today."

Still hoping to see Gabriella's car, Jesus looks up and down the street once more, but when she doesn't appear, he shrugs his shoulders and follows Mandy.

Knowing that Mandy's driver will be there soon, Randal walks back into the building.

Stopping a few paces down the sidewalk, Mandy looks around to make sure that Randal is gone before she turns to Jesus with an impish grin. Taking his hand in hers, she moves the boy's hand onto her chest once again. "My driver will be here soon," she says coyly.

Captivated by new and unfamiliar feelings, neither of the teens notices when a white van pulls up alongside them and two large men jump out. When they do notice, it's too late. Their mouths are covered, and they are swept up and shoved into the van.

When the vehicle's back door closes, Rocco Despirito slips out of the passenger seat and joins his men in the back.

"Let me go, you pricks!" screams Mandy, but her words are muffled as she frantically tries to bite the hand covering her mouth. "Don't you fucking know who my father is? Let me go!"

Determined to keep Mandy quiet, Rocco slaps her across the face. "Shut up, you stupid bitch!" he hollers. "Who the hell cares about your fucking father?"

When Mandy continues to yell, she is silenced by a gag over her mouth.

Confident that his new acquisition won't be making any other sounds, Rocco looks over at the other teenager his men captured today. "Well, hello again," he says to Jesus, who is clearly shocked at the sight of him. "I haven't seen you in a while. Too bad you hooked up with this bitch. How's your father?"

"*Por favor,* I don't understand!" cries Jesus, struggling mightily against his bonds.

"Oh? What don't you understand?" mocks Rocco with a leering look at the boy. "I'm so happy you're here. It's Jesus, right? You're going to be my boy now. Yes, yes," Rocco says approvingly. "I'm really going to enjoy you."

Randal Levy is home now. Holding a diet soda, he studies the board he tacked onto the wall of his spare room. With a red marker, he crosses out several names—"Mandy," "Calista," and "Jesus." Then, he draws a line toward "Tara" and circles it.

Randal is still analyzing the board when a loud sound startles him. Recognizing it as his front door being jimmied open, he pulls a Glock from his waistband and crouches down. Moments later, he finds himself staring at a wide-eyed Will Ballard pointing a gun at his head. With both of their guns drawn, the two men have created the classic standoff.

"Where the hell is my daughter?" yells Will over his gun sight.

"Calm down, okay?" declares Randal. "I can explain."

Will edges toward Randal. "Fuck you!" he shouts, refusing to be pacified. "You're not Randal Levy! That person doesn't exist! Who the hell are you? And where the FUCK is my daughter?"

Keeping his eyes on Will, Randal raises his free hand and lowers his Glock onto the floor with the other. "Will," he says softly, "reach behind that black picture frame on the table over there."

Holding his firearm steady, Will inches over to the table. Feeling something behind the frame, he grabs what's there and looks incredulously at Randal. In Will's hand are an official-looking badge and an FBI ID card with Randal's photo.

"Agent Adam Cohen? You're a fucking Fed?" Somewhat mollified, Will holsters his weapon.

Adam retrieves his gun from the floor and replaces it in his waistband. "I'm a special agent from Washington," he explains. "I've been working on a case about missing children for a while now, and it's led me here. Your daughter isn't the only one who's gone missing. All of these kids," he says, pointing to the names he crossed out on his board, "have disappeared in the last twenty-four hours. And they're all linked to the same person."

Will's mouth drops open in shock when Cohen points to a photograph of Judge Nicholas Handel.

"It's time to talk to the D.A.," states Agent Cohen.

When Christian and Jesus arrived at the Hoffman home, Christian insisted on taking care of all of the gardening, even though he wasn't feeling well. Today, as he works on Gabriella's prized rose bushes, he bends over in pain and collapses on the lawn. Under his bandages, a foul-smelling liquid oozes from his wounds.

While Christian lies unconscious at the Hoffman home, the white van holding Mandy and Jesus pulls up to a door at the rear of Rabbi Katzoff's Hollywood mansion. Sliding out of the van, Rocco Despirito watches eagerly as his men force Mandy and Jesus out.

Jesus is surprised again when he recognizes his surroundings. He's seen this house and the armed guards patrolling the yard before. When Rocco turns his back to the youths, Jesus whispers to Mandy, "I know this place."

Marching over to the teenagers, Rocco grabs their elbows and directs them inside the house. Then, he leads them down a hallway that Jesus remembers all too well. When he stops in front of an oversized door, he grunts, pushes the heavy door inward, and forces both youths inside. Within the cold room are three females and one male, all of them lying listlessly on the floor. Reaching over, Rocco removes Mandy's gag. "You two can chill out in here, as you kids love to say." Then, he pulls the door closed and locks it.

Scared and exceedingly angry, Mandy rushes to the door and bangs on it forcefully, screaming, "My daddy's gonna have your head for this!" However, the door is solid and the room is well insulated, so none of her protests are heard.

"I know this place!" Jesus shouts to Mandy.

Mandy gives Jesus an angry look over her shoulder. Enraged by her helplessness, she screams, "It's all your fault! You and your cute face distracted me, and now look at where we are! Fuck this! Fuck this! Fuck this!"

Jesus is confused. "Why do you insult my face?" he asks. "Why is my face make you angry?"

"Do you have any brain at all in that fucking head of yours? We were kidnapped, you stupid ass! And Mr. Levy's probably behind it! You know what he did to Tara!"

Mandy turns back to pound on the door, but Jesus drags her away. "MANDY! I know this place!" he insists.

"Don't touch me!" shrieks Mandy, pulling away from Jesus.

But Jesus won't give up. *"¡Callate la boca!"* he shouts back. "I know this place! *Mi Papá*—he was cut here!"

Finally, Mandy stops. "What the hell did you say?" she stares at Jesus. "What do you mean, 'he was cut here'?"

Jesus raises his shirt, and with one finger, draws a line on his abdomen to show Mandy where his father had surgery.

When Mandy realizes what Jesus is doing, her

face loses all color. For the first time since she got there, she looks around at the other children in the cold room and notices their bandages. "Oh, my God!" she cries. "This is... They take our organs here? Fuckin' shit! We gotta get out!"

This time, when Mandy pounds on the door and it opens, any relief the children feel quickly turns to fear when they see Rocco and two armed henchmen in the doorway.

Parading into the room, Rocco reaches for Mandy. "You, brat bitch, are coming with us!" he snarls.

Mandy tries to shrink away from Rocco, but the two henchmen grab her and tie her hands tightly in front of her. "What are you gonna do?" she wails fearfully.

"Don't you worry your pretty little head about it," sniggers Rocco.

Closing the door behind them, the men drag Mandy roughly down the corridor, but Mandy has other ideas. Stopping suddenly, she slams her shoe onto one of the men's insoles and breaks his foot, sending him to the floor cursing in Russian. Following up quickly, she head-butts the other man and slams Rocco in the throat with her roped hands.

While the men are incapacitated, Mandy runs through the hall and up a stairwell. Exiting one flight up, she spots a door with a key still in the lock. Turning the key, she enters the room and closes the door quietly behind her. Breathing heavily, she looks around and finds that she's not alone.

"Mandy?" calls Tara.

"They got you, too?" groans Calista.

Not believing her eyes, Mandy squeaks, "Holy shit! Help me, quick!"

Pulling and straining at Mandy's bonds, Tara loosens them enough to pry them off her friend's wrists.

When Mandy is free, Calista runs over and hugs her, something she never would have done only twenty-four hours ago. "Do you know where we are?" she asks hopefully.

"No, but we need to get out of here," Mandy replies, handing the key to Tara. "Come on. Let's get everyone out."

While Calista urges the others in the room to follow them, Mandy rushes to the door and flings it open, but runs smack into a tall and obese guard. The recoil flings her backward onto the room's sandy floor as several more guards appear in the doorway brandishing weapons pointed directly at her.

Like a bad dream, Rocco appears behind the men. Brushing them aside, he snatches Mandy violently off the floor by her hair. "You little fuck!" he bellows. "This is not where you're supposed to be! Time to go, bitch!"

Careful to avoid Mandy's writhing and flailing appendages, Rocco drags her by the hair through the hallway and down a flight of stairs into what looks like an operating room. Still gripping her tightly, he flings her onto a long table covered by a white cloth. Seeing their new patient, two white-clothed men jump to Rocco's assistance and strap Mandy onto the table.

Screaming and yelling at everyone in sight, Mandy tries to kick her way free, but it's useless. Her cries, heard throughout this wing of the house, are terrifying to Tara, Calista, Jesus, and the other children.

"What are you gonna do to me?" she shrieks. "Wait till my father finds out! He's gonna cut your balls off, if you even have any, you fuckers!"

Inured to the screams of bound children, Rabbi Katzoff calmly enters the room, followed by a man who looks like a doctor prepped for surgery.

As the rabbi watches, the surgeon grabs a pair of surgical scissors and cuts off Mandy's clothes. "What are you doing?" she howls frantically. "Are you going to rape me?" When there is no reply, Mandy understands. "Oh, my God!" she shrieks. "You people are monsters! And you, you're a fucking rabbi for crying out loud! You call yourself a man of God? You're gonna burn in hell for this!"

Smiling from ear to ear, Rabbi Katzoff leans over Mandy. "So will you, my dear," he whispers, "but your strong heart is going to remain here, inside a good girl."

Mandy spits in the rabbi's face, but the man just wipes the spittle away. "Take your time with this one," he says to the surgeon. "No anesthetic. We don't want to damage that heart."

Nodding in reply, the surgeon grabs his tools and starts with an incision over Mandy's liver. Proceeding up her torso, he is indifferent to the girl's screams and shrieks of excruciating pain. "Oh, my God, you're killing me!" Mandy roars. "Just do it! Get it over with, you bastards!"

On the floor above them, Tara, Calista, Jesus and the other children hear Mandy's blood-curdling screams. Some of them cover their ears while others tremble and moan in fear.

All too soon, the terrifying sounds are replaced by an equally chilling silence.

Abby is practicing her dance routine alone because Calista wasn't at school. Her friend is still not answering her cell phone, and there's been no answer at her home number, either.

As Abby goes into her favorite part of the dance, she collapses onto the floor without any warning. Before blacking out, she calls out for her mother.

Alerted by an odd quality to her daughter's voice, Gabriella rushes into the room, where she finds Abby sprawled on the floor. "No, no!" she shouts. "Hold on, baby! I'm getting help!"

Rushing back out of the room to get her phone, Gabriella catches a glimpse of Christian lying on the lawn outside through a large window in the living room. Baffled by the sight, she exclaims, "What's going on?" as she dials the county's emergency number.

When the 911 operator answers, Gabriella's voice trembles. "Please help! I need two ambulances! One for my daughter, and one for my gardener! Please hurry! Abby has a bad heart!"

In the Hollywood mansion, the surgeon, now covered in blood, removes Mandy's heart and places it into an aluminum case cooled by dry ice. When he's done, Rabbi Katzoff glares at Mandy's now-lifeless body and spits in her unresponsive face.

CHAPTER TWENTY-THREE

For several hours now, Darren has been rooted at his computer. He can't seem to tear himself away from scrolling through screen after screen of the files on Eral's flash drive.

Initially stunned by the familiar names that kept popping up, he is now resigned to the fact that the human trafficking problem that he thought was just a local one is actually connected to a much larger organization. The names he is seeing are members of state governments, federal employees, local and national politicians, prominent judges, and even clergy members. He has not been surprised to see that Rabbi Herb Katzoff and his own father, Judge Nick Handel, are mentioned prominently.

While Darren is familiar with the local challenges of human trafficking, until now he had no knowledge of the organ harvesting business that is apparently being run out of his own area. He was shocked to find records listing the types of organs that were sold to buyers around the world and the names of the children who were murdered for their body parts.

Although Darren is disgusted by what he's reading, he continues to review the contents of the small memory storage device. Plowing on, he eventually finds a subfolder marked "Gentlemen's Club" that draws his interest, but when he clicks on it, he is alarmed when a photograph of a large house with a Boynton Beach address comes into view. Scrolling down the page, he shudders at the names of many local influential men and women that appear under the heading, "Supporters." Scanning the list, his eyes widen at two names in particular—Fred Staten and Denise Handel.

Darren remains transfixed in front of his screen. When his phone rings, he answers it in a daze, listens absently and responds, "Yes, yes. I'll be there." Just then, an urgent sound from his computer grabs his attention-—an alert across the bottom of the screen flashes with the names of three newly missing children—Calista Ballard, Mandy Goldman, and Jesus Garcia.

Troubled by this new development, Darren makes a couple of urgent calls and prepares to leave the office. However, before he can shut down his computer, he receives a frantic phone call from Gabriella, who tells him that Abby is in the emergency room.

Now worried about his other daughter, Darren shifts his focus to the hospital. He is about to head out when Will Ballard appears in the office with Agent Cohen in tow.

"Will? What are you doing here?" asks Darren, surprised by the unannounced visit. "And why are you here, Randal?"

"Darren, this is FBI Special Agent Adam Cohen," says Will. "He's been posing as a school counselor under the name, 'Randal Levy.'" Will pauses and inhales deeply before he continues. "Darren, we have bad news.

Agent Cohen has information that links your father to the Rosenbaum case, and also to a large human trafficking ring."

Darren winces and runs a hand over his face. "Yes," he replies quietly, "it's all here on a flash drive that Rosenbaum gave me in exchange for a plea deal. But Will, I just got an amber alert, and I was shocked to see your daughter's name on it. I think I know where she and the other missing children are. And I also found out where Denise is."

"What?" exclaims Will. "You know where they are? Then why are you still here? Let's go get 'em and bring 'em home!"

"Listen," Darren says, holding a steadying hand out to Will. "I already spoke to the Palm Beach County sheriff and to Lieutenant Jeffers. The mansion in Boynton where Staten is stationed may be the center of it all, so we set up a raid there for tonight. Jeffers contacted BSO, and they'll be raiding Rabbi Katzoff's Hollywood mansion tonight as well."

"How can you be so calm!" yells Will, disturbed by Darren's outward composure. "We need to go now, and..."

Darren holds Will back. "Be patient, Will! Don't do anything stupid! I want to get Denise as much as you want to find Calista! Join the raid in Hollywood with Jeffers. I promise that you'll get your daughter back tonight."

As a police officer, Will understands the risk of rushing into a criminal situation haphazardly, so he reluctantly nods his head in agreement.

"Look," adds Darren. "Abby was just rushed to the hospital, so I gotta leave now, but I'm gonna leave my computer on. Check out the files on Eral's flash drive." Without a backward glance, he runs out of the door.

Curious, Adam sits down at Darren's desk and begins to scroll through several still-open files. When he finds the information he's been looking for, his face becomes grim. "Wow! We got a lotta work to do," he says. "I'll call your Lieutenant. I want to lead the raid on Katzoff's place in Hollywood."

Looking over Adam's shoulder, Will has also seen enough. "I need to get my baby!" he shouts fiercely.

Rabbi Katzoff has been keeping a close eye on the doctor as he packs Abby's new heart into its special case. He continues to follow it as Rocco carries it out the back door and into the van.

When Rocco drives off, the rabbi places a call to his partner. "Your granddaughter's heart is on its way to the hospital," he says dispassionately.

"Ah, that's great news!" responds Judge Handel from his Bentley. "I'm actually on the way to you right now to check out our newest merchandise and give it my seal of approval."

Although Rabbi Katzoff knows his partner well, his reckless and insatiable sex drive still amazes him. "When you get here, come to my office first," he instructs Handel coolly. "We have business to discuss."

It's been over an hour since Calista and Tara were moved into the cold room, a refrigerated meat cooler, and Mandy was taken out. As the children's body temperatures drop, friends Jesus, Tara, and Calista huddle together to keep as warm as possible while the other children do the same with those around them.

Suddenly, the cooler door opens and Harriet Petrov enters, flanked by two armed guards. Tara tries to hide her face behind Calista's shoulder, but the heartless social worker spots her instantly.

"Take those two girls," Harriet says, pointing at Tara and Calista, "and the others over there. Leave the rest for Rocco."

After the youths indicated by Harriet are whisked away, Jesus finds himself alone in the refrigerated room with two females—one alive, and one dead. Grateful that he was not one of the chosen ones—at least this time—Jesus closes his eyes and wishes that he was safe at home with his father. Slumping against the wall in a dark corner, he wraps his arms around himself and curls up in a fetal position to try to retain what little body heat he has left, but it is too bitterly cold in the cooler to do much good.

The young boy from Mexico has never experienced such frigid temperatures, and as time passes, he struggles to remain conscious. When he doesn't think he can stay awake much longer, Rocco enters the refrigerated room and drags him out.

As usual, the full moon over South Florida, a spectacular sight in the dark sky, draws people out of their lodgings to partake of the evening's offerings. This evening, the revelers are unaware of the police activity in Hollywood and Boynton Beach. Two SWAT teams directed by the FBI and members of local police departments are preparing for simultaneous assaults on two homes.

Connie Jackson, a young, female FBI agent, is in charge of the team in Boynton Beach, and Agent Adam Cohen is in control of the team in Hollywood.

In Boynton, Agent Connie Jackson is just about to begin her mission briefing as copies of a photograph are passed around the room. "That's Sergeant Fred Staten," she explains. "He's with FLPD, the Fort Lauderdale Police Department, for those of you who aren't from this area. Study his photo. Staten is undercover inside the mansion, so make sure he stays safe. If you see him, identify yourself immediately. He's on the mansion's security detail and he's armed. We don't want to compromise one of our own tonight."

"Agent Jackson, we have an in," interrupts Lieutenant Jim Baxter of PBSO, the Palm Beach Sheriff's Office. Deputy Steven Zambone has been posing as a Boynton Beach Administrator for a while now. He's attending the meet and greet at the mansion tonight and he's wired. We'll keep him informed, and he'll contact Staten to let him know what's going on."

This is news to Jackson, and she is more than

a little upset by the unexpected revelation. She nods her approval, however, but states testily, "I should have been told beforehand that someone was already in there. Maybe we should have had more planning; we put this together in a last-minute rush. But it's too late now, so let's continue. We'll mount two attacks, one from the Intracoastal and one from the front gate. I was prepared to blow the gate, but now that we have someone on the inside, I'd rather keep it on the down low. Get Staten to open it up for us," Jackson orders, with a glance at a rather uncomfortable-looking Baxter. "What now?" she asks.

"Um, we have a unique problem," Baxter says. "Any activity at the gate will be noticed immediately, and announced loudly."

Stymied again, Connie is almost ready to lose it but keeps her cool. "What on earth are you talking about?" she asks in as professional a manner as she can.

"Peacocks, ma'am. Nature's alarm. There's a mated pair on the grounds but we may be able to neutralize them. One of my men carries a rifle with tranquilizer darts. We can silence them, if we can find them."

"Fuck it all!" shouts Connie. "Find those peacocks! And have your man tell Staten that we'll storm the mansion at nine! Let's go! Surveillance from our overhead drone tells us that there are guards around the pool at the back of the house. Keep it safe out there, everyone!"

While the meeting was going on in Boynton, Agent Adam Cohen and his team in Hollywood were setting up a command post in an empty house still under construction two blocks from their target. The assaults are timed to occur together so that the conspirators at one location won't be able to tip off their associates at the other.

As lead agent, Adam Cohen plans to oversee the team that enters through the back of the house while Will Ballard heads up the frontal assault.

"All right, we go at nine," says Cohen. "There are armed guards out back, so we have to assume that there are armed guards inside as well. Let's be safe out there!"

Cursing in Italian, Rocco readjusts his grip on Jesus as he pulls him through the house. Although Jesus squirms with all of his might, his abductor is too strong for him. None of his struggles have even caused the man to break his stride.

Jesus knows what his father went through with these people, and his fright makes him wet himself. When the unpleasant odor reaches Rocco, he looks back at the boy in disgust and pulls harder. Still cursing, he rounds a corner and forces Jesus into the home's operating room, where he drops him onto the floor.

Jesus gags when he catches a whiff of the nauseating odors of blood, bile, feces, and urine that permeate the room. When he spots the lifeless bodies of a boy and a girl that he recognizes from the cooler lying on a wide table with their chests split open and their internal organs removed, he loses control and vomits repeatedly.

Repulsed by the boy's nausea, Rocco quickly lifts him onto one of the room's empty operating tables and backs away. While an orderly straps him down, Jesus whips his head around and sees the lifeless body of Mandy Goldman on another table. Horrified, he shrieks at the top of his lungs, "What did you do to *mi amiga? ¿Están locos? ¡Todos ustedes son monstruos!*"

"Your liver and kidneys are on their way now," says Rabbi Katzoff into his office phone as Judge Handel sits down heavily into a leather love seat.

While the rabbi conducts his conversation, one of the mens' henchmen enters the well-appointed office with Beth, a thirteen-year-old redhead in skimpy lingerie and a thick layer of makeup.

The burly man throws Beth onto the love seat with Nick, who pulls her close and fondles her aggressively. "Ahh," he says appreciatively. "I love sampling all the new stuff!"

When the rabbi ends his call, he slams the handset onto the cradle in annoyance. "Damnit, Nick!" he shouts. "Will you stop playing with the merchandise? You're going to use them up before our clients get a chance!"

"I'm just warming her up for them," replies Nick between kisses and squeezes.

"Focus, Handel!" Katzoff warns gruffly, pointing an accusing finger at the judge.

That gets Nick's attention. Pushing Beth

roughly, she falls onto the hard floor and uses her sudden freedom from the depraved man to scurry over to a far corner of the room. Safe for the moment, she cowers there, trembling with fear and loathing.

"Damn you, Katzoff!" barks Nick. "I was just getting started! You're going to have to compensate me for that! Give me a glass of your single-malt Scotch!"

"You know, Nick," the rabbi says coolly, "I got his daughter here—that Detective Ballard. He needed to be warned. He was getting too close."

Aghast, Judge Handel jumps up from the sofa and slams both fists onto Katzoff's desk, causing Beth to cringe at the outburst. "You mean the cop who got Eral? How can you be so fucking stupid?" he snarls. "He's way too close to my family! That girl is my granddaughter's friend, and the man knows my son, for Christ's sake!"

Exhaling deeply, the rabbi rises from his desk and walks over to a small wet bar, where he pours a single-malt whiskey neat. "Calm down, Nick," he says, "I got it covered. There's nothing to fret about." Motioning to Beth, he hands her the drink and orders her to take it to the judge.

Reluctantly, the frightened girl complies. When she reaches Nick, he grabs the drink with one hand and pulls the girl onto his lap with the other. "Well," he says after giving a long slobbering kiss to Beth, "if you got it handled, let's celebrate our victory. It's not every day that my granddaughter gets a new heart!"

CHAPTER TWENTY-FOUR

It's time. Thankfully, the full moon over South Florida will assist law enforcement's efforts this evening.

In Hollywood, FBI Agent Cohen leads his team down the Intracoastal Waterway in a marine unit patrol boat, while Vice Detective William Ballard and his men drive into the large compound in assault vehicles.

When Cohen gives the signal, his SWAT team at the rear of the mansion silently swarms over the seawall at the water's edge, easily surprising two unlucky guards, who surrender quietly.

At the front of the house, Ballard's team quickly breaks down the door with a battering ram and subdues the few sentinels who respond to the intrusion.

Most of the guards at the house are stationed in the ballroom and around the pool this evening to watch the guests at the social event taking place tonight, so the main security team doesn't know that police officers are now surrounding them.

In Boynton, Sergeant Fred Staten is on high alert. The brothel is hosting one of its frequent parties this evening, and he's on duty. As the guests mingle with the scantily-clad women and girls provided for the evening, he scans the crowd continuously, filing away descriptions of the faces he sees around his post at the French doors leading from the house to the pool and dock areas.

Already notified about tonight's raid, PBSO Deputy Steven Zambone is searching the crowd for Fred. Dressed in a new Armani tuxedo to reflect his faux position as a Boynton Beach administrator, Zambone is relieved when he spots the officer. "Sergeant Staten," he whispers, "my name is Deputy Steven Zambone. Like you, I'm working undercover tonight." Moving discreetly, he reveals a badge on his waistband. "FBI and Palm Beach Sheriff's units are raiding this compound in five minutes, and we need you to open the gate."

Although Staten is surprised, he keeps his face impassive. With an imperceptible nod, he replies softly, "There are four armed guards in the ballroom, and more out back. They will definitely engage, so be prepared. I'll open the gate and neutralize the ones by the pool." Not waiting for a reply, Staten weaves his way through the ballroom crowd to the gate controls in the foyer.

As Fred passes Debra, he overhears her talking to Denise, who seems to be high as a kite. "Go to room 2A, honey," says Debra. "A client is waiting for you." To keep his cover, Fred winks at Debra, and she happily winks back.

Still strapped to a table in the separate wing of the house of horrors in Hollywood, Jesus closes his eyes and expects the worst. Terrified, he prays the rosary in preparation for meeting his maker.

All too soon, Jesus detects the ominous hum of a surgical saw coming closer and closer. Terrified, Jesus closes his eyes tighter and races through his prayers. But an unexpected sound that is much different from the first causes his eyes to fly open. Turning his head toward the sound, his spirits soar when he sees a team of SWAT officers kicking in the operating room door. With one quick shot from an AR rifle, an officer dispatches the surgeon, and the saw crashes to the floor. The rest of the officers instruct the orderlies to surrender.

Relieved that he was able to prevent another death, Agent Cohen holsters the .45 he had in hand at the break-in and makes his way over to Jesus. On the way to the boy, he is shocked and angered to see Mandy's corpse and the bodies of two other children lying on nearby tables. "It's okay," Cohen assures the trembling youth, "you're in good hands now. "These men will take care of you." With a pat of reassurance, Cohen leaves Jesus to his squad members.

In another wing of the house, Rabbi Katzoff is still impatiently watching Nick Handel entwine himself around Beth. When the sounds of bangs and thuds overtake the judge's moans and groans, Katzoff stands and looks questioningly toward the door. "Nick, do you hear that?" he asks.

Before Nick can respond, the door is kicked in, and several armed men barge into the room. Beth covers her head protectively while Judge Handel jumps off the sofa and pulls up his pants. Smoothing down his hair, he shouts, "Thank God you guys arrived! That's him! Arrest him!" Always a quick thinker, Handel points his finger at Herb Katzoff, who curses and points a middle finger back at his partner in crime.

Ignoring the men's protestations of innocence, the officers quickly cuff them both. "You have the right to remain silent..." begins one of the officers.

"What the hell are you doing?" interrupts Judge Handel indignantly as Katzoff is led out of the room.

The officer continues, "... anything you say can and will be used against you in a court of law..."

"COURT OF LAW?" shouts Handel. "Don't you know who I am? I'm a respected judge in this county! I'm Judge Nicholas Handel!"

Clinging tightly to each other in the refrigerated room, Calista and Tara shiver in fear as Rocco cleans his gun and Harriet applies makeup to several of the other victims.

Unexpectedly, a loud pounding sound causes all heads to turn toward the door. When a bang shakes the door and flings it open, the victims are thrilled to see police officers rushing into the room in riot gear.

Unwisely, Harriet panics at the sight and pulls out a semi-automatic revolver from her makeup case.

The officers order her to put the weapon down, but when she points it at them instead, Agent Cohen drops her with a fatal wound to the head.

Rocco makes an equally bad decision. Determined not to give up easily, he tries to make a stand by grabbing one of the girls and positioning her in front of his chest with a .357 at her head.

When Cohen hesitates, Rocco has a few precious seconds to analyze his situation. Knowing that he would more than likely receive a death sentence if there is even one person left alive who could testify against him, the thug resolves not to leave any witnesses to his activities. Pulling on the trigger of his .357, he kills the young girl and another victim before taking a bead on Calista.

Fearing for his daughter's life, Will doesn't hesitate. He shoots Rocco in the head, scattering his blood and brains around the room in a pink fog. Not satisfied with only one shot, Will sprints over to Rocco's body and shoots him again.

Elated by her father's presence amid all of the terror she's seen since she was kidnapped, Calista jumps up from the floor and grips him tightly.

"It's okay, baby girl," says Will soothingly, cradling his daughter's head in his arms, "Daddy's got you. You're okay now."

Left behind when Calista ran to her father, Tara remains seated, but she is exceedingly puzzled. She has spotted the lead FBI agent and is studying him intently with widened eyes and a hand held against her open mouth. "Mr. Levy?" she inquires, looking questioningly from Cohen's face to his name tag. "Who are... Are you with the FBI?"

"Yes, Tara, I'm an FBI agent," replies Cohen. "I was working undercover as a guidance counselor at your school. I see you've noticed that my name isn't Randal Levy."

While the rescue was going on in the refrigerated room in Hollywood, Fred was unlocking the front gate at the Boynton brothel.

When that was done, he went out to the pool area. Calling to the guards, he raised his weapon and shouted, "My name is Sergeant Fred Staten, and I'm with FLPD! Drop your weapons and stand down!" When FBI Agent Connie Jackson heard Fred's shouts, she ordered her team into the pool area to back Fred up.

All in all, the ambush of the Boynton house was successful, thanks in part to the successfully tranquilized peacocks. The raid was a total surprise and no shots were fired. When the officers took control, the guests were rounded up in the ballroom for questioning, and all of the guards were led outside.

Outside with the guards, Fred answers a few questions and then reenters the house just in time to see Debra Connelly being handcuffed. Happy that the impossible woman in charge of the brothel is now in custody, he smirks, "Hope you like small spaces, Connelly, " 'cause you're gonna be in one for a long time. But I'm really gonna miss that Camaro."

"Oh, yeah?" pouts Debra over her shoulder as she's being led away. "But are you gonna miss me and all of the fun we had?"

Staten shakes his head at the brazenness the sex-crazed manager of this urban brothel and turns away. When he catches the questioning eye of Sheriff's Deputy Zambone, he raises his hand to him and says, "Don't even ask."

With the activity in the foyer in good hands, Staten runs up the marble staircase to Room 2A, where he comes upon a police officer restraining Denise's John of the evening. Denise is still lying on the bed behind them, naked as a jaybird, so Fred grabs a sheet and covers her. "Let's get you to a hospital and back to your dad," he murmurs softly, but Denise is generally unaware of what's going on around her. Her mind is enveloped in a foggy mist, and she is having trouble focusing. She didn't understand much of what Fred said, but she did understand the word "Dad," and that made her very happy.

In Hollywood, the front of Katzoff's mansion is now bathed in a sea of blue and red lights with armored vehicles, police cruisers, and ambulances positioned haphazardly along the winding driveway. Police, SWAT, and FBI agents are swarming all over the grounds for evidence, and personnel from the Medical Examiner's Office have now joined the group.

Outside the house, Agent Cohen is making himself useful by directing traffic and answering questions.

When he sees District Attorney Darren Handel drive up, he is too busy to greet him personally, so he keeps an eye out for a moment to say hello. However, Darren doesn't exit his vehicle right away. He remains in his car, looking out at all the commotion.

Cohen knows that Darren has spotted his father yelling and cursing in the back of a squad car and that the D.A. has also seen Rabbi Katzoff in the custody of an FBI Agent, so when the rabbi nods his head ever so slightly at Darren and Darren respond to him in kind, he is shocked. Then, when the D.A. turns his car around and drives away, Cohen's bullshit meter goes sky high.

In Boynton, the mansion housing the gentlemen's club is also blanketed in blue and red lights. While FBI and police personnel process the crime scene, police transport buses are filling up with the victims and their johns.

Parked near the buses, an ambulance waits to bring Denise to the hospital. She is lying immobile on a gurney inside the vehicle, hooked up to an IV drip.

"How's she doing?" asks Fred.

"She'll be fine," responds the young EMT attending to Denise. "She's a little dehydrated, so I'm giving her saline. Hey, I hear that she's the long-lost daughter of the Fort Lauderdale D.A. Is that true?"

"Yeah, it is. Listen, I got a request from the governor and the Palm Beach sheriff. You need to bring her directly to Broward General Hospital. Her father is there with her half-sister, who's in surgery."

The young technician shakes his head. "No can do. I can't transport her out of our area just on one cop's say so."

Nodding, Staten removes his phone from his pocket. Then, he punches in a number and hands the phone to the technician, who takes it and listens. Seconds later, the man hands the phone back to Staten with a sigh. "Okay, I guess I'm heading south."

Smiling, Staten melts into a sea of law enforcement personnel with single-minded purpose. Dodging busy officers and forensic technicians, he finally spots the car that Debra obtained for him as a perk of his security job and as a reward for his personal favors. Looking over the Camaro SS fondly, he runs his hand along the hood and sighs wistfully.

CHAPTER TWENTY-FIVE

Too often, the trauma center at the county hospital is a chaotic place, and it becomes even more so when the victims of the raid on Katzoff's compound arrive.

Because of the number of victims, uniformed officers and agents are pressed into service to assist in bringing the young girls and women into the treatment rooms.

As the steady stream of victims enters the unit, the ease with which the doctors, nurses, police, and EMTs work together underscores their senses of urgency and hope.

"Papá! Papá!" calls Jesus from a wheelchair. As a nurse rolls him past a bed in the hallway, Jesus reaches for his father, and the nurse stops her forward march.

"Ay, mi hijo! You are okay!" exclaims Christian with tears in his eyes.

"Sí, papi, pero... Why are you here?"

Wincing in pain, Christian answers with some effort. "These good people will fix my cut, and...*ayy,"* he moans, "take care of me. They say I will be okay, *gracias a Dios."*

Jesus smiles and then furrows his brow in mock

annoyance. "*Ay*, that is good! But *papi*, you must practice the English!"

Chuckling weakly, Christian holds his son's hand and allows his tears to flow freely. "Yes, I will do that. Thanks be to God!"

In Calista's treatment room, Will holds his daughter's hand while various doctors and nurses come and go. "I'm sorry, Dad. I screwed up," laments Calista. "Forgive me?"

"Of course I forgive you, baby girl. That's what a father does. But you know that you're grounded until further notice, right?" he admonishes.

In a separate room, Tara has been resting with her eyes closed. She was told that she would be held overnight for further tests because of vaginal bruising and because the medical team suspects that she has suffered a concussion. When she senses someone nearby, she opens her eyes.

"There's someone here for you," says Agent Cohen.

Looking past Adam's shoulder, Tara shouts for joy when she sees her mother walking through the treatment area. While Adam stands by, mother and daughter share a lengthy hug.

When the pair finally disentangles from each other, Jenny wipes her eyes and turns to Adam. "Thank you so much, Agent Levy! You have no idea how much you've helped us!"

"You're very welcome, but my name is actually Cohen," Adam responds modestly.

Looking at the agent, Tara asks, "Where's Mandy? Is she here, too?"

Although Adam fully expected the question, he can't seem to form the words to explain what happened to Tara's friend. So instead, he lowers his eyes and shakes his head.

At first, Tara is perplexed, but then, she understands Adam's unspoken communication. With a shudder that shakes her entire body, she covers her face and remembers the horrific screams that echoed throughout her recent prison cell.

When Darren arrives at the ER, he pays a brief visit to the trauma section and then goes upstairs to find Abby. Directed by the floor nurses, he finds her in bed, with Gabriella and her husband sitting nearby. "Abby, everything's going to be all right now! I did it! I got you a new heart!" he says happily.

Abby smiles in gratitude, but Darren can tell that she's nervous. "You all gonna be here when I get out of surgery?" she asks her family.

While the adults assure Abby that there's nowhere else they'd rather be, Will Ballard pops his head into the room. "Mr. Handel, can I have a minute, please?" he asks.

"Sure," says Darren, throwing a kiss at Abby. "See you later, pumpkin."

Will grabs Darren by the arm and leads him a few doors away from Abby's room. Turning to the D.A., he says in a low voice, "Denise just arrived from Boynton. You owe the sheriff in Palm Beach County a steak dinner for allowing her to be moved out of their jurisdiction."

The expression on Darren's face changes from relief to joy to anxiety at the prospect of seeing his older daughter again after so many years. "Can I have some time alone with her before you tell Gabriella she's here?"

"Sure, no problem," agrees Will. "You got all the time you need. Just let me know when you're ready."

Darren follows Will with some trepidation into the now-subsiding chaos of the ER. When Will indicates a treatment room at the end of the corridor, Darren walks on alone, but stops just before entering the room. Nine years of constant fear is threatening to turn into a stream of tears, and he desperately wants to keep the floodgates closed. Steadying himself, he peeks his head into the room, but Denise has already seen her father in the hallway.

"Daddy, Daddy! Oh, my God! Daddy!" she yells, and Darren ignores his free-flowing tears to rush to his daughter's side.

Looking on, Will can't tell who is crying more. Wiping his eyes with the back of his hands, he turns away from the happy scene to give the father and daughter some privacy.

Meanwhile, upstairs, Gabriella and her husband are watching a nurse wheel Abby out of her room. Gabriella puts a brave face on for Abby while clutching her husband's arm tightly in a desperate need for support.

With Darren's permission, Will is now on his way back upstairs to give Gabby the good news. As he rounds a corner, he sees her in the hallway, talking with her husband. "Excuse me, Mrs. Hoffman."

Gabby's eyes light up with pleasure. "Oh, Will! Jesus said Calista was found and that she's fine! Thank God she's safe!"

"Yes, I'm very grateful!" replies Will. "She seems okay, but I'm afraid she may have seen some things that will take her a long time to get over. As a cop, I've been exposed to awful crimes during my career, but it's hard to believe that this ring hid their tracks so well. No one knew that they've been operating right under our very noses!"

"Yes, it's all so horrible!" agrees Gabby. "Let me know if you and Calista need anything at all. We're here for the both of you."

"Thank you, Gabriella, I appreciate that. Look, I, um... I have some news for you. Uh...there was another raid this evening, in Boynton Beach, and, um..." Will doesn't know how to break the news about Gabby's older daughter, so he just blurts it out. "Gabby, we found Denise. She's downstairs."

Shocked, Gabriella gasps and her hand flies to her mouth. Staring at Will in wide-eyed disbelief, she shrieks, "You found my little Denise? I, I thought... I thought she was dead! Oh, thank you, Lord, thank you!" Reaching for Will, Gabriella grips him tightly, but Will gently pushes her away.

“Come on,” Will says, she’s waiting for you. Darren is already with her.”

Looking on, Ted Hoffman is a shocked as his wife, but he understands that Gabby will need to process this new development with her former family. He never met Denise, having married Gabriella after Denise went missing. “Go ahead, Hon,” he says. “You need to see her. I’ll wait up here for you.” With a quick kiss for her husband, Gabriella leaves the floor with Will.

For Gabriella, the trip downstairs seems to last a lifetime. When the pair reaches the ER, Will points out Denise’s room and she walks toward it alone, not knowing what she will find inside. When she enters the room, Denise and Darren are talking to each other so earnestly that neither of them notices her until she walks right up to the foot of the bed.

At the sight of her mother, Denise shouts, “MOM!” and breaks down into fresh tears.

Gabby can’t get enough of her daughter. She touches Denise’s face continually and asks her over and over, “Are you all right? What do you need? What can I do for you?” But to Darren, she mouths, “I’m sorry about everything.”

Watching his daughter and his ex-wife being so happy together, Darren sighs wistfully at what his family could have been.

CHAPTER TWENTY-SIX

A bright and sunny day in Fort Lauderdale means the temperature is already in the mid-eighties, even at ten o'clock in the morning. Accustomed to the morning heat, the crowd in front of the podium at the Broward County Courthouse waits patiently for the D.A. and the mayor of Fort Lauderdale.

When the speakers arrive, the crowd listens attentively to the mayor as he introduces Darren with a long political speech. While the mayor speaks, memories of the events that led up to this day are flashing through Darren's mind, along with several details he'd like to forget. Unbidden and unwelcome, a conversation with Rabbi Katzoff bubbles up to the surface.

Rabbi Katzoff: *"Did you find me some prospects?"*

Darren, standing in a courtroom hallway: *"Yes."*

Katzoff: *"Are they ready for pickup?"*

Darren: *"I'm working on it."*

Katzoff: *"Will it be soon?"*

Darren: *"Yes."*

Unnerved, Darren shakes his head to try to remove that conversation from his mind but more like it take its place.

Darren, at the Irish pub: *"Hey, Dad, I got your call."*

Judge Nick Handel: *"I heard you were with my new housekeeper."*

Darren: *"Yes, I took Lu Tang to the beach. The case went to the jury today. I think we got him. Another sex trafficking sleazebag is off the streets."*

Judge Nick Handel: *"You know how many cases my colleagues get because of trafficking? Are your efforts worth it?"*

Darren: *"Of course they're worth it. If I can save one child like my daughter—your granddaughter—it's all worth it."*

Judge Nick Handel: *"My boy, do you really think you can get them all?"*

Darren: *"Well, I can try."*

No sooner does that memory fade, than another fills his mind.

Darren, standing outside of his office: *"Hey, I have something for you."*

Katzoff: *"That's great, who?"*

Darren: *"Her name is Mandy Goldman. She's been bullying my daughter. I have her phone number right here."*

Katzoff: *"So, we're able to help each other after all."*

That memory ends, and another begins.

Darren: *"Hello?"*

Katzoff: *"Prospects ready?"*

Darren: *"The wheels are in motion."*

Katzoff: *"We're ready here."*

Darren: "*Good.*"

The unsettling memories finally stop when Darren hears himself being introduced amid enthusiastic applause. Clearing his throat, he approaches the podium and looks out over the crowd. While he waits for the applause to die down, he is not surprised to see Agent Adam Cohen amid the onlookers, texting furiously.

Darren begins his narrative when the crowd quiets down. "I've called this press conference today to update you on the state's case against Eral Rosenbaum. The state has agreed to a plea agreement in which Mr. Rosenbaum pledges to assist with our investigations into the sex trafficking and organ harvesting operations taking place in this area. The information Mr. Rosenbaum has already provided to us has resulted in numerous raids, and the resulting arrests have shut down a major sex trafficking ring with ties to the governor's office. Because of the plea, the jury was recalled, and the trial was adjourned.

"Mr. Rosenbaum pled guilty to multiple counts of kidnapping and child endangerment and was sentenced to ten years in our Apalachee Correctional Institution, a minimum-security prison in the Panhandle. He'll be eligible for parole in five years.

"On a personal note, my daughter, Denise, was found during one of those raids and is currently in rehab. Her mother and I thank God and the FBI for their help in finding her."

As Darren continues with personal updates about his younger daughter, Abby, Lu Tang lies in a tub of blood-stained water in Darren's father's mansion across town. She slashed both of her wrists and is now failing fast. Barely conscious, Lu calls out her parents' names and then closes her eyes for the last time.

At the courthouse, Darren is responding to questions from reporters. "Yes, at this time, I am announcing the start of my campaign for governor of the great state of Florida. I pledge to continue my efforts to stop this scourge against the youth of our state, and I ask for your support. May God bless Fort Lauderdale, the state of Florida, and the United States of America!"

While Darren waves at the crowd, Adam Cohen focuses on his cell phone, and his non-stop texting.

EPILOGUE

Life goes on. While many involved in the unspeakable crimes revealed by Eral Rosenbaum are enduring the harsh consequences of their actions, some of their victims are enjoying improved and hopeful futures, thanks to the heroic efforts of dedicated law enforcement personnel.

When Eral Rosenbaum was sentenced, two mansions and one high-rise condo were added to the list of exclusive properties for sale in the South Florida area. Although the owners were distressed at the thought of losing their flamboyant abodes, the profits of the sales will be shared by various organizations that assist in rehabilitating their victims.

As Lisa Berg predicted, Eral did not remain behind bars for long. After only one year of incarceration, he died in prison under mysterious circumstances. Eral's death was classified as a heart attack, but no autopsy was performed. Nick Handel and Herb Katzoff are both on death row and their appeals are being handled by Lisa Berg.

In Fort Lauderdale, the public was outraged when they became aware of the connections the homeless shelter had to the human trafficking ring, so the facility underwent a hasty change in ownership. Now operated by the City of Fort Lauderdale, the shelter was re-named after the state's new governor, Darren Handel, and Lorinda Vitale is proudly continuing her work there.

Mei Lan, one of the lucky victims, has fully recovered from her self-inflicted wounds and has been granted permission to remain in the United States on a student visa. She is trying hard to improve her English in preparation for getting her GED, and upon graduation, she hopes to attend Florida International University in Miami. Mei Lan feels blessed to have her college tuition and housing costs guaranteed through the Mandy Goldman Foundation, which Mr. and Mrs. Aaron Goldman set up in honor of their late daughter. She is also happy that Will Ballard has allowed her to live in his apartment while she studies for the GED. Although Will treats her as a daughter, he continues to keep a close eye on her and Calista.

Abby Handel is doing fine, and her new heart is strong. The only ones who know for sure whose heart is now beating in her chest are her father, her grandfather, and Rabbi Herb Katzoff. They have agreed among themselves to never let anyone else know the truth about Mandy Goldman's heart.

Despite everything they've gone through, Abby and Calista have remained close friends, and their determination to enter their school's annual talent competition has not wavered. They've devised a new dance routine and are practicing and improving it every day.

Thankfully, Jennifer and Tara Smith are once again a family. Through the efforts of Detective Ballard and Agent Cohen, Jennifer was able to find a well-paying, full-time job that enabled her to regain custody of her daughter. Although Jennifer has more time to spend with Tara now that she doesn't have to work three jobs, she is happy that Tara isn't at home as often as she was before. She doesn't begrudge her daughter the time she is now spending with her new friends, Abby and Calista.

Sergeant Fred Staten is no longer in charge of Fort Lauderdale's Vice Unit. In recognition of his work on the Rosenbaum case, he was rewarded with a promotion and is now the city's newest homicide detective. And along with a new job, Fred also has a new love life. When he's not fighting crime, he's driving around the city in a new Camaro SS, courting Denise Handel. He knows Denise has a long way to go to overcome her years of abuse, but she is going through therapy and seems to be adjusting well to resuming a normal life.

Although Judge Handel was convicted of several heinous crimes and is now on death row, he has never revealed his son's similarly atrocious offenses, and this left Darren free to pursue his dream of a successful political career. Currently raised to the level of governor, Darren Handel is doing everything he can to stop the sex trafficking plague that is continuing to infect the country. His commitment is solid—most likely a reaction to Denise's kidnapping and to the roles he and his father played in the related crimes. Darren is grateful for his father's silence on the matter, but he has had no contact with him since his incarceration. Darren is counting heavily on his father's silence continuing as he sets up a committee to explore a possible run for President of the United States.

Poor Lu Tang has not been forgotten. When she

died, the gentle and fragile girl was quietly buried in a ceremony attended by only a few persons, and ever since her burial, fresh flowers have appeared every month at her modest gravesite. No one knows for sure who has arranged for the flowers, but there are many theories among the locals.

Last, but not least, FBI Agent Adam Cohen now lives in Tallahassee, Florida's state capital. He is often spotted at Governor Handel's public appearances, and whenever he's seen there, you can be sure he's texting.

A NOTE FROM THE AUTHOR

This novel is a work of fiction based on the unique and terribly ugly experiences of the victims of human trafficking. Tragically, circumstances all too similar to those outlined in these pages take place behind closed doors in every type of neighborhood across the world.

Every year in the United States, between 600,000 and 800,000 human beings are sold into forced sex and labor. Sadly, a large part of those numbers is made up of children. Fully fifty percent of victims are estimated to be youngsters aged eleven to fourteen, with the internet playing a prominent role in their ordeals. It is estimated that seventy-six percent of transactions for sex with underage girls occurs online.

Since 2012, victims of human trafficking have numbered 20.9 million worldwide, with 1.5 million in the United States alone. Approximately 80 percent of women and children bought and sold worldwide end up imprisoned in forced servitude in the underground sex trade industry, with their lifespans averaging only seven years under those circumstances.

I would like to thank Ark of Hope for Children for these statistics. You can read about their efforts to combat child trafficking, child abuse, and bullying at www.arkofhopeforchildren.org.

www.ingramcontent.com/pod-product-compliance
Lightning Source LLC
Chambersburg PA
CBHW061937170626
46813CB00006B/2433

9780983680352